CRY TO THE MOON

CRY TO THE MOON

Joyce Stranger

Severn House Large Print
London & New York

This first large print edition published in Great Britain 2002 by
SEVERN HOUSE LARGE PRINT BOOKS LTD of
9-15, High Street, Sutton, Surrey, SM1 1DF.
First world regular print edition published 2001 by
Severn House Publishers, London and New York.
This first large print edition published in the USA 2002 by
SEVERN HOUSE PUBLISHERS INC., of
595 Madison Avenue, New York, NY 10022

British Library Cataloguing in Publication Data

Stranger, Joyce
  Cry to the moon. - Large print ed.
  1. Wildcat - Scotland - Highlands - Fiction
  2. Gamekeepers - Scotland - Highlands - Fiction
  3. Large type books
  I. Title
  823.9'14 [F]

ISBN 0-7278-7187-0

Printed and bound in Great Britain by
MPG Books Ltd, Bodmin, Cornwall.

Author's Note

This book is dedicated to all those who have helped to make my life special in so many different ways during my husband's recent very serious illness.

To all our family who made such noble efforts to help in spite of being busy and all living far away.

To Liz, my Home Help, who makes it possible for me to write and to help owners train their dogs.

To Richard next door who has kept weeds and grass at bay, which is no easy task on our patch.

To Katie McKay, my much valued agent who, among other kindnesses, sent an enormous bouquet to cheer me.

To the staff of *My Weekly*, who have been part of my life for so long, and Ian Sommerville and Harry Harrison who cheered me by their phone talks. I shall never forget the huge bunch of wonderful flowers which they all sent for my birthday.

To Megan Owen, who took me regularly to

the hospital and sat with my dog Troy in the hot car park so that the car windows could be open and who then took me shopping.

To Eryl Restall who in spite of a very busy life e-mailed me every day and visited with Bud and Kim and Hunny, and arrived on my birthday complete with lunch for us as otherwise I would have been alone.

To Michelle and John Clark, who are among the most regular attendants of the dog classes that I teach, and who also shopped for me, and whose lurcher Charlie always makes me laugh.

To others too numerous to mention who phoned, visited or sent cards, and to my many e-mail friends who also sent cheering messages.

It is so comforting to have so many good friends, and to know you are not alone.

Prologue

At first she was a shadow, half seen. She was a wild and eerie voice in the night, waking the sleepers with her cries. There had always been wildcats on the hills round the estate, but relentless keepers thought they had eliminated them. They wreaked havoc among the birds.

She was a force to be dreaded, with her stealthy hunt, her sudden pounce, her raking claws and tearing teeth. She was death incarnate. She was unwanted. She was wild, she was wary, and had learned that men were her greatest enemies. She took care not to be seen.

Winter that year had been wicked, with snow that lay for days, with bitterly cold nights and hard frosts, with ice that froze the water, so that none of the animals could drink. They licked the chilling surface, but longed for clear cool liquid that could be lapped by their eager tongues.

Even the cascades that leaped over the great rocks in the high hills were sculptured. The translucent icicles captured the light in diamond glitters, their movement stilled.

Here, where heather hid grouse, and capercaillie strutted, where hare and rabbit and mouse and shrew found sustenance, the wildcat came, seeking sanctuary. There were no houses in the high hills. No men and no guns. She was young, not yet two years old, and lacked experience.

There were those who thought she should be protected. There were others who did not care. She was death to their stock and death was to be her portion. If they could find her.

She had too many enemies. This was her second litter. Her first had been born on a dark and windy night, and she had been exhausted by the birth. A keeper had trapped her mate, caught in a snare, set illegally, but who was to know? A bullet, fired straight into the male wildcat's brain, ended his life as he tried to fight his attackers. Snares tortured but did not kill.

The female wildcat had much to learn. One kitten, exploring too far when his mother was hunting, fell victim to a prowling stoat. Another to the eagle, desperate for food for his own young, incessantly demanding, there on the hill. Yet another fell in the bog and drowned, while the fourth was caught as his father had been. His mother fought the noose to free him but it tightened round his small neck as he struggled. She lay beside him, trying to feed him. She drove

8

away the stoats and crows that came for bounty.

Death claimed him and she gave up. Not one of that litter had survived.

This time she knew better and would guard the kittens with her life.

She was alone, her second mate newly dead. The cold had driven them down from the hills and forced them to hunt round the houses, raiding the bins. Nature had no sustenance to offer.

The deer and wild ponies came down into the villages too, seeking for food in the winter-weary gardens. An irate cottager, incensed by the loss of four of his chickens, lay in wait one night, and his gun found one target but missed the other.

The female, terrified by the sound of the gun, did not wait for her mate. When three days had passed, during which she fed sparsely, she left the area and travelled over the hills, looking for a sanctuary away from man. Her kittens, as yet, were only a rumour of what was to come.

Spring flew in with a flourish of blossom, the late flowers seeming to make up for time lost so that they flowered out of sequence, bluebells coming almost on the heels of the snowdrops and primroses. Every creature revelled in the warm days and the ever-strengthening sun.

There were baby stoats underground, tiny

mice in hidden nests, their own little ones sucking. There were fledglings in the many nests.

The wildcat waited for the birth. She would need all her skill and cunning in the days that lay ahead.

She was surrounded by enemies, on two legs and on four, and on wings.

Fox and stoat, weasel and hawk, eagle and owl, all knew that soon there would be kittens in the nest. All had young to feed. Only the ospreys, fishing the lochs, left the mountain creatures alone.

Every creature on the hill was hunting.

Including man with his guns.

One

To those who came to walk on the hills, to taste the mountain air and watch the wild-life, the place they called 'the Micklemoor' was a sanctuary. It covered the slopes of the foothills, a mass of heather, carefully nurtured by burning off each year to provide the best habitat for the birds.

Foxes, hawks and other predators took daily toll. To those working there, it was a battle zone.

The once-thriving estate had been sold, on the death of its owner, to a syndicate. Most of the shareholders were men who came for a day's shooting but had little interest in the care and upkeep of birds or land. Once there had been a team of five, headed by Alastair McNeill. Now there were only two men, aided by Alastair's twenty-year-old daughter, Sheina. Her work was not acknowledged and she was unpaid, though she was skilled in the job, having been her father's shadow ever since she could toddle. They could not have coped without her.

Alastair had little time for modern ways.

'They expect two men to do the work of six. They don't pay for that work and they don't pay overtime. We work seven days a week and form night patrols. Do they think we're machines? They forget about the gangs that come from the cities to poach the deer.'

He said that over and over again at their shared midday meal until it had become a litany so that both Ian Benton, the younger man, and Sheina could repeat it for him.

'They grumble if the shooting is poor. They never praise when it's good. The laird's guests tipped us well. These men are unaware of any need. They should try our life, out in all weathers and at all hours. The hills are hard on a man.'

Ian was a newcomer. Few men stayed. The work was too hard and the place too isolated. Though he was shy, he had a quick sense of humour. Alastair's oft-repeated phrases drove him to glance at Sheina. They exchanged conspiratorial looks of suppressed amusement.

Ian had grown up on an estate in Southern England, owned by an earl. It had been a good place to work. His father, Jack Benton, was head gamekeeper. His mother, a city woman, had abandoned them both when the boy was only one year old. She was not a maternal woman and found his needs a nuisance. She longed for the bright city life that she had given up, too young, for an adolescent passion that she thought was for life.

She hated the isolation and a husband who appeared to prefer his pheasants to her. She was now married to a man who had called each week, bringing animal feed. Luckily the man she deserted adored his small son, and the other men stepped in so that at times Ian felt as if he had six fathers.

Ian had not seen his mother since she left and had no desire to meet her again. He loved the life he led with his father. Most of his time was spent in a wholly male society, dominated by the constant changing seasons and the pheasants that they reared.

It was hard work with the birds penned, the coops to clean, the feed to prepare, but he had enjoyed it. This Scottish estate was very different. The grouse were wild. There were no rearing pens. No eggs to hatch. He had never had to watch over deer. Although he was beginning to love the wilderness in which he found himself, he was occasionally homesick and at times he looked back with regret. He missed his father and his one-time companions. They had been good friends and splendid teachers.

It had been a wonderful childhood. The birds were his passion. He was charmed by the gentle hens and admired the brilliant cocks, splendid in their bright feathers. They were not blessed with much intelligence and needed constant care.

The shoots were successful, the five keepers well rewarded by an appreciative employer. Ian hoped to succeed his father as head keeper one day in the future. He did not like shooting but understood the necessity. He acted as beater, and did not use a gun himself, although he often shot at a target.

Life changed almost overnight, without warning.

The earl, not yet fifty, died of a coronary. His son had no desire to live as his father had. He sold the estate, and emigrated, buying a large property in Canada, saying there was no future in Britain.

Ian's father retired to a small cottage with a few acres of rough fields, where he opened a small nursery, specialising in 'pick your own' soft fruit. Nobody wanted a fifty-year old gamekeeper. He grew fruit and vegetables, kept bees, goats and sheep and lived comfortably on what he could grow for himself.

'Get yourself a city job,' he told Ian. 'There's no future on the land. Give it fifty years and they'll have forgotten how to manage it. The moors will go back to scrub, the fields be neglected, and the villages overrun with starving deer and foxes. There'll be nothing for them to eat.'

Ian had no desire for a city job. He could

14

not bear the thought of massed buildings, of hard pavements, of jammed traffic. He loathed crowded buses and trains and the stink of exhausts. He had visited London once and hated the taste of the tainted air and the thronging crowds that seemed to threaten him at every step.

His life from the age of one had not prepared him for communication with women, who terrified him. He loved wild places, enjoyed his own company and was unable to share the interests of his schoolfellows. They labelled him an oddball, but mostly left him alone.

They soon discovered he was no wimp, thanks to one of the keepers who had, in his younger days, been a champion boxer at his school. He taught Ian to defend himself. Nobody tangled with him a second time.

He intervened if other children were threatened, and they too benefited from his training. Nobody teased him. He only had to look at the girls if they tried to make fun of him.

'He has the weirdest eyes,' his schoolfellows told one another. 'He makes you feel as if you're not there at all.'

It was his only defence against what seemed to him like an alien species. He was used to open spaces and looking into the distance. Often, when he should have been concentrating on lessons, he was back in his thoughts at the rearing pens, or out in the woods with his Labrador at his heels.

His schoolwork suffered. He learned to read and keep account of his money, as both were useful skills, but saw little need for history or geography or languages. Why should it matter that Henry VIII had six wives, or that the Normans came to Britain in 1066?

He would not listen to his father's urging to look for somewhere safe. There was always a need for good mechanics, he suggested. Gamekeeping was a dying profession.

He was part of the natural world, as at home there as any of the wild animals. He had endured the shoots, saddened by the need to kill the birds he had tended so lovingly during the year, keeping away from people he did not understand.

He needed space. He loved his work, loved handling the dogs, and the satisfaction of watching the pheasants grow from tiny yellow creatures with tiger-striped backs into handsome cocks and dainty hens.

He could not find any work in the southern countryside he knew so well. Few estates still existed and they were laying off men, not taking them on.

He spent an uneasy twelve months with his father, feeling he was a burden and an unnecessary expense. He disliked this new way of life. He argued constantly with his father, who thought him a fool to cling to what was already a dead profession.

'There's always a need for social workers,' Jack Benton said. 'Or take a training course in computers. You'd never be out of work then.'

Ian ignored him. He hated machines. He yearned for the countryside, not for digging and planting and a few domestic animals in a small area, the town a whistle stop away.

He went, with trepidation, to the Highlands of Scotland, when Alastair McNeill advertised for a second keeper. The estate was isolated. The village, twelve miles away, was small and introverted, disliking strangers. It was hard to find anyone to help. But Ian, after more than a year of job seeking, had no choice.

He took the old Ford that had served him well for three years but was forced to leave his much-loved dog behind. Brandy was eleven years old and not fit for the hard life any more. He was better off with Jack.

Much to Ian's joy, his new home was a revelation and an inspiration. He had never been north before. He fell in love with the wide moors, the mountains dark against the sky, the streams that tumbled over boulders, and the totally different landscape.

He arrived in the autumn, when the woods were blazing with colour. The winter was bleak but even that failed to daunt him. His father had always referred to him as dynamo-charged. In his new home there was space and also occupation to work off his immense energy.

The snow-covered hills were a delight. One day he saw his first osprey, tussling with a surprisingly large trout. Behind it white-topped waves crashed, clouds gathered in a darkening sky, and the mountains rose to a soaring peak. He watched the bird trying to retain his lively catch. With a sudden movement the head of the fish was smashed against the rock, ending the struggle, and the hawk began to feed.

Maybe it had a mate and there would be eggs to guard in the spring. Ian was sure no one knew of the bird's existence here. He did not mention it. It remained a cherished memory.

Here, if he ever found time, he might fish. These were not the broad rivers of his birthplace, where he and his father caught trout. These were streams that rushed in a flare of white water down the hillsides. They might be shallow ribbons dancing over rounded rocks, murmuring to the sky. Then rains came for days, driving from the hills, soaking man and beast, and the innocent streams became raging torrents that hurled the thundering boulders skywards. It was impossible even to speak and be heard anywhere near the wild water.

There was nothing to equal the new-found thrill when he stood on the edge of a waterfall to watch the leaping salmon as they hurled their silvery bodies up the ladders to the spawning grounds.

'It's unbelievable,' he said one day, making a rare contribution to the conversation at lunchtime. 'To think of the distances they come, the hundreds of miles, and they still have the energy to force themselves up to what looks like an inaccessible place to reach the area where they were born.'

Alastair nodded agreement.

'Aye. I marvel at the swallows,' he said. 'Such tiny birds to take that long journey every autumn all the way to Africa, fighting the winds. And I never tire of watching the ducks as they skein across the sky, calling, and hearing the wild cry of the geese, bound for who knows where.'

Sheina glanced up when Ian spoke. She always concentrated on her food at mealtimes, leaving the men to talk. One word from her was enough to silence their new keeper for the rest of the meal.

He avoided her as if she were some strange animal that he was afraid might turn on him and rend him. Her father was taciturn but Ian was so shy that even being in the same room as him made her feel uneasy.

He was glad to escape from their company

and be alone again.

'Give him time,' Alastair said when Sheina commented on his behaviour. 'He had no mother and grew up with six men. Like growing up in a monastery. His father never took him anywhere.'

'He must have met people who came to shoot,' she said.

'I would rather think he took care to be well in the background and meet no one on those days,' Alastair said. 'Like you, he has two minds about the killing.'

He was busy cleaning his gun.

Sheina, equally busy at the sink, turned to look at him, the tea towel in her hand.

'He talks to you.'

'Only if I ask questions when we're on night patrol.'

Poachers were a constant threat and no one sensible ever went out alone at night. Sheina often did, but she was sure she could remain hidden. She had learned woodcraft from a master. She took care that her father did not know of her forays. There was more to see at night.

Ian was daily discovering a new world, so far from his placid homeland.

There was nothing there that could equal the plunge of the peregrine from the sky as he saw his prey; the flash of a deer as it raced through the trees, the lifted head and huge antlers of a wary stag, sniffing the air for news of danger. Nothing matched the dive of the eagle, shooting down the sky, in urgent search of food for himself and his mate. Nothing rivalled the lochs covered with wild duck that flew in at night, and then went off in the early dawn for some other destination.

He loved the spring and the sudden glut of young. Foxes might be his enemies, but the cubs enchanted him, as did the sight of a doe with her fawn. He could never put any of his feelings into words, though at times he longed to share them. He did not realise that the way he worked and the way he handled animals told his employer all he needed to know. The animals were his own, to be treasured as much as any family pet, and anything that threatened them threatened him.

Alastair was delighted to have a man with such passion. Sheina was less enchanted. She had hoped that, given the lack of candidates when the job was advertised, her father would let her achieve her ambition to follow in his wake. He, like Ian's father, saw no future in gamekeeping. At times he wished his daughter far away. She was too like her dead mother, reminding him of her with every turn of the head and every sudden smile.

He still missed Morag desperately, although it was now over eighteen months since her death. Cancer took so many

21

victims and she had delayed asking for help. A strong woman, impatient of illness in herself or others, she had never complained when ill but often carried on beyond all sense. It was a trait he now cursed daily. If she had only come to me a year before, the doctor said. It was an unhappy epitaph.

Sheina grieved by herself. Her father was unable to show his feelings and she was sure he did not care. She never guessed at the tortured thoughts that he held inside him. She knew nothing of the long sleepless hours when he tried in vain not to rethink the past and give it a different ending. He couldn't speak of the nights when his wife's name drummed in his head as he called her back to him in his dreams.

Morag. Morag. Morag.

He heard it in the wind and in the long calls of the hooting owls. He heard it in the rustling branches of the trees, and the sighing of the waves as they broke at the edge of the loch.

If only he had noticed and persuaded her to see the doctor. She had hidden her pain until it became unbearable. She thought it indigestion and simply took over-the-counter remedies.

It had been a good marriage and he only realised that now, when it was too late. Worse, he himself was not feeling well, and was doing his best to pretend there was nothing wrong with him. He hated doctors. They had not saved Morag, nor diagnosed her illness when it might have been possible to cure her. But it was difficult to ignore the fact that distances seemed longer, hills were steeper and everything he did left him weary.

Maybe it was just the effort of trying to keep up with Ian, who was less than half his age and had more energy than any man he had met before. Maybe it was a sign of growing older and nothing else. He was becoming cantankerous, and was aware of it, but seemed unable to help himself.

He knew that Sheina thought him cold and unloving. She missed her mother terribly. Morag had been warm and outgoing, a woman full of hugs for her family, quick to comfort anyone she thought was troubled. They had had visitors before she died. Nobody came now. Her father's brusque manner alienated them.

Sheina was sure he wanted to be rid of her. She was unaware that it was her future that worried him. He had nothing to leave her. Their home was rented, his salary barely adequate for their needs. If anything happened to him the syndicate would never employ a woman.

He had not told his daughter that he had suggested to the syndicate that she took Ian's post when it had fallen vacant. She was as good as any man and a far better shot than some. Their representative had made it very clear that that was not an option.

She never met any man who she might grow to love and marry. Ian had no prospects and was scared of women.

There was no future here and what else could she do?

At times he felt the world was unbearable.

'You should get yourself to university,' he told her. 'You have the Highers. You did well. Your head teacher thought you ought to get a degree.'

He felt guilty because Sheina had given up the idea of higher education to look after her mother. They had endured those last agonising months together. Morag had never complained and had worked until she was too weak to do so.

Alastair now said repeatedly, 'You need a good job with prospects. There's none here. If they stop shooting as well as hunting our way of life will end.'

'And the wilderness will come back,' Sheina said. 'Nobody seems to understand that the farms and estates of the countryside are what keep it as a pleasing playground for city people. It would go back to scrub and forest, and become impenetrable.'

It was an old grievance.

Sheina, like Ian, was passionate about the countryside. She thought she might, one day, work in conservation, but just now she

24

had all she wanted. She would not have gone to university even if her mother had lived. Now her father needed her to keep his home clean, to make meals for him and for Ian, and also provide food when the syndicate members came to shoot.

'There's rumours of the syndicate selling up. I canna think who to,' Alastair said one night. 'Then we'll be out of a home. I wish you would think about that degree.'

Sheina stared at him in dismay. Micklemoor House was her reason for staying. Without it, they would be rootless. And she could never live in a town.

That night she lay awake, fretting. Nothing had gone right since her mother died. She watched the moon chased by clouds. A calling owl was answered by his mate. Far away she heard a sound like a fighting cat, and wondered. Her father had killed a wildcat last year and driven its mate away. He had battled with them all his life. She did not want them to come back. It would be a death warrant.

Alastair was merciless when his grouse were threatened, and man-made laws did not stop him from killing the predators.

It was a very long time before she slept and then she dreamed that she had come home to a deserted house and was walking through its rooms calling for her mother.

Nobody answered.

Two

Micklemoor House had once been a duke's shooting lodge. Built of grey stone, it had been elegant, but time and lack of money had robbed it of its grace.

Then it was bought and the syndicate converted one end of it into a flat for the head keeper. The old keeper's cottage was sold. It was to be a weekend home for a rich city stockbroker and his family.

Alastair and Sheina lived in just six of the twenty rooms in one wing of the almost derelict mansion. There were times when Sheina, returning after one of her night-time forays, persuaded herself she saw ghosts walking on the ruined terrace.

Though the kitchen and bathroom had been modernised, the water for washing came from the loch. They were inland, far from the sea. Their rare visitors were entertained by a sieve attached to the cold taps that caught prawns and shrimps and tadpoles and some odd-looking creatures that were faithfully returned to their homes.

Drinking water came from a well fed by an

underground spring that would, the authorities said, be good enough to bottle. Nobody had time to explore that road.

Owls nested in the rafters and bats roosted in the rest of the building. That was open to the sky. The elegant rooms and the entertaining were now dim memories in the minds of the older members of the village.

'People miss those days,' Mairi McLeod, their nearest neighbour, told Sheina when she visited the old lady, longing for female conversation. Mairi was rumoured to be over ninety and most certainly was over eighty but was as active as many a younger woman. She had trained in both herbalism and homeopathy and her ugly little cottage was a focus for half the village, who came for healing remedies, for her ever-ready comfort, and her wonderful cakes and biscuits, which were sold by the local baker. Hector McCann was a dour man who made nothing but bread, but was glad to have the extra attraction in the little shop that adjoined the bakehouse.

His vast ancient stone oven, with the fire burning underneath, was never let out night or day and was a tourist attraction. On Sundays the older villagers brought their roasts to cook there, saving their own fuel. They also used Hector's oven when the power supply failed, as it often did in stormy or snowy weather.

Sheina called on Mairi, with whom Ian lodged, once a week, using her home as a refuge after putting fresh flowers on her mother's grave. Beulah, her spaniel, knew the routine and headed there immediately her mistress had finished her task.

Few visited the little cemetery now. Her mother had been one of the last to be buried there. There was no minister for the kirk. Three villages shared one man.

Mairi, like Alastair, had her own regrets.

'They say folk are better off now,' she said one morning, bringing out home-made lemonade and flapjacks that melted in the mouth. Though the outside of the cottage was stark, inside was bright with knitted throws, embroidered cushions and rainbow-coloured rag rugs. She had a vast collection of small model animals given her by grateful clients. An Arab horse occupied the centre of the mantelpiece, flanked by a number of owls.

'Folk are worse off and it's an uncaring world, whatever they pretend. Basic pensions are a pittance and you have to find all you need from them. When the Family lived there, folk were well looked after. We often had grouse and salmon and venison given to us.'

Mairi sighed, looking back over more years than she cared to count.

'If we were ill, there was always food sent

until we were well enough to manage for ourselves. When we retired, there was always food from the Big House, and they saw we lived well enough on our pensions. Not like now. Nobody cares.'

Mairi's mother had been cook in those long-ago days, and the old woman had many tips for Sheina. Morag McNeill had also taught her daughter how to make the game pies and the soups and sandwiches for which she had been famous. Nobody else could do it as well and it was part of her father's reputation that he provided splendid meals as well as one of the best days out for those who came to shoot.

Sheina had once thought she might take up cooking as a profession but the thought of working in hotels or restaurants daunted her. So many other people. So much noise and bustle and rush. She loved the wild too much to give it up unless forced. The thought of leaving Micklemoor hung over her like a giant black cloud, spoiling enjoyment.

'You can manage?' Sheina asked, suddenly afraid the old lady was short of money, and hoping the question would not give offence.

'Aye. I always was a saving body. I was thinking of those in the village. Their young canna look after them as they need money for their bairns, and the social may make up the pension with this and that, but it doesna cover food and clothes and heating, so there's little to spare for wee gifties to the grandchildren. It's not a dignified life. Folk feel it's charity.'

Sheina helped herself to another flapjack, wondering just who Mairi had in mind. People put a brave face on their difficulties.

'I do have good news. I've a buyer for the last of Gwen's pups,' Mairi said, knowing that the puppy money comprised almost all of Sheina's income. At twenty she could be earning a great deal more in a city job. As Micklemoor House was so isolated and visitors rare, Mairi took the pups when they were six weeks old to ensure that they met all kinds of people and visited all kinds of places.

Her fee was one puppy, as it was a very valuable service. She never took it until the last was sold.

Sheina now bred the springer spaniels and Labradors for which her father was renowned. The Micklemoor lines were coveted by those who knew their dogs. At £500 a puppy the income was very useful, but they only had one litter a year.

Gwen had produced eight pups last time. Money in the bank for Sheina to spend as she chose. She hated asking her father when she needed cash. There was little enough over when all the necessary bills had been paid. They had lived rent-free under the old laird.

'The syndicate give with one mean hand and take away generously with the other,' Alastair commented when they sent him the first demand for the rent, asking him to pay quarterly.

The sturdy fell ponies, fortunately, were considered a necessary part of the business, as they carried down the shot deer. Their keep was assured, and all other expenses. Which was as well, as they were geniuses at presenting vet bills. A turned hoof, resulting in lameness, was so easy on these rough hills.

The ponies were also Sheina's responsibility and she thought of them as hers. Dainty black Corrie, who spooked at paper bags, was her favourite. She played up when the men groomed her but stood still for Sheina.

Bracken, their second pony, the colour of the fern in the autumn, was expecting a foal early in August. It was the first ever, and it had taken Sheina four years to persuade her father to buy a mare young enough to breed. The syndicate had agreed, since Corrie was old and would be retired within a year or so.

Sheina had schooled the third pony, Tarn, herself, and taught him to suffer the deer that were loaded on to his back. They were her family.

If they had to leave here the ponies would be sold. Sheina could not bear the thought of missing the birth or the growing up. The foal, like the mare, was syndicate property but at least she would have the fun of watching it grow up. If they did not have to move.

She sat on the wall outside the stable the day after that on which she first heard they might lose their home. Bracken nosed her shoulder. Ian had seen a dying stag high on the hill and the two men had taken Alastair's dog Bosun to help track him so that they could put him out of his pain.

Sheina hated the killing, but it was necessary. She had never forgotten walking by herself down the glen and finding an old stag who lay, too weak to rise, too weak to eat with his rotting teeth, his eyes pecked out by crows, but still alive. The memory returned to haunt her.

She had been ten years old. She ran home crying. Alastair took his gun and put the old warrior out of his misery.

'He's at peace now,' he said, comforting her, when he came home. She wanted a funeral and they buried the stag and put a cross on top and her father said a prayer.

That day remained memorable. In the evening her mother had brought out an old book of poems, once the property of her own mother. It was well read and falling apart.

Sheina could still hear her voice, feel her strength as she sat cuddled up against her.

Her father listened too. It was a late autumn evening, the chill in the air and the quiet punctuated by the impatient stags, challenging for territory.

'They all come to the same end,' her mother said. 'Nothing alive can escape it.' She stroked the book. 'This is a very long poem. I'm not going to read it all. You can do that for yourself. It's about a bull, not a stag. But the story is the same for both.'

She began to read. Even the Labrador at her father's feet seemed to be listening. Sailor, Bosun's father, was old and privileged to sleep indoors and live in the house. He too was failing. He died two months after Morag, adding a further blow for her daughter and husband. The dog had been part of the family for fifteen years. Alastair was determined not to get so fond of any of his other animals.

Sheina thought often of that night, of her mother's soft voice, of the shadowy room, lit only by the glow from the burning logs.

'Dreaming, this old bull forlorn,
Surely dreaming of the hour
When he came to sultan power
And they owned him master-horn
Chiefest bull of all among
Bulls and cows one thousand strong...'

He had been young once, that sad old warrior, lying alone and forgotten by the other deer. The small girl thought life very cruel. Why did everything have to die? She had lost her three remaining grandparents in the previous two years. She wondered often where they had gone. How could people who had been alive and vital suddenly just not be there? They had to have gone somewhere. They could not just cease to exist.

Her mother's arms tightened round her. That night would be a memory to treasure.

A log slipped in the hearth. The fire always seemed to Sheina a symbol of contentment. She loved the flickering shadows in the room when the lights were off, as they often were to rest the noisy generator. Oil lamps lent a serenity that was lacking with electricity. They changed a few years later to butane gas which was quieter.

Alastair had been a much easier man to live with then. He had taken up the story and told her of the stag's life. Of the tiny calf born on the hill, who grew to power, and became a magnificent animal, bearing his huge head proudly, defying his rivals.

Her father told her how that young beast had become master of the herd until another stag ousted him. He was the biggest of them all, with the most massive antlers, well worthy of his place as Monarch of the Glen.

That picture had pride of place above their mantelshelf. As a small girl Sheina loved to curl up on the battered old settee and look at it, savouring it, drawn into the scene of wildness and magnificence.

The autumn roaring was part of their lives. The air was filled with excitement, with the challenges and the rage of the great beasts. Sometimes they heard the clash of antlers as the huge stags fought for the chance to produce a future generation.

The patient hinds waited, mild-eyed, for their lords to come and claim them. The old great-grandmother, barren now, watched over the herd and stamped a warning if danger threatened.

Sheina listened, loving the stories of the wild animals about them. Sailor yawned and eased into a more comfortable position, revelling in the warmth of the fire. He tucked his black head under his tail, dreaming away his last few months. He had puppy days to remember, days of walking the hills, days of pride when a bitch was brought to him.

He had joined so many others, buried in the tiny graveyard at the edge of the wood where neat crosses bore the names of all those long-lost and much-loved dogs.

Her mother began to read again.

'Pity him this dupe of dream,
Leader of his herd again
Only in his daft old brain.
Once again the bull supreme
And bull enough to bear the part
Only in his tameless heart.'

Sheina felt safe, tucked up between her parents on the settee.

'So many sons and daughters keep his memory alive,' Alastair said. 'Now he's gone where all of us go and all the beasts as well, to a world where he's young again, and proud again, and not a feeble creature, slowly losing all that once made him so great.'

Between them her parents had exorcised the memory of the dying beast that had so upset her, fitting him into a scheme that belonged through time immemorial.

Now, when her father seemed a different man, she tried to hold that memory alive. He had loved her once. She had always longed for brothers and sisters and now she did so more than ever. They would have been there to share.

Some of the past keepers had been very young men missing their own families and she had enjoyed their teasing and played football with them. One taught her to sail on the loch. Another taught her to shoot at a target. She took part in clay pigeon shoots and distinguished herself. Nobody ever seemed to remember she was a girl.

In the years that followed she learned that much of her father's work with the deer was saving those who were weak and old from such a fate. It was also necessary to watch for poachers. Alastair was afraid that if Sheina should meet some on her own she would be harmed.

Sheina longed to work with the two men when they were about their business, but her father prevented her, finding her jobs elsewhere. It was bad enough to see her in the evening, when she constantly awoke memories of her mother. He could not bear to have her around him all day, keeping his grief alive.

Sheina felt more and more unwanted. They spoke little, and seemed to grow further away from one another. Often Alastair took his gun and went out into the night, saying there might be poachers about. He came home in the early hours and went to bed to lie awake, listening to owls call and foxes cry. He wished he could follow Morag.

Ian, like Sheina, suffered from Alastair's constant faultfinding. Neither of them realised that frustration at his inability to work as hard as before was making the older man angry. He seemed to be ageing fast and changing almost daily. Ian was worried about him, and confided one evening in Mairi.

'He is missing Morag, his wife,' the old woman said. 'It's only eighteen months since she died.'

She filled Ian's plate with vension stew made from steaks Alastair had given her that she stored in her deep freeze. She was near enough to the village to benefit from the power lines.

'That was a good marriage. Morag could manage him, and keep him sweet. Sheina looks like her mother and that's no help, and a daughter canna comfort her father as a wife can. Bear with him. It should pass.'

She stroked the black cat that had jumped on to her lap, green eyes on her plate, one paw lifted to snatch. She put him down on the ground.

'No, greedy one. You come later,' she said.

There was a long-drawn-out banshee yowl in the air; a spine- prickling sound that made Ian pause with his fork halfway to his mouth. The cat, fur fluffed up, ran to the window, parted the curtains with his paw and looked out, hissing.

'What in the world—?'

'Wildcat,' Mairi said. 'You won't have met them. They seem to come and go around here. She is crying to the moon for her lost mate.'

Ian had heard tales of them and the damage they could wreak on a kept moor. It was spring and there might be kits. It would not help Alastair's temper but he couldn't keep the news to himself. Ian had spent most of his life battling with foxes. This was a new enemy.

He reported the news the next day. Alastair tightened his lips. The cat would have to go. She was too big a threat. A family hunting on his hills was unthinkable.

Sheina saw her first. Her father had forgotten his sandwiches and flask, and she took them up to him. It was a warm day, the spring sun promising heat to come.

Beulah scampered ahead of her, nose down in the new greenery that succeeded the burning off of old growth. Here she ran free, though always quick to respond to a whistle that signalled the need for her to be at heel. She dived into the long grass, which bore memories of a fox that had run through the night before. Following his trail, she found a wonderful smell and rolled in it.

Sheina, who did not like the spaniel out of sight for long, called her back and was rewarded by a greeting from a happily stinking dog that made her catch her breath. She cursed the fox that had led Beulah to such ecstasy; a bath was now needed.

Suddenly the dog stiffened and Sheina followed the line of her focused eyes.

The cat, high above them, was tearing at her latest victim. She was alerted by their scent, borne on a fitful breeze that constantly changed direction. The mountains caused eddies and air currents that seemed to have no reason or sense, and made stalking difficult.

The wildcat was basking in the first spring sunshine, appreciating the warmth after one of the coldest spells of the year. She stood, guarding her kill, as the woman and the dog came into sight.

Sheina caught her breath. The animal was magnificent.

She was an enormous tabby tiger, black stripes vivid against the grey. Her domed head was also striped, her laid-back ears flattened. Her mouth, open in spitting hatred, revealed her red tongue and pointed teeth. The thick striped tail lashed in anger. Glowing eyes glared. She challenged them, arrogant. The grouse lay beneath her bloodied jaws. Her body betrayed the imminence of her kits.

Sheina stood still, her heart racing. For a moment she thought the cat might launch herself down the hillside and attack her or the dog. Beulah could never stand up to such a creature.

There was a swift flash, a hiss of fury, and the cat was gone, taking her booty with her, to eat undisturbed in a safer place. Sheina whistled the spaniel to heel. She did not want the youngster chasing after the wildcat. It would mean certain death.

She decided to keep her discovery secret. If she told Ian and her father, both men would be hunting with their guns, especially as the quarry had been one of their precious grouse. The birds were scarce enough last year, after one of the worst springs in living memory. They hoped for better results this time.

The syndicate was hard to please, its representative without understanding of country ways. He was a surly, fault-finding man who never gave praise. They all dreaded his visits.

It was a day to charm the gods. The sun shone from a bright blue sky. The cat had chosen to eat on cliffs that bordered a mountain burn. White water thundered over black rocks and fell in a sparkling stream into a large pool.

There was no way that Sheina could condemn the cat to death. But, in the next weeks, she could not keep her presence secret. She didn't see her again, but there was evidence of her kills. So many little heaps of tell-tale feathers, blowing in the wind, told their own story to the two men.

Sheina, remembering German lessons at school, christened her Hexa, the witch. She led a charmed life, always evading them. She was swifter than the swooping hawk and

41

twice as cunning as any fox. Ian and Alastair hated her and yet they admired her. Sheina wished her well, but she knew that the two men would be even more determined when they found out Hexa was going to have kittens.

She had a sudden absurd longing to steal one and make it her own. She would have to hide it. Her father would not have cats of any kind, wild or tame, about the place.

Nobody could tame a wildcat kitten, but Sheina was determined to try.

The dogs were aware of the cat at night. They were restless in their kennels, barking and whining, annoying Alastair.

Sheina's second sighting surprised her. It occurred when she was taking flowers to her mother's grave. She had picked a huge sheaf of the daffodils that grew profusely all over their neglected garden.

She did not realise that the wildcat haunted the little cemetery. Few people came there and Hexa felt safe from prying eyes. There was a dry hiding place among the tumbled stones of the old wall that had long fallen into disrepair.

Hexa was now so slow that Sheina saw her as she crept into hiding. Aware that the cat hid in the churchyard, she brought food and left it for her, taking care than nobody saw her.

Mairi too knew that the cat was there and

the two women conspired to keep her fed. If she were not hungry, she would not prey on the grouse.

It was a faint hope. Hexa was ravenous, needing to feed the kits growing inside her. The food left for her was not enough to satisfy her growing appetite, and in any case she had to leave her sanctuary to exercise and find water.

The men patrolled at night, carrying their guns, dogs at heel. Their chief concern was poachers, who were growing bold and came in vans with dogs and guns, and were a threat to those they met.

They watched for the wildcat. Human dwellings offered temptation. There were ducks and chickens. She changed her habits, hunting by day, her need to survive overcoming her nocturnal nature.

Long-legged, bushy-tailed, wide face alert, swift to savagery, ears pricked and green eyes glowing, she was beautiful. Yet she was death on four legs, threatening any small creature that came within her range. She was wicked, a she-devil incarnate in muscled body and tawny fur.

Ian grew to hate her, finding daily evidence of grouse that had died to feed her. His grouse, that he protected, trying not to think of their future as targets for the guns. He saw Hexa once, far below him, as she wandered at the edge of the loch, turning over the seaweed to find food hidden beneath. He did not realise she was about to give birth; she was too far away and he had left his binoculars in the van. He had brought his flask and sandwiches so that he could eat looking out over the loch. It was his favourite view.

Sheina glimpsed Hexa more often and continued to daydream. The wildcat would live and she would study her and her kittens and one day write a book and astound them all. So little was known.

Meanwhile she devoted herself to keeping Hexa fed and safe from Ian and her father, and felt guilty as she did so.

Three

Alastair McNeill had killed her first mate, but Hexa eluded his gun. She was a demon, sent to torment him, a hellcat, possessed of uncanny powers. Sheina and Ian shared their anxiety; he seemed to overreact to almost everything that happened. Mairi, hearing from her lodger about what was now a growing problem, became concerned.

Daily he ranted, his temper growing worse as he found new evidence of the wildcat's hunting. Sheina listened in dismay.

He said it at every meal.

'The hell's spawn must die.'

For much of the time the wildcat haunted the woods and took small birds. Just before the kittens were born she raided the ducks, hunting in daylight. She was slow and clumsy and these were easy pickings.

There were three lakes on the estate, and at times the keepers felt as if every creature in the wild needed little ducks for food. Hawk and owl, weasel and stoat, wildcat and fox all took such toll that few of the broods survived. Even the pike in the lake considered them as bounty, and the bigger ones took the adults too.

A friend in the Lowlands gave Sheina and Alastair two black swans. Hexa took one at dusk and came back next day for her grieving mate.

The gamekeeper found the tell-tale mass of feathers in the morning and swore immediate vengeance. Ian too felt anger. He loved birds of all kinds.

'She's a killer,' he said to Sheina later that day. 'Your father has a point. She needs to be shot. There's no place for her here. I doubt we can drive her away on to the high moors where she'll find other game and leave us in peace.'

Sheina had no intention of letting the men shoot the cat, which she had come to regard as hers. She bitterly regretted the death of the swans. They were lovely creatures, both very tame, coming to her each day for a hand-out of bread. It was hard at times to reconcile the needs of the wildcat with their own needs.

Sheina did not mention that she had seen the killer, or that Hexa was almost certainly due to have kittens, which she intended to tame. They would be fed so that they had no need to kill. She had no intention of allowing the men to destroy a beautiful animal who was only obeying her own wild nature.

Surely wildcats were protected by law.

Birds of prey certainly were, though there were keepers who had accidents. When the needs of the predators became excessive, the birds on the estates suffered. Nature was not always well balanced.

Hexa was worried by the presence of the two women who came to tend the graves each week. In spite of the food they left, she found herself another home.

Sheina looked for the new den. She found it by accident one day, at the edge of the woods, in a converted earth abandoned long ago by a fox. Relentless hunting had driven him to seek a new home.

She began again to leave food nearby. She took care that no one saw her.

With only a few days to go until the birth, Hexa's hunting was often unrewarded. The bounty brought her kept her strong. She only moved when evening spilled its shade. Mouse and beetle and earthworm gave little comfort to a craving appetite.

She ate the food left under the bushes, although it was tainted, smelling of man. Sheina brought all the leftovers, taking care to cook more than was needed. Some she took from their store, hoping no one would notice. The cooking was left entirely to her, as was the shopping, and her father was too obsessed with the need to kill Hexa to notice bigger bills for food.

She did not enjoy her shopping trips. She

had no friends of her own age and the bustle and noise reminded her of schooldays, which she preferred to forget. Home had been a sanctuary and she could not wait for the end of each day. The other girls did not understand her and many were cruel.

She had felt so alone. Her classmates were unaware of the simplest things. How could anyone not know that the hare dropped her leverets in several different places, far apart, and left them alone, to make it less likely that all would be killed by other animals?

Nobody shared her excitement when she watched eagles courting, cutting through the sky, swooping and soaring, the great wings beating the air as they sped towards one another and then chased away.

In those long-ago days she was always out with her father. If he had time he went fishing. Those days were rare and were holidays. They took a picnic and she and her mother sat by the river bank, enticing the little ducks to come to them for crumbs. They tamed the wild foals. Sheina learned that if she stayed as still as the trees themselves, they came and investigated her.

She loved watching the herons standing immobile in the water, watching intently till, with sudden movement, the fierce beak speared its quarry and the bird ate.

Once, on holiday, around her fourteenth birthday, her father went mackerel fishing in a sea loch. He hired a small boat but she and her mother remained on shore. Morag wanted to explore the town, a rare treat for her. Even then Sheina hated shopping.

The sea loch was very different to their own inland waters and she wanted to savour every moment. Small waves lapped against the land, bearing immense bounty. Orange seaweed coloured the shore, lying in wild tangles.

She found an entire sea urchin. There were fan shells, glittering in the sun, and turret shells, tiny and perfect. She loved the intricate shapes and the delicate colours that were brought to life when they were dipped in the sea. She held a rainbow in her hand.

The tide was on the turn, leaving a few feet of sand. She rounded a corner. There was a family of herons fishing in the creaming waves that broke round their long legs. Out in the loch the mackerel were shoaling, feasting on every creature they could find. The small fry fled to the edge of the water, straight into the jaws of the herons.

The young birds were entranced. They were miniatures of their parents, half the size, and had not yet gained the handsome grey and white adult plumage. Never had food been so easy to find. Never had such a feast presented itself. Excitement mastered them. The slim beaks dipped and grabbed and ate until they were over-full. Even then they could not give up fishing. Each bird had beside it a pile of glittering scales.

As dusk approached the parent birds flew towards the heronry on the other side of the loch. Their offspring were too engrossed to follow. The parents called without result. They flew on, still calling.

The youngsters could not leave their feasting.

Sheina watched them, highly entertained, as the parents turned back. On their arrival both disobedient youngsters were buffeted with wing and beak until they reluctantly left their trophies and flapped heavily across the loch. They had eaten so much that Sheina thought they would fall out of the sky, but they managed to fly safely back to their nest. She watched them through the binoculars she had persuaded her father to lend her.

There was a big heronry, she discovered, with nests in the trees, and on each nest birds sat with their wings covering their young. Some of the necks stood up like thin branches. She had never seen so many birds in one place.

When she reached their tent, which was on a farm near the sea, her mother was already cooking mackerel. She entertained her parents with her description of the small birds and their fascination with the teeming fry.

When term began her class was set an essay. They were to write about an event that occurred during the holiday. She achieved an A+, and was asked to read her story aloud. It was unique but she was aware, even as she read, that it did not interest any of the other children. There were sighs and whispers and fidgeting.

Many had travelled abroad, and had stories to tell of air trips and hotels. Of meals eaten out and dances and discos. They described new clothes. They had new boyfriends.

Afterwards in the playground one of the girls in her class came up to her.

'You know what, Sheina McNeill. You're nuts.'

Few lessons interested Sheina. The teachers themselves were mostly city-bred, but her English teacher loved the wild hills and the beauty of the world around her. She shared Morag McNeill's love of poetry. She was entranced by the wizardry of words that could describe a sunset or bring a deer, running on the hill, to instant life.

Sheina did not make any real friends. The other girls seemed only interested in clothes and boys and make-up, and the lives of their heroes. Sheina found it all pointless and sordid. At first the boys teased her mercilessly. She learned to say nothing and stare at them in silence with a stony face. This they found so daunting that they gave up.

She had an unusual face, far short of beauty, but it arrested many adults when they saw her for the first time. Rich copper-coloured hair contrasted with dark brown eyes, inherited from her father, and black lashes and eyebrows. Her manner and her appearance combined to put off the boys, they were attracted by more conventional looks.

Her shopping trips, which for the first part of the day were a change and an escape, invariably brought her younger days back to her. She could not wait to escape and drive home. She longed for solitude, and for Ian and her father, both of whom were able to talk about the things she loved.

By the end of the day she was tired of the busy crowds. She was not used to so many people and felt threatened, although everyone ignored her. She did not relax until she saw the distant hills and knew she was nearing home.

She needed the high peaks and the heather, the grouse moors and the lakes. If she were lucky, while driving, she might glimpse deer at the edge of the woods, or a hare bounding across a field. She could never live in a town.

She treasured each sign of spring. She revelled in the first snowdrops, nodding under the hedges; in the bright golden flare of the first crocuses in the tiny garden she and her mother had made together. She watched for the deep purple dwarf irises that speared bravely in the wind. They had been her mother's favourite flowers and while they bloomed she made tiny posies to carry to the kirkyard and perpetuate the memory.

They grew in the little walled garden that Alastair had made for his wife to celebrate their fifteenth wedding anniversary. The red bricks held the heat from the sun and kept even fragile flowers safe. Sheina cherished the garden still, taking time that should have been spent on other chores.

Then came the daffodils. When she was a tiny girl she and Morag spent afternoons planting bulbs all around the house and in the woods. They had spread until great masses welcomed the day with their vivid flowers, flirting with the wind.

Sheina and her mother picked huge bunches. They flaunted in the dark corners of the house. Then came the bluebells. As yet nobody had rifled the woods and here there were seas of blue, the flowers growing so close it was impossible not to trample them when she and the men walked among the trees.

She thought the kittens would be born as the first bluebells opened their buds. She spent much of her allowance on extra food for Hexa. She felt as if the cat were her own, a creature to be cherished, even if she could not catch her. She rarely caught more than a glimpse of tabby fur.

Such an animal should not be tamed. She belonged to the wilderness. Man did not. What right had humans to covet the world and desecrate the wild places?

Beulah always accompanied Sheina in the old Discovery on her trips to the town. The little bitch wore a dog car harness to keep her safe. She loved to sit on the front passenger seat and look through the windows, often alerting her mistress to something she had not seen for herself.

Twice during these journeys, once at the end of March and again in mid-April, Beulah gave her excited soft yelp. Each time Sheina, braking, saw the wildcat. Hexa was prowling.

The sun of a late April day slid behind the peaks and darkness ate up the world. That night was wicked with cold, a late frost silvering grass and trees. Hexa was racked by pain. Pain that made her gasp and wail as the first kitten fought his way to life.

She looked down at the tiny creature lying beside her. Memory flooded her mind and she began to lick him. She had to massage him to warmth with her tongue to encourage the wee creature to breathe, to cuddle him close so that he could find his goal and suck strength into his body.

When a grey dawn revealed the small leafed trees, there were three sturdy kittens lying against her, burrowing into her body, taking warmth from her dense fur. Their eyes were closed and their minute pads, like their noses, were pink. Later they would be as dark as their mother. Both blind and deaf, they were safe in the deep underground, away from prying eyes.

She licked each small body, removing all traces of the birth. She stretched luxuriously as they sucked. She washed them devotedly, forcing them to excrete. They needed her massaging tongue. She tucked herself round them, relaxed and warm, sheltering them from the wind and the slash of rain that crept into the hole.

She savoured the taste of them, the sight of them, the sound of them. She watched each movement, overcome with a passion she had forgotten. Her first litter had not survived long enough to trigger this wild delight.

She purred softly. Small paws padded against her. Tiny mouths drew strength from her. Mairi's herbs and vitamins and Sheina's food had produced very healthy little animals and also ensured a plentiful supply of milk.

As yet, blind and deaf, they did little but feed and sleep. Two weeks later, they opened their eyes. They saw the strange world about them, and soon could hear sounds, some of which startled them so that they jumped and burrowed close into Hexa's deep fur.

Sheina's bounty ensured that the wildcat did not need to leave her family for more than a few moments. She was aware of enemies everywhere. She needed to guard her little family well and teach them how to survive.

The cold weather had gone. The sun shone and warm winds from the south brought rapid growth to the newly opened leaves, brought a flush of bright flowers to the woodlands, brought new heather to cover the burned ground. The now defenceless stags sought solitude in the high hills. They were careful of the sensitive velvet that covered their budding antlers. It would take all summer for regrowth. The young of other creatures found the cast horns and took them as trophies and pleasant objects to chew.

The hinds, now giving birth, were wary. The little ones played, butting and bounding, overcome with the joy of living.

The kittens were growing fast. Their newly opened eyes were a vivid blue. They were quick to spit and hiss if something alarmed them. They also cried for their mother if she went out of sight, however briefly. She answered them, a reassuring mew, which quietened them. Others heard and knew there was bounty. They were never left alone for long. The patient watchers knew that

Hexa was a formidable enemy.

The kits began to move about, on unsteady legs that often betrayed them but that grew stronger daily. There were two females, one gentle and biddable, one who was bolder. She was the strongest and soon made the others do as she wished.

Hers was the teat that gave most milk, and she pushed her litter mates away. If they did not move she used her sharp teeth to make them obey. She had the right to greet her mother before the others.

The little male was born with deep curiosity and a longing to explore. Even when he could just crawl, he went too far from the nest. Hexa was forever lifting him, protesting, in her jaws and carrying him back to dump him beside his sisters. He fought her with kitten anger that could never prevail. When they were safe together again he burrowed deep into her fur, looking for comfort, and patted her with gentle paws as she nuzzled him.

Sheina continued to provide for them, but more was needed. The kits would soon have to learn to hunt for themselves and for that live creatures must be brought back to the nest. Hexa began to forage again.

One night, when the moon was a slip of its former self, painted on a midnight sky, she left her new family briefly. A pool of fresh water had collected in the rocks around the tree roots. She drank thirstily.

There was half a cooked chicken in the hollow where Sheina put food.

Hexa picked it up, intending to take it into her den to eat. A faint but urgent sound reached her; the mew of a frightened kitten calling her home. She dropped the bounty and raced to her nest.

The two little females were crouched, fur fluffed, hissing and spitting. A surprised intruder faced her, the third kitten in her jaws. The watching weasel knew the kits had been born. She had seen the wildcat leave the lair. She had young of her own to feed.

Hexa sprang, snarling. The weasel dropped her trophy and fled, one ear bleeding, her shoulder slashed deep by a raking paw. She knew she could not fight this furious tornado of protective mother love.

Their home was no longer safe. Hexa needed to find sanctuary elsewhere.

The rescued kitten had teeth marks on his neck. She let him feed, then picked him up by his scruff and left her den. He shifted his head, whimpering with discomfort. Owing to his own curiosity he was used to this mode of travel but he did not like it.

Urgency mastered the wildcat. She was hungry but she forgot the abandoned food. She needed somewhere hidden, somewhere much safer than this invaded lair. Where one had come, there would be others soon.

Shadowy clouds hid the moon and rain threatened. Hexa began to climb.

The small weight hampered her. She was anxious to hurry, in case the weasel returned for another kitten. She crossed a tiny stream, using the stepping stones that humans had laid for their own convenience.

She reached the edge of a foothill, covered in bramble and brush and heather, a few sparse pines straggling in undergrowth that choked them. Few humans ever came here. The burn slid across the rocky flank, where the earth was thin and sandy, and trickled over lichened rocks. Above them was a small cave, the floor covered in fallen leaves blown in by the wind.

She laid her firstborn gently behind a boulder that blocked the entrance. She could leap it, but her son's lack of strength would not allow him to stray. It would be at least two weeks before the kits had the power to climb out of their new home.

She left him, trusting his safety from those who could climb the rock to the brambles through which she had pushed her way and the loss of scent where she had walked through water.

He whimpered, alone and afraid, thinking he had been abandoned in this strange place with its unfamiliar smells. He was cold and needed the warmth of his mother and sisters. The bitten area on his back hurt. He curled up small and cried softly to himself.

Fear walked beside Hexa as she fled down the hill, desperate to move the rest of her family.

Four

The moon was an enemy, revealing Hexa to any prying eyes. The path she chose was tortuous, hiding her and her burdens. Though small, they were heavy and she had to stop often, to listen and to test the wind for the scent of would-be attackers.

Hunger tormented her, as did her overflowing milk. Yet she dared not rest long enough for the kits to suckle and bring her relief. She had moved two of her babies and was carrying the third when she heard the thunder of human boots on the vibrating ground and the pad, pad, pad and pant of two dogs.

They were very close. If they caught her scent, or that of the two she had already hidden, they would bring instant death to her newborn.

She was lucky. The two men, who had driven from the city, were looking for deer, not for wildcats. They were trying to walk silently, unaware of the sensitive ears that could catch the sound of a beetle stroking one leg against another.

61

The wind was kind and blew their scent to her. They passed on. Not even the dogs caught a whiff of her. Hexa crouched flat against the ground, hardly daring to breathe. The kitten was silent too. One mew would alert them.

When they had gone she ran fast, afraid that her other kits would betray their new nursery, calling out for her, hungry for milk. She was hindered by last year's untidy heather, which no one had burned off. Her fur was caught by thick brambles. She had to climb the uneven rocks littering the hillside, tumbled there by a past landslide.

Once she froze at the sound of a big body moving over the ground. The stag paused and stared at her. His size intimidated her. He snorted, kicked up his hind hooves and was away. With his new antlers as yet only irritating buds, he felt vulnerable.

Finally she was safe, all her kittens cuddled close. She licked each one, and fed them, purring. She curled around them, her body relaxed and warm, sheltering them from an intrusive wind that whispered its way into her hiding place. She lay near the entrance, ever watchful.

The boulder that prevented the kits from climbing out gave her a sense of security. She relaxed, allowing herself to purr softly. She washed each kitten devotedly, savouring their small warmth. They fed and slept. They were full and comfortable. She was aware of their breathing, of the murmurs each made, of the minute paws that stretched and pushed against her as they moved in their sleep. She looked at them with proud eyes.

This was why she had been born. This was her birthright.

A young moon silvered the water and cast long shadows that worried her. They moved as the branches moved. There were sounds she could not identify. Any noise might be a danger, alerting an enemy. She had never before heard the far away rumble of thunder. Nor had she previously seen the lightning zig that flashed across the sky, terrifying her.

The storm muttered in the clouds, but died away leaving only rain and hail. The cave reached back into the rocks, and she shifted herself and the kittens out of the flailing stones that stung her face. She did not want to leave them, even briefly, but she needed food to enable her to rear them. She needed water to drink.

She was aware of other creatures nearby. Some would provide her with the strength she needed. For the moment she needed to rest. The kittens were heavy – the way to their new home had been difficult – and she was exhausted. Her jaws ached; they had been awkward burdens. Hunger had to wait.

She slept on and off all day. The kits woke and fed and she cleaned them. They slept and woke again. Hexa too woke, to a raging hunger that could not be denied. She left her new lair just before dusk and the wakeful birds called an urgent warning.

Cat! Cat! Cat!

It spread from tree to bush to tree, preceding her. Chatter and caw and angry chirrups alerted the hill and fear and anger stalked before her. Small beasts hidden in the undergrowth froze, feigning death. A tiny mouse, caught in the open, scurried to hide beneath a leaf.

The bird calls became more insistent, alerting every creature on the hill to her presence. They preceded her, picked up by those in the distance. They had not yet seen her but her coming was predicted as the cries were broadcast.

She is here, cried a hidden watcher, high in the dead pine that lightning had struck the year before.

She is coming, called another, and the mice hid.

She is near. She is passing through the bushes. There was now a chorus.

Watch out.

Hexa crept on, using the dense undergrowth to give her cover.

Rabbits heard the warning and thumped on the ground, fleeing so that nothing was there when she arrived. Only the tantalising scent and the memory remained.

Murder has come, the birds called. Even the grazing hinds vanished, terrified by the wildcat and the ·size of her, knowing that their own young, if weak, would become her prey.

A small bird fluttered from a bush, unaware that she was close. She slashed him out of the air. She crouched and fed, a morsel to fill the enormous hunger that now urged her to find larger prey.

A stoat met her in the half-light, hissed and swiftly vanished. She had no ill intentions towards him. He could inflict a nasty wound. She tested the wind and stalked towards a small group of young rabbits that were unaware of her presence and had not heeded the warning given by their elders.

Her swift pounce ended life for one of the disobedient. She fed and returned to her young. Soon all were feeding.

They grew, and the world behind the boulder ceased to be enough for them. Small legs might not jump, but they could clamber, and they wanted to see the world around them. As week succeeded week, Hexa began to feel more secure.

There was food in plenty, and she had regained her former skill. She watched her small family learn how to hunt. Their world was one· of wild excitement. Movement stimulated them and they reacted quickly to the twitch of a tail, the bowing of a grass stem, the run of a beetle along the leafy trails between the new seedlings.

Their unsteady legs betrayed them when they tried to pounce and ended in a tumble. If they were near one another this ended in a mock battle, patting with inexpert paws, twisting and turning, till Hexa stopped the play lest they alert all the creatures round them.

When she was sure all was quiet she rolled on to her back, exposing her soft underparts to the sun, basking in warmth. Nobody seeing her now would believe that she could turn in an instant into a raging fury, ready to defend herself and her young with her life.

They were shielded from prying eyes, and the heat tempted her, so that they spent part of each day in the sunshine on the little plateau. They learned the sounds of the wild: the soft whisper of running water in the distance, the calls of the birds, the hoot of the owl calling to his mate. If these changed, the cries turning to alarm and becoming urgent, then they ran for shelter, now leaping the boulder, to reach the den behind it.

All three now were becoming wary, learning from their mother. Any unexpected sound was greeted with a hiss. They fluffed their fur so that they appeared to be far bigger than they were.

The little male was Hexa's torment, as he forgot his lessons and was apt to wander.

She was forever tracking him, answering his sudden terrified cry, and carrying him back to the nest, protesting. In spite of his adventurousness, when he found himself alone and had forgotten the way home, he was always frightened and sent out an urgent distress signal. Hexa was afraid this would bring new enemies.

On one of his forays he came face to face with a tiny roe deer, lying in the bracken. The little animal, only a few hours old, stared at him. He had no idea that it could be food and, curious, nosed it. The nearby hind stamped her hoof in anger, butting her baby away from danger.

She was immense and the kitten bolted, calling urgently for rescue. Hexa, when she found him, had no idea what had so alarmed him. He kept close to base for several days after that.

His mother was busier than ever. It was time to wean her young and teach them how to hunt for themselves.

Sheina, finding the wildcat had moved yet again, spent the next week exploring, hoping to find out where Hexa's new lair was. She took food with her, but there was no trace.

Spring had brought so many new babies. She discovered a litter of foxes down by the stream and crept out at night, watching the cubs, now five weeks old, playing in the moonlight.

Dainty and kittenlike, they pounced and tugged and wrestled, chased shadows and teased at long grasses. One found a quill feather and carried it everywhere he went, defying his litter mates to take it from him.

She told no one of their presence. Her father would not tolerate them near his birds. She brought food for the vixen in the hope that it would stop her from hunting.

Once, while hiding as the cubs played, she saw three men with dogs climbing the steep hillside below her. The vixen heard them and hissed a warning. The cubs vanished, leaving an empty clearing and a lone feather that blew in the wind.

Ian and Alastair were patrolling. Sheina was hidden, high above all of them, but moonlight revealed their presence.

One of the intruders spotted the game-keepers as they came over the hill. Both men carried guns. The invaders were unarmed. They vanished into the darkness, not wanting a confrontation. A few minutes later the sound of their van, driving away, echoed on the night air. It had been well hidden and nobody was near enough to either see the colour or get the number. It was a still night and sound carried over a distance. Its head-lights did not come on until it was on the road that hugged the loch edge, well away from the scene of their projected crime.

Sheina hurried home, anxious not to be discovered.

Only five nights before Alastair and Ian had found a badger that had been killed by dogs. With dog fighting banned, the baiters came at night to look for other sport. The estate was far too big for two men to patrol efficiently, but Ian wished he could have caught the men and given them a taste of suffering. The need to obey the law was at times a penance. Why should men like this get away with such actions and be treated with respect after inflicting such cruelty on an innocent beast?

'They say the law is an ass,' Alastair said when Ian voiced this opinion. They sat over coffee. Sheina had just had time to make it before their return. 'Most asses have a great deal more sense than the lawmakers.'

Sheina spent most of the next weeks night-hunting for Hexa. There was no sign of the wildcat and her family. She began to fear that the men had found her and killed her and her kittens. She took care to walk warily and hide at the slightest noise, though often it was only an animal rustling in the leaves as it hunted for food, or one of the big stags passing on his way to find new grazing. They were swift to flee if they saw or scented her.

She had her own small adventures, some of which were more alarming than others. One night, walking along a tiny track, well hidden by overshadowing trees, something walked beside her in the bushes. Whatever it was kept pace with her, not troubling to be silent. The path she was on was a deer track, well hidden and unknown to most people. Though the moon shone, it was very dark under the trees. She was aware of the wind song, of a distant owl calling to his mate, of a sudden flurry as an unseen bird took fright at her presence and flew from its roost.

She was afraid for the first time. She dared not call out. Suppose some man was stalking her with rape in mind? She realised her father had a point when he told her not to wander alone at night. Man was not the only danger.

Mairi had told Ian only the day before of two sheep killed on a farm below them. They had been torn to pieces by some savage animal that left huge paw prints. These were nothing like those of a large dog or a domestic cat. The farmer thought it might be one of the huge black felines that were so often reported but never found. Many feared these were actually pumas or maybe black leopards.

There were tales of escapes, of people who had tried to keep an exotic animal as a pet and then when it was grown had taken it into the countryside and released it. There were stories of the huge cats breeding. Would such an animal attack and kill a human? It was certainly capable of doing so.

Sheina's thoughts raced. She was off the known paths, following a deer trail. Would anyone even find her body before it was reduced to nothing but a pile of bones? Even those might be taken by foxes.

The big cats could climb trees, so there was no escape there. Surely Hexa wouldn't behave like this? Mairi had said the paw prints were far too big for those of even a wildcat. Neither Ian nor her father were anywhere near. Her mouth was dry and her heart racing. Maybe it wouldn't attack. The creature was much too heavy and incautious for a wildcat or a small animal.

She stood still and the sounds stopped She walked on and there was the rustle of a big body pushing through the undergrowth, and the crack of a trodden twig. She came to a fork in the path and decided to walk down towards the loch road. Surely there she would be safe.

At the edge of the road the trees ended. She reached clear ground lit by a brilliant moon and so did her stalker. She stared, even more afraid, at a headless body that walked towards her, half hidden by shadows, a weird-shaped animal with one white hindleg beginning halfway down. Its tail emerged from nothing, and part of its back was also missing.

A ghost would surely not make so much

noise, but what in the world was it?

Her legs refused to move. She stood still as it walked towards her and then came into full view. She laughed. Her ghost was Domino, the piebald pony that was often tethered at the roadside. The black parts of his body did not attract the moonlight. They blended with the shadows so that only his light patches showed. He belonged to an old man who travelled around with a cart, selling firewood. The end of his rope trailed beside the animal, who was now eagerly nosing into her pockets, unable to believe she had nothing for him.

He had been frightened and lonely and needed company but had been unable to find a way through the dense undergrowth to Sheina who he knew and who, he was sure, would protect him.

He pushed at her, wanting sugar or a carrot. She always had something for him when she passed him. But he had no business here. He was miles from his home ground. How on earth had he got here? Morris needed him or he would be unable to do his round. Had something happened to the old man?

She took him home with her and put him in the spare stall. Her own ponies greeted him happily, calling to him, their heads over the half-doors that she had left open as it was warm. She would have to tell her father that Domino had wandered up here on his own.

She rewarded him with a carrot. It was a good job she had found him. Others might not have recognised him or known who owned him.

It took most of the next morning to walk with him to his home, over three miles away from hers. He was slightly lame. Morris was frantic, sure he had lost his horse. Drunken louts on motorcycles had cut the rope the night before. Two had chased the frightened animal down the road. The others had spent time teasing their human victim, threatening to pile his logs round the wooden shack in which he lived and set light to it.

Morris was sure they had meant major harm. Domino had been terrified and bolted into the trees where his tormentors could not follow him. He had kept on running, which was why he had been so far away.

The old man promised Sheina a load of free logs. He was an odd figure, wearing an army greatcoat that came down to the ground. It was never shed. His untidy grey hair was topped, summer and winter, by a dirty red woollen hat. His heavy boots were steel-capped, he said, to keep off the idiots who made his life a misery.

Sheina didn't go out at night after that for over a week. But nothing had really happened and, when Ian reported finding traces of a wildcat kill at the edge of the mountain stream above them, she did start looking again.

She found the little family on a moonlit night when the kittens were nine weeks old. Restless and unable to sleep, she climbed higher than ever before. It was warm, with little wind. Spring was flourishing. The ground was starred with flowers. There were multitudes of tiny mice and rabbits. Hexa had little need to venture anywhere near the keeper's home.

Sheina thought that Hexa had chosen her nest site well. There was a stream nearby where she could drink. There were overhanging rocks to give shelter. There was a flat grassy area just outside the den that was perfect for the kittens, and safe from all earthbound intruders. Tomorrow she would return with food.

A hunter's moon, high in a clouding sky, shone down on the little family. One chased her mother's lazily moving tail. Another sat and patted the teasing grassheads. The third was washing himself, but this was a new skill and he was still a little unsteady. He fell over and got up again, indignant, mewling.

It was a misty night, the moon veiled intermittently by wispy clouds. The wind was little more than a rumour, gently shifting the sliding leaves, dried memories of an autumn long past. The kittens were enchanted by them.

Sheina crouched as still as Hexa herself. The wildcat's ears were alert, her head moving to catch every sound. The youngsters, as yet untouched by fear, played on, oblivious. There were sudden rustles and swift furtive movements in the bushes. The stream was a murmuring background, lying low between its banks. A few hundred yards away, its voice grew to a roar as it spilled over the cliffs.

The small bodies tumbled over one another, teasing at tails, biting at ears, hiding and pouncing. They looked as pretty and as harmless as their domestic cousins. The faint moonlight was bright enough to distinguish them. Sheina was used to the dark. Torches scared off wildlife.

The kittens were learning to hunt and kill. It was difficult to remember that as they played. Even so, they often paused and their small heads lifted as noses tested the air. Read the news on the wind. Is an enemy hidden? Is the weasel waiting to pounce? Watch for the shadow of the hunting owl, flying, ghostlike, on silent wings, ever ready to swoop. Freeze as a startled herd of deer gallops by in the distance. Learn the shrill call of a bat, harmless to them.

Far below, startlingly clear, came the sudden bleat from a distant farm. A lamb had woken and could not find his mother.

The reassuring baa followed and then there was silence. Hexa relaxed. Restless sheep might mean that a fox or a dog was hunting. Vigilant men drove them away and they sought for food higher on the hill.

Sheina prayed that the wind would not change. She was an unseen presence, and the cat could not scent her. She was cramped but did not want to move. She might never get the chance to see the little ones at play again.

She amused herself by giving them names. She could not see which were male and which were female so decided jewel names would suit either sex.

One she named Jade. She was an enchanting morsel with an impish look about her as she teased her sister. Sheina could imagine that she might be a little minx. Amber's fur was yellower and the kitten was bigger than the rest, and a bully. The last, more adventurous, and as yet unnamed, toddled towards Sheina, unaware of the watcher in the shadows. He wanted to explore, to discover what there was under the trees.

She longed to reach out and pick him up and cuddle him, but she knew that these kits would not tolerate human hands. She would suffer bites and scratches. She was cramped and as she moved her foot there was an instant angry spit. She looked at the mite, amused to see his rage.

Hexa, returning from the hunt with a young rabbit for her family, saw Sheina although she had thought herself well hidden. She hissed and the kittens vanished.

For a moment Sheina stood, terrified, sure that Hexa would attack her. She dared not move. Then the wind changed and brought her familiar scent to the wildcat. It was a scent that Hexa recognised, since it had been on the food brought to her. She relaxed, picked up her bounty and disappeared.

It was later than Sheina had thought. The sun was already lifting over the hilltops, revealing the world in all its colour. She ran home, afraid that her father might see her.

Hexa and her family were safe. She hoped they would thrive now, hidden from the men. If she took food then there would be no need for the wildcat to come hunting as the family's needs grew.

She thought of a name for the last kitten as she went to bed to snatch some sleep before another night-time sortie. She called him Topaz.

Five

Although not the biggest, Topaz was the most adventurous kitten, giving his mother more trouble than the other two put together.

Once they were weaned the little tom outstripped his sisters. The world fascinated him. So many things moved, waiting to be tapped with an inquisitive paw or tested with a tongue.

It was a world peopled by giants. Enormous trees towered above him; titanic two-legged creatures shook the ground when they walked; behind them came huge dogs, nose down on a trail that might lead to disaster but usually ended at the rabbit warren.

The ground itself had its own fascination. Smells changed daily. There were days when it was wet, and on others it was dry. He did not like water; nor did Amber, and both kits trod with delicate paws, shaking at every step. Jade did not mind.

There were scents that caused Topaz to fluff his fur as his mother did, though he did not know what had made them. The scents of the prowling fox, roaming weasel and hopeful stoat all intrigued him but he and his sisters learned that when those smells were thick on the ground, wise kittens hid.

Hexa guarded them when they played. The craggy rocks that bordered the stream made fascinating hiding places. Here one could lurk and then, as one of the others passed, leap out and engage in mock war. Their cries as they played attracted attention so that they were often interrupted with a sudden hiss, learning to vanish fast and leave behind only a hint of their presence. A tossed feather, lying crumpled and dirty, or the scut of a rabbit, long gone to satisfy their increasing needs, bore testimony to those who knew the signs.

Lichens grew on the boulders, and patches of moss. Clumps of bright flowers presented nodding heads for small patting paws. There were no trees close to the stream, but a hundred yards back there was deep cover.

Pride mastered Hexa as the kits tumbled over one another, lashing out in feigned anger. Sometimes this turned to genuine rage: the small teeth were sharper now, the claws were harder and could inflict a nasty wound. Excited kits did not always remember to keep claws sheathed and only nibble with their teeth.

They often played together, but sometimes

each became absorbed in some ploy of its own. Topaz collected feathers: long shining ones from magpies, speckled ones from grouse. They sometimes teased their mother's waving tail but received a sharp box on the head if they bit too hard.

Hexa dismembered her kills now and gave parts to each of her young. They learned to worry at a leg or shoulder, to remove feathers and tear at the meat, to gnaw happily on the bones. They guarded their food from one another and any kitten that dared to try and steal from another soon regretted the attempt.

They learned to lap at the puddles in the channelled rocks. Hexa kept them away from the stream. The water was a threat. She never understood how the placid gentle murmur could turn overnight into a raging torrent. She only knew it was best to stay well away.

Sometimes she was able to catch fish in the shallows, pawing them out of the water, impaled on her claws. She had regained her former skill and was swift and relentless.

When the kits were playing, she always placed herself where she had a wide view. Her favourite lookout post was a wide plateau. Some hundred yards away above her the water rushed in creaming foam over outcrops but near her den the pool was placid and shallow at the edges and it was safe for her to drink.

Other creatures came to drink too, offering easy prey, so that she did not have to leave the kittens for long. Jade and Amber wrestled endlessly, but Topaz had a great need to know what was over that boulder, what was round that corner, what was hidden in that crack. He was stubborn, hating to be interrupted if he were attracted to some unusual sight. When his mother hissed to warn them of danger, the two little females vanished fast, but he always had something else that he needed to see. He was too big to carry but she chivvied him, nipping him, slapping him, ever more angry. Freeze when I tell you. Hide when I tell you, or you die, her attitude told him. He was too eager, too full of life, urged on always by his desire to find out more about this wonderful world in which he found himself.

Jade was the most timid, keeping her mother in sight if she could. As yet their small legs would not carry them far. Jade was the first to greet Hexa when she came home from her forays. She lifted her small nose and nuzzled her mother's cheek and then her lips and nose, stimulating Hexa's urge to feed her offspring. Jade sought the warmest place in the nest, curled close in the dense fur.

Above them the eagle watched, looking down on his territory. Amber and Jade learned to run and hide when the huge shadow crossed the ground, but Topaz was too fascinated to heed, unless his mother was there to herd him into their den.

He sharpened his claws daily on the big old tree, and then realised that if he clung to the bark, he could climb. He swarmed up the trunk, enticed by a bird above him. Up he went, never looking down, never heeding, until he reached a thick branch, high above the ground, and crouched on it. Only then did he begin to appreciate the vast distance between him and the familiar solid ground.

He was very high, very small and very frightened. To add to his fears, the early morning breeze was strengthening to a blustering monster, intent on bending the trees to its will.

He cried out, calling for his mother. It was several minutes before Hexa realised where he had gone. She sprang up the tree, climbing swiftly, and gripped him in her jaws. She came down backwards, slowly, anchoring herself, hampered by his weight.

His sisters stood at the foot of the tree, anxious eyes on their mother. They dared not follow. A passing fox, intrigued by the calls for help, stood watching, one paw raised, his eyes bright. Hexa turned to face him, dropped her kit and snarled. The fox, seeing the immense fluffed-up body and the spitting hate, decided that discretion was wise and vanished into the bracken.

Dawn and dusk were playtime. There were twigs to tease, cast-off feathers to carry and stalk as the wind blew them. Dry grass stems bent and bowed. Dead leaves rustled. They were not at all pleasant eating, as each kit found in turn.

Hexa showed them the wild ways and the deer paths. She demonstrated how to crouch and hide. She taught them to vanish like smoke when danger threatened. They learned to fear the call of the vixen, the harsh eagle cry, the slithering threat from the wicked little snake that could kill with one bite.

Topaz found a slow-worm. He tapped it languidly and watched it writhe away from him. He pounced and caught at the tail, which separated from the body. The tail continued to wriggle, and Topaz hunted it, unaware that its owner had slipped down a hole, away from its tormentor. Tails grew back easily and saved many a life, but soon became disappointing playthings, lying like a discarded piece of string without a twitch or a tremor.

Night fascinated the kittens, especially when the wind was wild and dark-streaked clouds fled across the moon, which seemed to be playing an endless game of hide-and seek in the midnight sky.

Amber saw the big globe of the moon

reflected in a small pool and spent half an hour trying, with immense patience, to claw it out of the water. Her dabbling paw broke the golden ball into a thousand ripples but, if the kitten remained still, then it formed again, tempting as before.

She gave up and lapped, drinking deep. Behind her Hexa lay, stretched on a knoll, eyes and nose and ears all working overtime to catch the faintest hint of danger.

Here it was easy to vanish, to hide in a dense-growing patch of blueberry bushes or seek shelter among thick brambles, to duck into thick rank grass. They had not yet learned which were foes and which creatures could be ignored. On one exploration they found a crude wooden cross above a small grave. The name 'Max' was painted in wavering letters on the wood. All three fluffed their fur and spat until certain it would not move and attack them.

The kittens loved the dusk. Great moths fluttered silently by, to be zapped by small paws which gradually gained in dexterity. The skittering bats fascinated them but were never likely to be targets. They learned to ignore the distant hoots of hunting owls but to take shelter if the birds came close.

Topaz became more wary as he grew, so that his explorations were often exhausting. He fluffed and spat at an odd-shaped rock, at a bush that bent towards him in the wind, at the wind itself, running unseen through his fur, so that he turned, startled, trying in vain to discover who was so familiar with him.

There was so much to startle them. The pounding hooves of stampeding deer, running from intruding men; the wild screams of the vixen calling to her mate, the squeals of the screech owl, the thump of a rabbit's hind leg on the ground and the immediate scutter as the colony took shelter.

They were conscious always of birdsong, though more often what they heard was a wild alarm system, sending news before them, warning all that danger stalked on many legs as they began to hunt.

Now they needed food in quantity. One small rabbit did little to allay their fierce hunger. Hexa killed where she could. Rabbit and grouse, ducks on the loch, unguarded chickens. She left more than one man swearing to end her life, laws or no laws.

One night, crossing a main road on her foraging expedition, she found unexpected bounty. Here, she learned, were many kills, but she had to be swift, since racing demons with giant searchlight eyes roared out of the darkness and threatened her. She did not bring the kittens with her on these forays. She watched a young buck rabbit die beneath the wheels of a Jaguar and learned fast that it was not wise to tarry on the road.

She profited from his mistake. She seized her chance, disappointing the waiting fox who had also learned about road kills. It was his chase that had sent the rabbit to his death, trying to escape the hunter and unaware of the speed of the traffic on the road.

Hexa took her trophy back to her den. She dropped it in front of the kits. This time they were to dismember it themselves. It was small and not sufficient food for them. She left them arguing over it and went off to find more.

The road provided for her almost daily. Rabbit and hare, hedgehog and a baby badger, and once a deer calf. That she dragged to the verge, and took back in pieces to her young. It did not last long as it was shared by many others. Fox, weasel, owl, and crow were among those who took advantage of the slaughter.

Hexa was away hunting one evening when Topaz went wandering. He followed a tiny trail made by small animals finding their way to the water. There was a family of badgers further down the hill, one little sow with the same curiosity about life as Topaz.

Nobody had warned the kitten about badgers, and the baby badger knew nothing about cats. They met nose to nose and backed away, startled. The little sow grunted in surprise and Topaz hissed and began to fluff his fur.

The little sow was undaunted. She cocked her black and white striped head and stared at him. She nosed him again, and then the two of them began to play, rolling and tumbling as they did with their litter mates. They were much of a size and not yet old enough to be aware that the other presented a possible threat.

The game did not end until Hexa returned with a grouse that had found death under the wheels of a bus. Topaz heard her imperative summons and abruptly stopped their play. The sow returned to her own family.

Badger and wildcat coexisted peacefully; Hexa and the old sow were aware of one another but unprepared to fight for territory. Neither mother knew of the unlikely companionship, but Topaz began to look for the little sow and she lay in wait, greeting him with a soft throaty rumble, while he purred. The infrequent meetings and games continued for almost a month and then events parted the badger cub and the wildcat kitten.

The kittens were well grown and almost sixteen weeks old when Hexa saw a large hare dancing alone in the dusk. He would be very useful bounty, as they now needed a vast quantity of food. He was mesmerised by his own movements, leaping and turning, rolling and bounding in enormous leaps in an ecstatic celebration of the sheer joy of being alive.

He was young and had forgotten wariness. As time passed, the rising moon lightened the sky. Hexa waited and watched, crouched low, hidden in undergrowth.

She could smell his scent on the wind. He could not smell her. He knew nothing of her presence. He leaped once more, covering an incredible stretch of ground. His landing brought him almost into her waiting jaws. She pounced and he died with a violent kick of his legs and a sudden panic. He did not have time to understand what had happened.

She found his body a burden but dragged it up the hill. It would provide good food for all four of them. The kittens attacked it at once. They were still feeding when daylight flooded in. Colour returned to the trees and bushes and flowers. A vivid sky promised a sunny day.

Topaz always managed to get the largest portion and carry it away to gnaw on it by himself. His two sisters had to be contented with whatever he left. He was too engrossed with his meal to notice the shadow on the ground that grew blacker and larger until it covered him. With one swoop, the eagle had him in his talons.

Hexa saw her son about to be lifted off the ground and fury carried her fast over the ground. She leaped at the great bird, slashing upwards with ripping claws. He was slow to rise, hampered by the weight of the kitten. He dropped his prey and raked at her with his beak, catching her on the cheek. The searing claws that tore at his underparts sent him high into the sky, torn with pain. Blood dripped from him and he wanted only to escape.

The shadow lifted. The air was clear.

Hexa lay beside her son, licking the wound on his neck, her own injury forgotten. Fur mixed with savaged flesh where the talons had dug deep. It was some hours before he recovered enough from shock to try and suck. The milk was almost gone, her teats nearly dry, but she gave him what comfort she could.

Next morning he was stiff, moving with reluctance, fearful of the world outside the den. He refused the food his mother brought him. Nor did he join his sisters when they went out to play.

He curled in the dead leaves that lined the cave floor. His mother licked at the wound, cleaning it as well as she could, but her tongue was not enough to heal it. Over the next few days it began to fester and the kitten grew weaker. His sisters avoided him, but Hexa did her best to keep him warm and alive.

Her own wound healed. It was time to take

them hunting, but Topaz could not follow. She went off with Amber and Jade, leaving him on his own. He lay, mewing softly, his world dominated by pain. The unheeding moon looked down on him as he weakened by the hour.

Six

The McPhee farm had been a mystery throughout Sheina's childhood. Although only two miles away, hidden by one of the smallest peaks, the families never had contact and if she mentioned them she was told to be quiet. They were not the sort of people anyone wanted to know.

'We don't talk about them,' her mother said when Sheina, then only five years old, had asked. 'Don't mention them to your father. Ever.'

There were no young children. There was just old man McPhee and his son, who had been around twenty years old when Sheina was born, so far as she could find out. Seven years ago the young man had been killed in a car crash and soon after that his father had died. Nobody seemed to know who inherited the land, but there were known to be heirs. Meanwhile the farm was rented.

With her own home over twelve miles from the nearest village, Sheina knew few people and had little time to spare. Her shopping expeditions were only once a month and hurried. There was always work waiting, more than they could manage.

The only visitors they had came during the shooting season. She had little to do with them and nothing in common with them. They were wealthy people who did not know the meaning of hardship. No longer were their patrons lairds and men who had inherited estates, but men who paid for a single day's shooting and went back to opulent offices and luxurious homes. To them she was part of the set-up, a servant to wait on them, in charge of their food, ensuring they had all they needed. She sometimes wondered if they knew she was human or, at times, even visible. A smile would have helped, or a thank you, but these courtesies were rare. 'A new breed,' her father said. 'Not like those who came in the old days. And they can't shoot. They miss more than they hit. They wound and don't kill.'

Sheina found it increasingly hard to talk to anyone but Ian and her father. Their conversation was limited to work, with an occasional burst of interest when the gun catalogue came. She sometimes wondered if she was impossibly shy, or just out of practice, lacking friends and with no other family.

They were always busy, and so was she. The chores were endless, and they never caught up. In her free time she was happiest alone on the hills, watching the animals, her dog beside her. She felt safe there. With people she was uneasy.

She could talk to the ponies when she groomed them. She loved the way they listened to her soft voice, their ears flickering towards the sound, now forwards, now back. She could talk to Beulah when they were alone on the hills. The spaniel sat in front of her, eyes fixed unblinkingly on Sheina, her head cocking first to one side and then to the other as if trying desperately to understand.

Ian was so shy and awkward if accidentally left alone with her that she was uneasy with him. She was unaware that she haunted his dreams, but that he regarded her as out of his reach.

He had never been able to talk to women. Those who came to help his father were elderly, grandmothers all of them. They were undemanding and only wanted to mother him. The younger women went out to more interesting work.

Sheina increasingly had as little to do with him as possible. She would have been horrified had he told her of his feelings. To her, he was just part of the estate. She was not even sure that she liked him. Life was miserable. Her father was increasingly critical, constantly finding fault or dictating to her.

Ian now found it easier to talk to Sheina, so long as her father was there. His unease with her was no longer due to his shyness, but to his growing fondness for her and the knowledge that this was not reciprocated. Only Mairi, seeing his expression when he talked of the girl, knew how he felt.

Sheina needed space for all their sakes and her sorties to the hills became more frequent. Maybe she should go away, she thought and find work elsewhere, but she knew that her father could not manage the shoots with only himself and Ian. She was trapped.

Hexa continued to leave traces of her kills. The kittens were always ravenous and her needs grew daily. The men were obsessed, determining to put an end to her life. Sheina was equally obsessed, determined to save her.

Her father grew daily more morose. Mealtimes were filled with brooding silences. He would not discuss anything with Sheina, though she knew there was still talk of selling the estate. What would become of the three of them then? As yet it was only a rumour, but fewer people came to shoot each year and they were no longer making a good profit. It was more difficult to keep up their former high standards of management and grouse were becoming scarce.

Summer was almost on them. Sheina had a rare free afternoon, and decided to climb into the hills and see if she could find Hexa and her kittens. She was just coming out of the house when someone shouted, ' Hey, you!'

She stared at the ancient Land Rover that had skidded to a stop. The door was flung open and the man who had addressed her so unceremoniously leaped out. He grinned at her. She had never seen him before. He was a very noticeable figure, over six feet tall, his head crowned by a tawny mane of curly hair cut to just below his ears. Vivid brown eyes surveyed her as if assessing her. His blue jeans were topped by a remarkable multi-coloured jersey, patterned with all kinds of farm animals. It reminded her of Joseph's coat of many colours.

'I've just moved in next door. Well, a month ago. To the old McPhee farm. I've got a crisis and need an extra pair of hands. Used to animals, are you?'

'Since my father's the head keeper here, I'd say yes,' Sheina said, irritated by his manner.

'Good.' He opened his passenger door. 'Hop in.'

This was going too far.

'I have no idea who you are,' Sheina said.

Both men were busy elsewhere and she had not yet released Beulah from her kennel. Alastair would not have another dog as a house pet after his treasured old Labrador had died. Morag had insisted the old boy would suffer from cold on winter nights in a kennel, but Sheina could not persuade her father to change his mind.

The visitor spoke as if he were cheating time and had to spill out all the information fast.

'I'm Rob Vincent. Perfectly respectable. My grandfather was a bishop if that's any recommendation. Not a white slave trader. Been trying to move some of my animals. Wretched donkey's fallen into a small pit. Can put a ramp down and lead her up. Need someone to convince her that I haven't invented a new form of torture.'

Sheina was not at all sure she would like to trust herself to either this complete stranger or his singularly ancient vehicle, which looked as if it would break down any moment.

'Please,' he said. 'I know it sounds odd, but the postmaster said you'd help out. I don't have any other neighbours near, and Semolina... that's the donkey... is about to foal.'

Anyone who had a donkey by the name of Semolina might be more than halfway mad in the nicest way, Sheina decided, and hoped he really was harmless. A foaling donkey in a pit sounded like a major disaster. It was time to be practical. 'Do you need tools, or ropes?' she asked.

'No. Just someone to hold big juicy carrots and I've got those.'

He started off almost before she had fastened her seat belt. She decided, as they turned out of the lane on to the road that led to his new home, that it was unlikely they would arrive in one piece. She rarely travelled in this direction. Last time it had been bleak but now the leaves were unfurled, bright with summer colour, and masses of yellow flowers starred the banks. She had never even seen the McPhee property.

'I didn't know the farm was being let again,' she said. 'It's been rented so long. Mairi thought the Hunts, who used to live there, would probably buy it, if they couldn't find an heir. It must be five years since old Angus McPhee died.'

'Six years and seven months,' Rob said, as he turned into the track that led to his new home.

The track was deeply rutted and Sheina felt as if she were being jolted from hummock to hummock. The ground on either side was moorland. Distant trees shone in the sunshine and masked the slopes of the faraway mountains.

There was a sudden whine from the rear of the Land Rover. The large black Labrador had been so quiet up until then that Sheina hadn't realised he was there. They had hit an even bigger bump that jolted her in spite of the seat belt, and the dog had skidded across the slippery unmatted floor at the rear of the vehicle.

'Sorry. It's an old river bed,' Rob said.

'Nobody's ever bothered to turn it into anything like a decent track. I might one day.'

A cold black nose thrust itself into Sheina's neck.

'Meet Pocohontas. Poco for short,' Rob said with a grin. 'He's a lot wiser than I am.'

Sheina was becoming even more bemused. 'Pocohontas was a woman, not a man,' she said.

Rob grinned. 'Not many know that. Little details like that never bothered my mother. She liked the name and pointed out that Hilary can be male or female, as can Evelyn. Poco sounds male enough.'

'Why did she call a donkey Semolina?' Sheina asked.

'That wasn't Mum. It was my three-year-old nephew, who thinks it's a lovely name. His dad farms and Paul chooses the animal names. As you may gather Paul is sold on milk puddings. Only way his mother can get him to drink it. She adds weird things to it, like cochineal or saffron. Or alphabet biscuits.' He laughed.

The track was lined with trees, and at times the branches brushed the top of the windscreen. Sheina began to wonder if they were on a road to nowhere, and if she had been conned.

'Very earnest, my sister. Doesn't believe in convenience foods, and cooks for the family still. Paul really does throw her at times. Would you believe he named her prize bull Victoria Tapioca?'

Sheina laughed. She suddenly felt light-hearted. This man was fun.

'Did they call him that?'

'Mark felt that if he registered a bull under that name they would send a little yellow van for him.' They hit another huge bump. 'Whoops. Sorry. Can't help it. He's register-ed as Majestic Victor. He is, too. Majestic. Glorious beast. But not an animal to meet in a cul-de-sac on a dark night. Temper like a wildcat.'

'Do they live near you?'

'Fortunately not. They live in Suffolk. Couldn't do with them here. Paul's a one-man destructive force. Worse than any puppy. Anything he sees he has to take to pieces. Including his own cot once, and my sister's washing machine outlet. The cot fell down with him inside it and the kitchen floor was awash, which the little monkey thought wonderful. He floated his boat in it.'

Rob laughed again as he drove on to a rela-tively smooth track towards the farmhouse. 'He looks like a cherub. An enchanting little face, with big blue eyes and fair hair and such a solemn expression. Till you catch that glint. Then watch out! Nobody believes he can be such a handful. I pity his school-teachers when he's old enough to start.'

'What made you choose to come and live here?' Sheina asked. 'It's so out of the way.'

'I inherited it. I'm a sort of second cousin by marriage twice removed, or something, to old Angus McPhee. One day I might find time to write it out. Suffice to say I turned out to be the next of kin. I was in Australia when the old man died. They spent time tracing me. I'd had a row with my dad and gone off in a huff.'

'What about your parents? Weren't they next of kin?'

'My father died while I was in Australia. My own mother died when I was two. Mum was my stepmother and no relation to the McPhees. Lizzie isn't either, as she's my stepsister. Mum was married before she married my dad. Modern families are very complicated, aren't they?' He slowed down as they turned into a drive nearly as overgrown as the river bed and bumped from pothole to pothole. 'I lived with my stepmother for a year while they sorted it all out. Got on very well with her in the end. We thought it was a run-down old place... a millstone. It was a complete surprise – none of us even knew Uncle Angus existed.' He slowed down and a second Labrador that might have been Poco's twin came racing to meet them, his tail swinging frantically from side to side. 'House came at a good time as I lost the lease of my place in Suffolk,' he concluded. 'Would have had to give up farming as I couldn't afford the sort of place I need.'

They had arrived at the farmhouse. The second dog padded beside the Land Rover while Poco tried to get through a window that was far too small for his stocky black body. He barked and was answered, the deep bays echoing.

'Shut up, dogs,' Rob said as he climbed out and waited for Sheina to join him. To her surprise they were instantly silent.

'Needs a lot of work on it, but luckily the barns are all in good repair with decent roofs. Had good tenants. Fortunately they wanted to leave anyway. I would've felt bad about turning them out, but my own need was desperate. Place was let furnished so I don't have to bother about that. A bit antiquated, but I can get by.'

Briefly Sheina felt worried. Did the Mc-Phee taboo extend to the new owner? What would her father say when he discovered where she had spent the afternoon? She wished she knew the cause of the trouble between the two families, but nobody would tell her. She wondered if Rob knew about it. He wasn't really a McPhee.

'Hey, Nin, Poco. Into the house with you. We don't need you to help make even more of a mess of things.'

'Why Nin?' Sheina asked. She liked

reasons for everything and Rob's names seemed crazy most of the time. She expected to be given some grandiose explanation. Ninevah?

'Short for Nincompoop. Mum bred him. He could lose himself on his way to find milk from his mother, hunting under her ear, trying to suck from the tip of her tail. We despaired of him and decided not to sell him. He's a lovely dog but no more brains than a pea. He gets lost regularly. Doesn't seem to have any sense of smell. And that's on home ground. I leash him when we're out. Often wondered if dogs can be retarded. He sure ain't normal.'

He led the way through a cobbled yard. 'He's Poco's brother. Poco got the brains, but Nin is the sweeter dog.'

The capacious farmhouse was built of stone. An ungainly building, it had been extended over the years and no longer seemed a coherent whole. Beyond it was a large field, the grass mown. It was dotted with a number of empty cages, many only half built.

'It's old,' Rob said. 'May go back to 1500... not had time to find out. Never time. Additions are Georgian. Not been added to since.'

A large tortoiseshell cat weaved round his legs, fixing questioning green eyes on the newcomer. A colourful mallard drake sat in a remarkably small puddle and glared at them with beady eyes. Sheina wondered what they were named.

'There's a lake for him across the fields – well, sort of. More like an enormous puddle. Needs work on it,' Rob said. 'He ignores it. Likes company. Like most of my animals Tussock seems not to know what he ought to be doing, and so does something quite mad. Like master, like man,' he added.

'Tussock?' Sheina asked.

'That's where his daft mother laid her eggs. In a large tussock right away from the house. At my mother's, last year. A fox took her. We salvaged the eggs and put them under one of the hens. Only one hatched. Hence Tussock. Seem to attract potty animals and birds.'

Sheina had a problem keeping up with him, even though she walked fast herself.

'Problem is time. Never enough,' Rob said, opening a gate into a second field. A shaggy animal galloped towards them. Sheina stared. She had never seen a llama on a Scottish farm before. She wanted to run, but Rob seemed unconcerned. It stopped, braking at the last minute, just as she was wondering whether to run.

Rob produced a handful of mints from his pocket, which were taken eagerly. The animal's top lip was split into two halves which he seemed to use like a finger and thumb. Not content with that, he pushed against Rob, trying to dip his nose into the man's pocket. Rob rubbed the shaggy head, and was rewarded with a butt.

'My latest acquisition,' he said. 'He's only a baby. Not yet a year old. His mother and the rest of the herd were battering him. Kicked him and bit him. Poor mite. Just one problem. He spits at people he doesn't like and it's pretty copious. Luckily he doesn't seem to mind you.'

Since he was the size of a small pony Sheina felt that the term 'mite' was inappropriate.

Rob was now leading the way towards an area of ground in yet another field in which all that could be seen was a donkey's head, her chin resting on the grass. The rest of her was invisible until they reached the pit. Forlorn brown eyes looked up at them. She was a pretty animal with a soft woolly grey coat, the cross on her back very visible.

'How did she get in there?' Sheina asked.

'Napoleon... that's the llama... hates her and chased her and kicked her in. I forgot they didn't like each other and didn't shut the gate on him when I unloaded her.'

The far side of the pit had a wooden incline covered in straw. 'She's lucky,' Rob said. 'It's mostly rock at the sides and bottom but I'm filling it in and have put down a load of earth so she fell soft.'

The donkey took up most of the area.

'I just can't persuade her the ramp's safe,' Rob said. 'I'll go in and you can pull her while I push her. She usually adores these.' He handed Sheina a large bunch of carrots. 'Maybe they'll persuade her we don't have evil intent.' He walked down the ramp. 'Look, Semi, old girl,' he said. 'If it's safe for me, it's safe for you. Come on, now.' He turned her and Sheina leaned over, holding a carrot. Rob had made a makeshift halter out of rope. He passed the end to Sheina.

'She's never had any harness on,' he said. 'Usually she follows me. Mum's had her since she was a foal. She's three now.'

Sheina enticed and Rob cajoled and Semolina dug her small hooves in, brayed and refused to move.

'She says she doesn't want carrots. Can't think what else to get her,' Rob said, trying to push her and entice her into moving. She had no intention whatever of being forced to do anything. She kicked, and Rob climbed out of the pit, rubbing his shin, his eyes watering. He sat on the grass nursing his leg.

'Dear Heaven. I thought she'd broken it, but I think it's just a massive bruise. What do we do with her?'

'Are you sure that's not broken?' Sheina asked. 'It was one hell of a kick.'

'It's a restricted space so I didn't get the full force. Let's go and have a cuppa and think. She won't hurt for another few minutes.'

'What is that pit?'

'Nobody's sure if it's a bomb crater or due to a meteorite,' Rob said. 'It's been a farm feature for ever, according to Mairi.' He limped beside Sheina. 'My own feeling is someone quarried a bit of rock for a stone wall and never filled it in again.'

The farmhouse surprised her. It was Georgian, almost as much of a mansion inside as their own home. Although they only had a few rooms, all of them were very large. Here, the immense hall had several small recesses, in each of which was a large cage. These were, at the moment, empty.

Sheina looked round her. Carved banisters bordered a wide staircase, the gleaming treads polished. The walls were hung with pictures, row on row, as if in an art gallery. Many were modern, little more than wild blocks of colour, plastered on without any apparent care. Sheina hated them on sight.

'When I've time I think they'll end on a bonfire,' Rob said. 'Frames'll fetch a few quid. Old McPhee fancied himself as a collector. Hadn't much taste and even less skill. Most of them are originals but worthless, by unknowns who never made it. There was just one that was worth selling. That helped pay the death duties. Nice how we all work so hard for the government to throw our money down the drains, isn't it?'

He opened a door. 'Have a dekko.'

She had expected ugly, old-fashioned furniture but found herself staring at what looked like very valuable antiques. She wondered if Rob knew what he had and how anyone could have leased the farm to tenants with such contents.

'I've not got all the furniture back yet,' he said, almost as if reading her thoughts. 'Do you know, they think the old man never knew what he had. He lived like a pauper, in the kitchen and one bedroom.' He stroked the case of the grandfather clock that stood in one corner. 'People who dealt with it when he died were completely gobsmacked. They couldn't believe it. Like finding treasure at the bottom of an old pit. Even this is worth a small fortune. It's a long case clock and was made somewhere around the early 1700s.'

Sheina felt as if she had been transported into a museum.

'It cost a bomb in death duties. Luckily the smaller items covered that, and some antique farm equipment, just shoved away in one of the old barns by one generation after another. All collector's items. It was incredible, unearthing it, they said. I wish I'd been here. Must have been so exciting.'

One door after another revealed more treasures. The dining room was sombre, the wallpaper dark and in need of renovation, with heavy velvet curtains smelling of dust.

'The old folk never changed the furniture from one generation to another. The solicitors dealt with everything and put it all in store till an heir was found. I've had myself a ball cleaning it all up. I've had expert advice.' He stroked the shining top of a small ornamental table. 'That's Jacobean, like most of the furniture here. The old folk used this room as a parlour. For weddings and funerals only. It's a museum. Stuff ought to finance me over the years, selling it piece by piece.'

He led the way back into the kitchen, which was extremely modern. It might have come straight out of the pages of an ideal homes magazine. Sheina found herself envious.

'What a wonderful room,' she said, and then thought that maybe he would feel she was belittling the rest of the house. It had been wonderful but she could never live there. She would be terrified of damaging one piece or another. The custom-made cupboards, the big pine table with benches either side and the mass of storage space were all far more to her taste.

The microwave oven was so complicated that it looked as if it was part of a space programme. She walked over to examine the computer-like operations.

'It grills, roasts and bakes,' Rob said. 'I'm single-handed and need every time-saving machine I can find.' He stroked Nin, who had come to butt against his leg. 'I live in here mainly, when I can find time. The rest of the place is a showpiece. You can't feel at home in it. But they advise me not to sell it all now as it could appreciate still further in years to come.'

He opened a small cupboard, took out a dark brown bottle filled with liquid and applied it to a large white pad, which came from a drawer filled with all sorts of dressings. He took a wide bandage and fastened the soaked pad neatly round his leg.

'Arnica. Can't beat it,' he said. 'Get rid of that bruising in minutes.'

Though tall he was a neat man, moving with a deft competence that was unlike either Ian or her father. In spite of his slight limp there was soon coffee powder in two mugs, a kettle coming to the boil, and a cake tin and butter, plates and knives on the table.

Sheina straddled one of the benches. 'If only we had equipment like this.'

'Been very lucky. A Welsh dresser paid for the kitchen,' Rob said. 'Decided I need to be super-efficient. Doesn't go with the rest of the house, but in time I'll modernise every room. Meanwhile, that furniture is my nest egg.'

There was a movement behind Sheina, and a small noise. She turned her head.

'What is that?' she asked, looking at a large cage in which some kind of animal was shifting in its sleep. She thought at first it was a dog. She walked across the tiled floor and found herself looking down at a tiny roe deer calf, its hind leg in plaster.

It was the size of a small collie dog, its soft greyish-brown furred back blotched with white stripes. The fragile ears were turned back to reveal the pink, almost translucent, inner part, and the eyes were closed.

'Dapple was found on the road beside her dead mother. Whatever hit the hind hit the baby too. We guess she's about a week old.'

Sheina wondered who the other part of 'we' was. There had been no sign of anyone else.

'We?' she asked, wondering if perhaps she was unwise to ask questions.

'Don't suppose you've met our new assistant vet yet. Tom and I were at school together and when he heard of a job going right on my doorstep he applied. Good to know someone in a completely new place.'

He grinned again. 'Did my best to influence him. Nice to have brains to pick. He's a bit crusty at the moment. Wife upped and left him six months ago for someone with a nine-to-five job. High divorce rate in the veterinary profession. Like doctors

110

and policemen.'

He looked down at the little deer, and reached a finger through the bars to stroke her soft cheek. She stirred slightly, straightening the uninjured hind leg. She lay, almost unmoving. Only the rise and fall of the fur on her chest showed that she was alive.

'Old Morris found her yesterday and brought her to me. She had to have that leg pinned this morning. She isn't out of the anaesthetic yet. It's affected her more than we expected. I'm a bit worried about her.'

He went back to the kettle and poured boiling water on to instant coffee. They both drank it black, with one spoonful of sugar.

'I'll give her another hour and then ring Tom. I don't want her to die on me. There you go.' He put a mug of coffee in front of her and opened the tin to reveal a store of fresh-baked scones.

'Mairi McLeod has adopted me. She brings me sustenance and healing herbs for the animals.'

'Have you many?'

'More than I care to count. All sorts. And in case you're going to ask, yes, I inherited them too. From my stepmother. She had a wildlife sanctuary that opened to the public. Only the man who rented her the land discovered the rugby club would pay much more. So, when Mum died last year, he refused to renew the lease, which ended a few weeks back. I had to find a new place quick, and this turned up. Who says there aren't guardian angels?'

'And you have one?'

He grinned again and buttered a scone lavishly. 'Mum had one. He was an Indian chief in the seventeenth century called Listening Bear. Don't ask. You can see why I'm considered nutty. Even though she and I weren't related.'

Sheina was mesmerised. She had never met anyone like Rob in her life. Her father would hate him. She wondered what Ian would make of him.

'We're a nutty family. My dad wasn't, but I gather my real mum was a bit of a card. Dad seemed to be attracted to dotty women. He was an accountant. Sober sort of man... no sense of humour, which Mum found tiresome as the unlikeliest things tickled her. Which tended to annoy him. Like the day he fell through the ceiling trying to mend the cistern in the loft.' He laughed. 'He landed on a bed and lay there looking bemused with plaster falling all round him. Mum had told him to get a plumber... but he wouldn't listen. Was livid when we all laughed. He looked so funny. Cost a lot more than if he'd got the plumber.'

He put sugar in his mug and stirred the coffee. Sheina sipped thoughtfully.

'Mostly nuts on Mum's side too, except

112

Lizzie, my stepsister, who takes after her dad. He was down to earth and sensible. Though she did go and marry a farmer.'

He pushed the tin at Sheina and she took another scone. She felt as if she had wandered out of her own world into one touched with magic. She wished she need not return.

'Paul, my little nephew, seems to have inherited all the family barminess. Which is awful for poor Lizzie as she's so conventional it's painful. Mum horrified her. And so does Paul. I only hope his new brother, who's due in a couple of months, won't be in the least like him. Poor Lizzie just couldn't cope with two of them.'

'What about Paul's father?'

'He has more patience than any man I know. He's a wizard with animals. I'll miss him. He was a great help and if Mum hadn't room for a newcomer to the sanctuary there was always space in one of their barns. They lived quite near to her. Mostly I dropped in and out. Bit of a rolling stone. Not the pop group,' he added hastily. He stood up. 'Time we went to try and rescue Semolina. Maybe she's got sick of being stuck down there and will come out happily.'

Sheina glanced at her watch. She had already been gone longer than she'd intended.

'I'll drive you back. Not to worry,' Rob said. 'Mairi's told me about you and your dad and Ian. Like to meet them.'

That wouldn't be a good idea. Ian maybe. Her father definitely no. And how in the world would she manage to persuade Rob of that?

They reached the donkey's prison. They looked down. Semolina saw them and brayed. Beside her lay a minute foal, squashed up against the side of the pit.

'And just what do we do now?' Rob asked, staring down at his latest acquisition. 'It hasn't room to stand. It can't reach her to feed and if we don't get them out fast it will die. If it's actually alive.' He ran his hands through his hair so that it stood up even more wildly from his head. 'There just isn't room in that pit for me and Semolina and her foal. I'll be putting my big feet on to it. All I can think of doing at the moment is screaming.'

Seven

The weather had changed while they were indoors. The sky had darkened. The mountains had vanished, lost in a mass of black cloud streaked by occasional flashes of lightning. Distant thunder rumbled in the hills, its echo prolonging the drum rolls. Rain lanced the ground, the drops falling so hard that they rebounded when they hit. Within seconds they were both soaked.

'Great,' Rob said. He sounded as if he meant it.

Sheina looked at him in astonishment. She wondered if he was being sarcastic. But he seemed genuinely pleased.

'The gods are on our side. Semolina is terrified by thunder and loathes rain,' he said. 'She's an absolute wimp. Watch.'

The little donkey shook herself and trotted up the ramp as if she had done it daily for years. She shook again, her ears making the most astonishing flapping noise, then galloped past them as if they did not exist, intent on reaching the sanctuary of her stable.

'I don't think she even realises the baby's

there,' Rob said, as he walked down into the pit and lifted the little animal. The ramp, which was improvised from a very heavy old door, slanted against the edge at the top. It did not look at all secure.

'Don't touch him,' he said. 'She may refuse to nurse him if he smells of a stranger. As it is, I think she may need coaxing.'

It was a hazard Sheina knew well. Many a ewe rejected her lamb because humans unknown to her touched it, trying, mistakenly, to help.

Rob laid the baby on the ground before he climbed out. 'He's still slippery. She hasn't attempted to lick him and he needs milk, soon.'

The rising wind drove the rain into their faces. They ran, heads down, towards the kitchen, Rob carrying the tiny newborn.

'Is he breathing?' Sheina asked.

'Yes, but he's cold.'

Once indoors Rob seized a rough towel and massaged the small body, rubbing hard.

'We're going to have to work to make Semolina accept him. He's her first and she doesn't seem to know what it's all about.'

Sheina was feeling light-headed. In spite of being soaked she could not remember having enjoyed herself so much since her mother died. Rob was so easy to talk to and such fun to be with, while her own home seemed always to be dominated by brooding silences. This house was filled with laughter. Rob made light of difficulties, accepting them as challenges which he enjoyed meeting.

She wondered if the place had been like that when old Angus McPhee was alive. As always the thought niggled. Why did his name make her father so angry? Why had she never been allowed to visit?

She glanced at her watch. She was going to be very late home. They might worry about her absence. She ought not to have come at all. But how could she have refused?

Worse, if her father knew where she had spent the afternoon he might be furious with her. Did his anger extend to anyone who owned the McPhee farm, or only the old man himself?

'Jago,' she said to distract her thoughts.

Rob had stopped rubbing the little donkey, and was staring at him thoughtfully as if wondering what to do next.

'Come again?'

It wasn't familiar phrase to Sheina but she guessed at its meaning. Rob's English accent was unfamiliar here where everyone else was a Scot.

'His name. Jago.'

'Why?'

She grinned at him.

'It rhymes with Sago. Which goes with Semolina. I don't think Sago would suit him,

117

really. Nor would Tapioca.'

Rob laughed. 'You're as nutty as I am.'

He picked up the little foal. 'Come on, young 'un. Time we did something to make your mother feed you,' he said. 'Out here.'

The little animal lay in his arms without protest.

Rob led the way out of the kitchen, through an archway into the old scullery, its walls newly whitewashed. The rest of it was a mixture of items from another century and expensive modern equipment. The enormous brown sink must have been there when Angus McPhee was a toddler.

'It's useful for all kinds of things, even if old-fashioned. You couldn't buy a modern one as large or deep,' Rob said, noticing her glance at it. 'I can bath the animals in it. Especially when I get some that have been caught in an oil slick.'

There was also a large deep freeze, as well as a big washing machine. A huge elderly Aga dominated and warmed the room.

The old quarry tiles needed renewing. The battered wicker chair might be comfortable but it looked as if it had been rescued from a tip. Improbably, a hen was curled up on the cushioned seat, looking as if she belonged. She glanced up at Rob, cocking her head on one side, her beady eyes inquisitive, then fluffed her feathers and settled herself more comfortably, apparently unbothered by Sheina or the donkey.

'She's laid an egg,' Sheina said in astonishment, having glimpsed one as the hen moved.

Rob laughed. 'She's broody and it's china. It keeps her happy. I hoped to get her to look after a clutch of duck eggs, orphaned by a fox. But she wants her home comforts so one of my Rhode Islands is doing her best.'

One corner housed a large modern television set.

'Not the best reception here,' Rob said. 'But Myfanwy likes it. She's not too bothered about funny-looking pictures.'

Sheina looked at him, now convinced she really had strayed into cloud cuckoo land. 'Who is Myfanwy?'

'The hen. She belonged to an old Welsh lady who made a pet of her. She frets outside. They used to look at TV together. When she died, Mrs Owen left her and her TV to Mum, knowing she'd be looked after properly. Couldn't put her in a run, could we?'

'Why did the old lady have a pet hen? Why not a cat or a dog?'

'She had a farm which she sold when her husband died. She was over seventy and it was too much for her on her own. She retired to one of the farm cottages but kept six chickens for their eggs. The other hens died off one by one and only Myfanwy was left, and she was lonely so she was allowed in the house. She began to regard that as her home and finally had a box in the kitchen where she slept. As she does here.'

'Does she ever go outside?'

'Oh yes. She likes a good scrabble, like any other hen. My other hens pick on her, though, so she has to keep near the house. And Doodle Doo hates her.'

'I suppose Doodle Doo is your cockerel and Paul named him?'

Rob laughed again. 'You guessed it. If you want peace and quiet you don't argue with young Paul. Not that I reveal the cock's name to just anyone, mind. I do have some desire to appear sane to the community I live in. Difficult if Paul is around, though.'

Sheina contemplated a very odd world. She wondered what Ian and her father would make of Rob. They would probably decide he was madder than any March hare.

There were several cages in the scullery, all but one empty. That contained a ginger cat with four kittens, two like herself and two a mottled marmalade colour. Sheina walked over to look at the kittens and was rewarded with a snarling spit.

'She was found living wild at the edge of the housing estate in the village,' Rob said. 'Tom brought her here three days ago. Kittens not got their eyes open yet, so must be less than ten days old. He had to put a sedative in her food to get hold of her. She's as fierce at the moment as any wildcat.'

He put the foal down on the thick matting and opened the door of the Aga, piling in more wood. The tiny donkey lifted its head, staring straight at Sheina with remarkably bright eyes. She wished she could take him home.

Rob was still looking down at the cat, who regarded him with malevolent eyes.

'Tom had been feeding her for some days. He saw her when he was out on a farm call. Living in the hedge nearby and stealing what she could from the farm cats, who chased her off. She was pregnant when he first noticed her but he couldn't catch her before the babies were born.'

'Has she a name?' Sheina asked, expecting to hear something outrageous.

He grinned. 'I did think of Venus, but Mairi persuaded me to call her Ginnie, which is short for Ginger. Got some taming to do there.'

'Why Venus?'

'Why not? She's a very handsome animal now she's beginning to look cared for.'

That seemed both satisfactory and unanswerable.

'Like a kitten?'

'I'd love one. But cats are taboo in our house. Dad says they go for the grouse.'

'I see.' He looked at her, one eyebrow

raised. She wondered what he was thinking. She also wondered, not for the first time, if her father realised she was now adult, and not a little girl to be ordered about.

Rob left the little donkey and walked over to a cupboard that was remarkably like her father's gun cupboard. Inside, however, there were no guns. Instead it had been shelved and was filled with jars of all kinds, plus a vast number of tiny phials. Rob took one of these, and two of the jars.

'Rescue Remedy. Also salt, I think, and honey. Hold them for me.'

'What's Rescue Remedy?' Sheina asked, looking at the tiny brown phial.

'A miracle worker. It's an essence of several flowers. A doctor named Bach found they had a wonderful effect on both people and animals.'

Sheina looked at it. Her father would definitely think this man was a complete crank, if not worse. He had no time for those he called idiots who believed in homeopathy and acupuncture and other such nonsense. She wasn't sure. Mairi had some remarkable results with her herbal brews and healing touch, often when vets and doctors had given up or their medicines had failed to work.

Rob lifted the foal.

'Use the flower remedies all the time. For shock, for newborns, for the newly delivered.

For me if I'm overtired. Give you a phial. Useful for your bitches, especially when they whelp. Pups due soon? Mairi said you have good ones and I'm in the market for a spaniel pup.'

'Not for some months,' Sheina said. She had only recently sold the last lot of pups. Beulah was not yet quite old enough, but would be mated next spring. Gwen needed a lay-off for at least two years after her last litter. They always avoided producing puppies near Christmas.

The rain eased as they walked across the yard. The uneven cobbles were slippery and, though the torrential downpour had changed to a thin drizzle, the night-black sky still hid the mountains in a dense veil.

Rob put the foal down in the straw. Semolina stood at the back of the stable, showing no sign of even wishing to investigate her son.

Watching Rob, Sheina began to wonder if she was looking at some mystic ritual, maybe smacking of witchcraft. He opened the little phial and dripped five drops on to the baby's forehead, rubbing them into the fur. He then took a handful of salt which he sprinkled liberally over the small body. He completed the task by pouring honey over Jago's head and back and rubbing that in with his hands.

'Messy,' he said. 'But usually effective.'

He walked over to Semolina and held out his hands. Tentatively, she tasted them with an exploratory tongue, flicking it out delicately, as if afraid she might not like what she found. She became more enthusiastic, liking this odd mixture. She licked again and again.

Rob brought the baby to her feet, and she lowered her head and sniffed him. He smelled of the wonderful concoction that Rob had on his hands.

She began to lick, and a change came over her expression. Rob held the baby so that he could find the overflowing udder. She went on with her ministrations. When he had fed Rob laid the foal in the straw. He made feeble efforts to stand, his legs apparently made of rubber, so that he straddled and fell.

Semolina was fascinated by him. She nosed him. She licked him again. She watched him, ears flickering as she heard his small noises. When they finally left the stable the two were cuddled up together, the grey donkey savouring her first taste of motherhood.

'Never fails,' Rob said, satisfaction in his voice as he closed the stable door. 'At least, it never has yet. She'll do fine now. Let's look at the little deer.'

Sheina glanced at her watch again. Beulah needed exercise and was still in her kennel.

The dogs needed feeding. The men would also be expecting food, and she wasn't there. Worry flared. She should never have come. What on earth had she been thinking of, to go off like that with a total stranger?

'I really ought to be at home,' she said. 'I'm neglecting my own tasks.'

'Just a check,' Rob said. 'I'm sorry. Wasn't thinking – but I couldn't leave Jago mother-less. Your father would surely understand that?'

'It isn't that.' She didn't know how to explain.

'Surely he isn't keeping that old grievance alive? Mairi did tell me there was some feud and the two families haven't spoken for years. She wouldn't say why. Said it was best forgotten and she didn't want to rake up old woes.' He led the way back into the scullery. 'Just make sure Dapple's OK and then I'll drive you back.'

Nin and Poco greeted him as if he had been away for ever, wriggling their black bodies, waving wild tails, their bodies ecstatic with welcome, but never jumping up.

Rob laughed.

'Enough. Settle, both of you.'

Meekly, heads drooping with disappointment, they returned to the rug by the Aga. Myfanwy clucked. There was a second egg on the chair. Rob took it, grinning.

'An egg for my tea. She pays for her keep.'

The outer door opened. Mairi walked in, carrying two old-fashioned wicker shopping baskets, both loaded. She was a tiny woman, her white hair curling softly round a face marked by laughter lines. Her deep-set eyes were heavy-lidded and almost black. Her velvety trouser suit was a rich garnet colour.

She made her own outfits, complaining that no shops ever had anything suitable for her age group and that nobody wanted to see an eighty-year-old in a miniskirt or any of the other strange garments that were considered clothing these days.

Her yellow hand-knitted jersey was adorned with a heavy Victorian amber necklace. She frowned as she looked at Sheina.

'So there you are. Your father and Ian are looking for you. I met them on the way up here. Very worried, they are. Said you'd been missing for over three hours and you haven't got Beulah with you.'

'It can't be three hours,' Sheina protested, but when she looked at her watch she knew that Mairi was right. She had never known time to pass so fast. 'They were on the hill. I didn't think they'd be back till now.'

'Craig got a bad cut on his pad. They came back to get something to cover it before Ian took him to the vet. And found you missing.' She walked through the archway into the kitchen and put the basket down on the table. 'I'd better drive you home.'

'I will,' Rob said. 'It's my fault. I kidnapped her to help me get Semi out of the pit. Napoleon kicked her in.'

'She wouldn't come,' Sheina said. 'So we had tea and then she had had a baby and she wouldn't touch it... and it sort of went on from there.'

'It might be better if your father didn't know where you spent the afternoon,' Mairi said.

'That old nonsense. It's high time it stopped,' Rob said. 'I don't know what started it but it has nothing to do with me. I'll talk to the old man. He'll be reasonable.'

Sheina looked at Mairi. Reasonable was not a word you used in conjunction with her father. Pig-headed, her mother used to say, and that was now an understatement. He had become far worse in these last few months.

'I think maybe I should go with Rob,' Sheina said. 'It's quicker, for one thing. Your car can't possibly take the short cut. It's not much use hiding the fact that I've been here. And maybe Dad will forget the feud.'

Rob was looking down at the tiny deer. Her eyes were open, and she showed no sign of fear of this vast man who stood above her.

'I'll stay with her,' Mairi said.

'Why won't anyone tell us what the trouble was about?' Sheina asked, her thoughts

127

focused on her return home.

'I only know the gossip,' Mairi said, 'and that might not be the real truth. I'm not even sure your father knows the whole truth. It happened before he was born. It was his mother's tragedy. It's long ago and ought to have been forgotten.'

'Surely your father won't bear an old grudge against me?' Rob said. 'I'm not even a direct descendant of the family ... just related by marriage.'

'Get her home,' Mairi said. 'They're still looking for her.'

'Haven't they got mobile phones? We could ring.'

'My father hates them. He and Ian keep in touch with a two-way radio system. He says if you have a mobile you're at the constant call of all the world and his wife. You can't have them ringing if you're stalking a deer and nearly on top of him. Or just about to land a salmon.'

The journey back was silent. Sheina wondered what Rob was thinking. He must find her family very odd.

'Maybe Mairi could soothe your father,' Rob said, as Sheina's home came into sight. 'She has a way with people.'

'Not with him. He says what she does is like the old witches. Building a reputation with herbs and simples and pretending to have a healing touch.'

'That's only massage,' Rob said. 'My mother did it too and taught it to me. It's a special kind of movement ... it really does help both animals and people. It works wonders on young Paul once we get him to sit still long enough.'

He braked as Ian came down the drive towards them.

'We've been hunting for you everywhere,' he said, looking accusingly at Sheina. 'Your father thought you'd fallen and hurt yourself somewhere. He's in a real state. Especially as we also found the remains of three deer. They left the parts that won't make meat. They might have been there in daylight when we were the other side of the hill. We thought we heard shooting. If you met them—'

'I didn't think you'd miss me,' Sheina said.

'Your father's bothered by the poachers,' Ian said. 'The wildcat's been hunting. We found the remains of a grouse. And there's a rumour that the estate has a buyer. He isn't very rational just now. Try not to provoke him,' he added, desperately. He had been finding the last few weeks very difficult indeed.

Rob drove the last few yards and pulled up, wondering just what they were about to face.

The front door was flung open so violently that it hit the indoor wall with a slam.

Alastair exploded from it as if he had been pushed from behind and came up to the Land Rover, his expression thunderous.

'Where the hell have you been?' he asked Sheina and then turned to her driver. 'And who in hell are you?'

He looked as if he might drag Rob from the driver's seat and lay into him with his fists.

'I needed help with one of my animals,' Rob said, speaking softly in the hope it might defuse the man. 'I couldn't find anyone else. I'm sorry if I've kept your daughter too long. She thought you would be busy for some time and not worry.'

'I suppose you're the lunatic that's inherited the McPhee place,' Alastair said. 'Everyone in the village knows about you. Get off my property and don't ever come back. If you do I'll see you off with my gun. I'll not have any of that devil's spawn here.' He turned to Sheina. 'And you, get indoors. I'll talk to you later.'

'But, Dad—'

'Do as I tell you,' Alastair roared.

Sheina went indoors.

Rob reversed the Land Rover and drove away, feeling it was unwise to provoke the man further. He wondered if the gamekeeper was unbalanced. He had enjoyed Sheina's company, and hoped she might be able to help him with his animals. He was now very worried about her. He had had no idea his request would lead her into deep trouble. He had thought it a good way to get to know his neighbours.

He resolved to try and find out just how the feud between the two families had begun. Meantime the only thing he could do for her was to keep away. For all that, he carried away with him the image of a small slender girl with a mass of curling copper-coloured hair and expressive eyes almost the same green colour as his black cat's.

The last image he had of her was of a shadowed expression, overlaid with fear. The memory he wished to keep was of her sudden smile and quick laughter at the names bestowed on his animals.

He chided himself for idiocy. For a romantic notion of carrying off the maiden, away from the dragon. He had only just met her.

He wondered about her father. Somehow, Rob felt, he had to break down the long-standing antipathy between the two families. He had every intention of seeing Sheina again, but not with Alastair's fury threatening both of them.

Sheina heard the Land Rover drive off and ran to her room. Her father had never been as angry as this before. The pain of her mother's death overwhelmed her. She sat on the edge of her bed, afraid of the rage she had provoked. Life was becoming unbearable.

A moment later, her father was shaking the locked door. ' Sheina, let me in,' he shouted. She was too frightened to move.

Eight

Hexa was reluctant to leave her son alone, but his sisters were appetites on four legs and perpetually famished. She could not bring enough for them. Nor could she persuade Topaz to eat, though he sucked at her almost dry teats for comfort.

Everything she brought back was devoured within minutes, the two little females fighting for the best parts of each kill. She had no choice but to take them and begin to teach them hunting skills. They would soon need more than she could provide and she herself was now always hungry.

The demands for food were vociferous and could bring danger near. She was aware of the watcher above them, of his silence as he scanned for movement, of the shadow of his vast wings as he dived through the air, seeking fodder for his own clamorous youngster. He had already caused Hexa immense trouble and she did not want that to happen again. Luckily Topaz, hidden at the back of the cave, was safe from him, though not from others. Danger walked on four legs as well as on sweeping wings.

The little family left just before sunset. Amber and Jade, close behind their mother, were tiny shadows, echoing her need for wariness. They could already pounce, although their aim was poor. They learned on their mother's twitching tail and one another and on the small insects that were found in abundance round their home.

The eagle watched them go, but he was fully fed, having raided the rabbit warren earlier in the day. He stood on the peak, poised, a feathered engine of destruction, looking down the long sweep of pine trees and coarse grass to the distant shimmer of the loch.

He saw Hexa slip through the bushes, the kittens behind her. If she waited till daylight to return he might find bounty at her heels. Beyond him was his nest, the growing eaglet now asleep, his belly full. The mother bird brooded above him, spread wings sheltering him. She was as silent as her mate. Two eggs had hatched but the firstborn, stronger, had pushed his sister from the nest.

The untidy jumble was laced with interwoven twigs and branches that the female camouflaged with torn leafy twigs from growing trees. These unlikely adornments gave a little shelter to the youngster if both parents were hunting. As yet he was an ugly little creature with growing feathers and an ever-gaping maw perpetually screaming for food. The mountain loured above, fierce-cragged, its top hidden in cloud. A sheer cliff protected the eggs from thieves. No man could reach the nest, nor could the wildcat, the bird's only real enemy.

Time and again during that day the eagle had winged ever more wearily over the wood, and swooped to the rocky barrens and the rough land that bordered the loch. He returned bearing comfort to his young. He was enslaved by its needs, as are all other parents in the wild.

Hexa, far below him, crouched where tumbled rocks met the trees and bracken offered shelter. Unseen by others, she waited, Jade and Amber close beside her, aping every movement. They stalked when she stalked, sidled as she did. Then came a sudden soft hiss, warning them.

Freeze. Not a twitch of one whisker; death is near us. The stoat passed on, on the wrong side of the wind, unaware of their presence. Jade and Amber memorised its scent. In future they would both know that the beast was a threat.

There was movement in the bracken. The eagle noted it, but did not yet need to hunt. Hexa waited.

The deer calf was newly born. His mother was watchful, in spite of her preoccupation with her first baby. She was the wrong side of the wind, so she had no warning of danger. The two little cats waited, still as their mother.

The hind cleaned her son's coat. She nosed him, pushing him down, anxious to ensure he was well hidden in the undergrowth she had chosen for his resting place. New bracken, thrusting through tangled roots, helped to hide him, but a fly landed on one of his ears and the flick as he shook off its tickling presence alerted Hexa.

Further up the hill the main herd fed, their calves skipping at their mothers' sides, or dashing off to play games of tag and of head-butting, in wild abandon, heedless of danger. The old hind, the great-grandmother, now barren, kept watch. She had borne many calves and knew of too many dangers. Dangers that could come from the two-legged creatures that had no fur and were strangely shaped. They carried frightening sticks that spat fire, that made a terrifying noise, and brought quick death to the fortunate. Those less lucky endured slow torture and a lingering death from starvation if maimed instead of killed. Dangers that could come from the spitting wildcat. Dangers that could plunge from the innocent sky in a wildness of wings, tearing talons and a raking beak.

Alastair and Ian often saw the old hind guarding her charges. They christened her the Auld Yin. She stood, listening, her gently moving ears asking for tidings from the rustling grasses and the whispering trees, from the birds around her, as yet unalerted.

Her head, uplifted, smelled the air, seeking for news of a possible problem. The wind, blowing from the herd to Hexa, was a traitor, giving the guardian a false sense of security. Instead it brought information to the wildcat, telling her of a newborn, not yet able to stand and run, resting after those strenuous minutes that had brought him into the world.

She waited for her opportunity, endlessly patient. Amber, tired of being still, scratched her shoulder. Her mother slapped her with sheathed claws, and hissed again softly. Be still. Do as you are told. This is how we hunt. Give our quarry notice of our presence and we go hungry. Her expressive body told her daughters all they needed to know.

The Auld Yin, always uneasy, moved to another lookout post and listened again. She heard the soft rustle of the feeding herd. She heard the plash and play of wind-teased waves on the rocky beach. She heard the plaintive sound of faraway gulls, calling to one another. She heard the sigh of the wind in the shivering leaves.

Jade saw an unwary mouse running within inches of her. She forgot her schooling and pounced, her small body emerging into the dying sunlight. She missed her prey. It dived fast down a hole.

The air came alive as the birds called their rage. Cats. Cats. Beware. Take care. Hide. The call went on, endlessly, growing ever louder. The Auld Yin stamped and the startled herd fled, the outliers crashing noisily through the underbrush.

The new calf was not ready to run, and the hind was exhausted from the birth. She stood over her newborn as Hexa was sure she could defeat the young mother. She had no choice if they were to eat that night. She did not realise that the Auld Yin had not followed the herd. She raced to rescue her charges.

Hexa sprang, concentrating on her quarry. She did not see the approaching danger until it was too late. Two hard hind hooves delivered a tremendous double kick that caught her in the ribs. She lost her balance, tumbled down a small grassy slope and lay, bruised and breathless, at the bottom.

The ground was covered in thick moss. Jade and Amber crept towards her, terrified by her absence. Their small paws slid on the treacherous ground. They nosed their mother and she greeted them, reassuring them. They cuddled up against her, but she felt too battered to give them the comfort they needed.

Hexa recovered. The attack infuriated her and that gave her strength. She climbed the slope. Neither the hind nor the calf had yet had the strength to move. The old hind stood guard, watching over them.

In spite of her aching ribs, Hexa sprang again, this time at the Auld Yin. She was ravenous and hunger and fury made her braver than the mountain lion. She had her own family to feed and defend.

The calf was rich bounty. He was hers if she could drive off his protectors. There would be food for the three of them and some to carry back to Topaz. The Auld Yin was the main enemy. The mother had little strength and the calf was too new to protect himself.

The wildcat launched herself at the cause of her injury, this time dodging the kicks. Hexa clung to the hind's back with gripping teeth and clinging claws, but the old deer sped on, in spite of the fury that rode her. The Auld Yin had tangled with wildcats before. She knew many tricks.

Jade and Amber crouched together, close to one another, as their mother and her quarry raced past their hiding place and vanished.

The calf raised his head. He could smell milk. He stood on unsteady legs, and fell. Each movement brought strength until he was able to reach for the warm udder and begin to feed, comforted by his mother's presence. She licked him, sure they were safe for the moment. No news of the two kittens reached her and they were too tiny to be a threat even if it had.

The Auld Yin was waywise, and she still had strength. She did not attempt to shake Hexa from her grip. Speeding hooves cleared rocks and heather clumps and startled every animal in sight or sound. Birds called their protests and small beasts cowered and hid.

The hind leaped a crystal-clear beck where water chuckled over a shingle bottom and minnows lurked in the rainspecked swirls. Up on the hill the kittens crept into shelter, afraid to move alone.

The Auld Yin saw her target. It still stood, defying the weather. She had used the same ploy years before when she had her own calf to protect. She hurled herself towards the vast old dead tree, which stood, bare branches low and spreading, leaning towards the water.

She ran beneath it. Hexa was torn from her back and fell. The blow from the hard branch and the resulting crash to the ground as she fell from the back of the speeding hind added to her injuries. She did not recover for some time.

The old hind ran back up the track and joined the waiting herd, now more than half a mile away from the two kittens. The new calf found his legs and his mother, now with her companions, grazed near as he rested after his first journey, deep in another bracken clump.

It was well over an hour before Hexa found the strength to get back to her kittens. The kicks had cracked two ribs and the tree had bruised almost all of her body, but nothing was going to stop her from finding Amber and Jade. She climbed painfully up the path to the place where she had left them.

Jade and Amber huddled together, unable to manage on their own. Hexa dropped beside them, and they nuzzled into her fur. The rain swept over their inadequate shelter, adding to their misery.

The downpour eased as the first light painted the hilltops. The sun, emerging from dense cold, brightened the dawn. Hunger racked all three cats. Hexa could not hunt. She needed time to rest. She ached all over.

She dared not retrace the punishing path back to the high top where Topaz lay. It was challenging when she was fit. Now it was impossible.

Below her was the churchyard where she had sheltered before the kits were born. The tiny den was big enough for the three of them. The two-legged being that lived near had never threatened her. She had left food in plenty. Perhaps she could find food again. Memory tempted her. The path down the hill sloped gently. The food provider was in her garden, hanging out the day's washing.

Hexa began the painful descent, stopping often to rest. The hungry kittens pushed against her, mewing, unable to understand why she did not provide for them. This time her need to keep hunger at bay was drowned by the pain. Once she tried to pounce on a mouse, but could not bunch her muscles. Her ribs hurt when she breathed.

They did not reach the churchyard until lunchtime. It was necessary to keep under cover, to stop for frequent rests, to challenge the pain that racked her. She crept into hiding, Jade and Amber following her.

Mairi had gone out for the rest of the day. Nobody saw the wildcats arrive. At nightfall the two kittens went out by themselves to hunt the shadowed churchyard for insects. Both heard mice but could not catch them. Unsteady pounces invariably failed. Hunger raged within them.

A terrifying flash of lightning and a long reverberating rumble of thunder sent them flying back to their mother. By the time the storm died they were too afraid to venture out again. The moon hung above them, and they cried to it, forlorn, as if praying to some deity to provide them with the food they needed to survive.

Nine

Sheina sat on her bed, hands clasped round her body, listening. She was thankful that the doors were thick. It was ten minutes before her father gave up hammering and shouting. She sat, shaking, terrified that he might break down the door, and afraid of what he might do. He seemed to have gone beyond all sense.

Ian went home after trying to remonstrate with Alastair. He earned nothing but hard words and a flung boot. He was afraid that if he stayed he might make matters worse for Sheina.

He was now as frightened of his employer as Sheina was. He had never before seen him in such a rage.

He worried as he drove. He wondered whether to bring Mairi back to reason with the man. Or perhaps to offer sanctuary for the girl. He did not know what to do. He wished he were twice his size and possessed of the type of bravery that would have challenged such fury. Maybe Alastair would calm down and be more reasonable within an hour or so.

Halfway home he stopped in a lay-by, still worrying. Was Sheina safe? Surely Alastair wouldn't harm her? He reversed into a gateway and turned back. When he reached the house he stayed in the car but looked through the window. The curtains were open and the light was on. Alastair was sitting in his chair, the whisky bottle beside him.

Sheina's bedroom window was dark. Ian decided it might be wiser to return to his own home. She was probably in the kitchen at the back of the house, preparing a meal. He did not want to face her; they would both be embarrassed. He wished it were Saturday so that he need not return to work in the morning. He wondered what would happen next day. Perhaps Mairi would help him decide on his own behaviour. It would be hard to pretend that nothing whatever had happened.

Sheina felt as if she had been sitting still for hours when at last she heard her father's footsteps moving away. She sat in the dark room long after he had gone, crouched on her bed, as if she could disappear into nowhere. If only her mother were here. She had always calmed his anger. Yet, even immediately after Morag's death, Alastair had never behaved like this. She could not stop shaking. Fear had robbed her of her voice. What would her father do if she let him in?

When, after more than an hour, there was no further sound from him, she put on her warm outdoor clothes, pushed open her window and stepped out into the night. She was thankful that the whole of their flat was on the ground floor so that he would not know of her escape.

Maybe he would be recovered by morning. Meanwhile, she needed to get away, but there was nowhere to go. She would try and find Hexa and her family. Her thoughts were bleak as she began to climb. Perhaps it would be better if she left home and found work elsewhere. But while the estate was still functioning, the two men could not manage without her.

The moon was almost full. She paused for a while and sat on a rock. She had never felt so alone in her life. She longed for her father as he had once been. He never kissed her or held her close any more. In the last few months he had become a distant stranger.

Micklemoor House looked strange from above with its one sound wing. The rest of the roof had been removed so that they would not have to pay full rates. Those would have been astronomical. She saw it as a visitor might see it: a vast ruin, with one tiny corner where her own family lived. A house that had once been a home.

The need for her mother was a vast ache that engulfed her whole body. Sheina tried to distract herself by imagining Micklemoor House as it had been long ago. It must have been beautiful then. She and Morag had spent one afternoon in the library, trying to find photographs, but nobody seemed to have kept records. They thought maybe the laird had some, but they dared not ask him.

Moonlight shadowed the long terrace, its balustrades broken. It had once been lined with life-sized statues, but these had fallen into disrepair and been taken away. Sheina remembered one in particular that had terrified her as a tiny girl, as it was headless.

The relatively small garden that she and her mother had rescued from the long-neglected grounds held both a sundial and fountain, where a carved boy held a torch aloft. She loved him. He had been made by a man who revelled in his work and put his soul into the little statue. Every feature of his face, every finger, down to the tiny nails and the locks of hair, were lovingly carved. The water pump had not worked for years.

There was a light in her father's den, a room he often retired to at night, leaving her alone. It had once been her mother's sewing room. Alastair had taken it over after Morag died.

Sheina wondered what her father was doing. Would he turn for comfort to the whisky or take his gun to roam the hill, looking for poachers? She had to make sure she did not meet him. She could not face him yet. She did not know what to say.

She was cold. She huddled into the down anorak she had put on before leaving her room, wishing she had thought to bring gloves and a hat to keep her warm. At least the unlined hood kept the cold wind out of her ears.

The hills were alive with noise. Nearby a young badger blundered into the wrong territory. Snarls and growls and yelps rent the air, reminding Sheina of two immense dogs, snapping and biting as they hammered at one another, just out of her sight.

After what seemed like endless minutes the loser pushed noisily through the bushes. The winner whimpered somewhere very near as he licked at his wounds. She thought of Dapple and wondered how the little deer was faring.

She was cold and stiff and needed to move. The steepness of the hill made climbing difficult. She clambered over rocks. She was too near the stream. It had recently brimmed over and the ground was slippery. Above her the trees were dark shadows, moving eerily as the breeze strengthened. The night was alive with noise.

She was aware of the rustle of small animals hunting for food. The call of the questing owl. The eerie scream of a lone vixen.

147

The moon glimmered on a rushing torrent which dived over a small cliff, the cascading water silvered with light. She approached the falls, where the sound of water drowned all other noises. Rain had swelled the streams.

She had to tread carefully as the mud was treacherous. She wished she had brought Beulah for company, but she had not yet decided if she were going home. She could not add a dog to her problems.

The water had been much higher here only a day or so earlier. Though it had now receded she had a sudden fear that it might have flooded the cave and drowned the kittens.

Her thoughts raced, out of control, the memory of her father's anger still making her shake. What was the matter with him? Why had he changed so much? What had she done to deserve this, other than speak to a neighbour? What could have happened all those years ago to provoke such a reaction? Why would no one tell her?

Maybe she would climb for ever and never go back. Just lie at the top of the hill waiting for death to overtake her. Or jump over a cliff and die in the loch.

Her thoughts shocked her back to her senses. She was twenty, not thirteen. It was time she grew up. Maybe she would walk down to the main road in the morning and hitch a lift. Just vanish. She could easily find a job in a hotel or as a waitress if she went to one of the big cities. She could lose herself in the crowds. Perhaps, if she disappeared, her father would be sorry. She climbed on, fighting tears.

The little plateau was empty. There was no sign of Hexa. Sheina wondered if the wildcat had moved her home yet again. She walked over to the little cave and looked inside. A moonbeam fingered the leaf-strewn floor. There, curled up, whimpering softly, was Topaz, the ugly wound on his back now infected. He could barely move, but he heard her and opened his eyes. His feeble hiss was no challenge to the intruder.

Sheina was appalled. She forgot her own problems. If she did not help him he would most certainly die. She knelt by him. He made no protest at all. She wrapped him in her anorak.

She couldn't take him home. She couldn't leave him. She hadn't the slightest idea what to do.

Ten

There was only one person whose help she could possibly enlist, and that was Rob. It was too far to the vet's. She dared not take their Discovery without permission. Her father would hear the engine start.

The little body was so thin she could feel all the bones. She wondered if his mother had abandoned him. If not, she hoped Hexa would not come back to him till they were well away, as that would mean big trouble. The wildcat would not take kindly to someone stealing one of her kittens.

The way up the hillside and then down and across the fields to the McPhee farm was far more difficult than she had imagined. She struggled through overgrown gorse bushes, fighting her way, every sense alerted. Suppose Hexa hid ... and sprang?

Once at the top she had lights to guide her as Rob was still busy. Nobody had tended the land since the old man died, and here, on hills once grazed by sheep, bracken and furze had taken over. Last year's dead growth was tangled with the new green shoots. The old paths had vanished. Even the deer had forsaken the area, preferring the kept grounds where the feeding was plentiful.

She tripped a number of times, almost falling. In places dead weeds and ferns were chest-high. She thrust her way through them. Giant thistles pricked at her hands and face. She was able to see the farm below her, and the few grazed fields. Bramble trails caught at her ankles, scratching her.

Her trials were the results of years of neglect, as none of the tenants had farmed more than three or four of the fields. Sheina thought of stories of the jungle claiming the old cities long ago, and eliminating them entirely. She had not realised it happened so fast. Old man McPhee, according to Mairi, had had a well-kept farm of over two hundred acres. Also there had been another estate, where the wilderness was kept at bay. But that was looking for a buyer and nobody had worked there for several years.

She had a new fear now: she would arrive on Rob's doorstep with a dead kitten in her arms. His small breaths were shallower and weaker. She had to get there fast. She could not be in deeper trouble at home, so what did it matter that she was going to the man her father hated for help?

Rob had cages in which Topaz could be put while he recovered. He would care. Maybe

151

they could get the kitten well enough to return to the hills.

The sky was clouding over, the moon almost hidden. Sheina was bruised and aching and more miserable than she had ever been in her life, but the little animal she carried needed her.

She wondered what other animals Rob had around his home. She hoped that Napoleon had a stable, as she had to cross his field. There was no sign of him. A new worry began to needle. What would Rob say? Her father had made his feelings very plain. Would she be unwelcome here after the scene that afternoon?

She closed the field gate behind her. Its creaking provoked a sudden wild barking and Rob came out of the kitchen into the yard, the dogs beside him. They ran at her, and then, recognising her, greeted her with ecstasy.

She had no words. She held out her anorak. Rob looked down at the tiny animal and took it from her. He drew in a sharp breath.

'It's touch and go,' he said, leading the way into the house.

Sheina followed him. He put the kitten, now barely conscious, on the big pine table, dripped Rescue Remedy into him and laid him, very gently, in a cardboard box lined with a soft thick piece of old blanket. A padded hot water bottle was put in for extra comfort.

'We need Tom,' Rob said, walking across the tiled floor to the phone.

The dogs settled in their usual place on the rug. The little deer watched them as if curious. Her ears flickered, and she turned her head, following the two of them round the room with her enormous brown eyes.

'Do you think he'll live?' Sheina asked, as Rob put down the receiver after a brief conversation. She voiced her other worry. 'That isn't a gunshot wound?'

He looked at her, frowning, guessing her reason for the question. 'Definitely not. It's due to some animal. Whether or not he'll recover—' He shrugged. 'Anybody's guess. You don't look so good yourself. Care to tidy up? Plenty of hot water. I'll make us a drink when Dapple's had her bottle. Take Tom half an hour to get here at least.'

The bathroom had also been modernised. The thick cranberry-coloured towels contrasted with the pale green bath and basin and shower cubicle. Sheina wondered who had designed it. She also wondered if Rob did his own housework or if someone came in to help him.

She washed her face and hands and combed her hair, thankful that her pockets served as a handbag, an object she never carried.

Her hands were sore from scratches suffered as she tried to move the brambles out of her way. Rob offered her a small jar of cream as she came into the kitchen. He gave her another measuring glance as she took it from him.

'Magic potion,' he said. 'One of Mairi's little secrets. It'll take the sting out of those scratches. You did punish yourself, didn't you?'

'I tried to come too fast,' Sheina said. 'I was so afraid he'd die before I got here. I couldn't think of anyone but you to help. Mairi's too far away.' She hesitated. 'I was afraid you'd tell me to go away.'

'With a dying animal? Though I don't work miracles,' Rob said, as if embarrassed at her certainty that he could cure the kitten. He was sure that she had come too late, but did not want to upset her more. Her presence, especially at that time of night, troubled him. Her father would be even angrier if he learned of her second visit. He did not know how to approach that topic.

He brought her a huge mug of hot soup. 'Tom can give you a lift home,' he said, watching colour return to her cheeks as she drank.

She did not know what to say. She was not going home. She could not face her father. 'This is good,' she said, delaying the problem.

'Poacher's broth.' Rob grinned at her. 'I keep the pot brewing all the time as my gran used to do and add to it whatever comes. I get organic vegetables from the farm the other side of the village. Rabbit, venison, hare, all legal. I have a good supplier. Everything goes into the pan and gathers flavour daily.'

'I'd have thought it would lose it. Is it hygienic?' Sheina asked, with visions of food poisoning.

'It stays at the boil for hours. Kill any bug going.' He laughed suddenly, wanting to lighten the atmosphere. Sheina looked like a waif, her face white, her eyes dark and shadowed. She sat in the big chair by the fire, huddling up as if she would never get warm again.

'My gran had a saying that maybe might apply if you weren't careful,' he added. 'When I was small if I asked what was for dinner she always said Kill Me Quick. And if I asked what was for pudding the answer was Wait And See.' He laughed again. 'I must have been about three or four then and it was years before I realised what she really meant.'

'Mum and I once stayed for a week with my gran and grandad when I was very small,' Sheina said, looking back down a long tunnel of time. 'Right up the hill on the other side of this place. Grandad was head keeper before Dad, when the old laird owned the estate.' She sighed. Life had seemed wonderful then. It had all changed when her mother died.

'Dad used to help out on the estate even when he was a tiny boy. They lived in the cottage then. We did too when I was small and Dad was head keeper. Before the laird died. Gran always made stew from neck of mutton and I used to think of it as Splinter Stew.'

It was years since she had thought of that. Both grand parents had died the next winter, killed by flu that turned to pneumonia.

'There wasn't a bathroom. You had to go to the earth closet down the garden. Only if I woke in the night would they let me have a potty so I wouldn't have to go out in the cold and dark.'

They were both silent with their own memories as they finished the soup. It was rich and comforting and tasted delicious, Sheina thought.

'There was a huge tin bath. Gran filled it with hot water and bathed me in front of the fire. The towels were put to warm ... it was wonderful. Nobody ever modernised it till it was sold as a holiday home.'

'There are still places like that,' Rob said. 'Where does your water come from? Mine's from the stream and a very good well.

Electricity has reached here – we're not far from the main road.'

'We have a butane gas tank,' Sheina said. 'We once had a generator but it was noisy and always breaking down.'

Rob walked over to the box in which Hexa's kitten lay and looked down at him. 'Something made an awful mess of him,' he said. He frowned. 'That needs cleaning, but I think he ought to be sedated first. I wonder ... maybe the eagle tried to take him. He has a little one in the eyrie, and has been punishing the rabbits.'

Sheina was sure that Topaz would die. She wondered if Hexa had abandoned him or if she would hunt for him, trying to find out where he had gone. Were the other two kittens alive or had the predator that tried to take Topaz taken them too?

Topaz was just aware of his surroundings. He did not like the unfamiliar feel of the blanket under him or its smell, but appreciated the comforting warmth that soothed his chilled body. He was too ill to protest.

He wanted his mother. He needed the warmth of her dense fur, her comforting tongue and any milk that was left in her. He wanted his sisters, lying against him, all of them secure. Fear and pain together dominated him. The bright light hurt his eyes. The giants around him terrified him.

He was too ill to resist the liquid that was

dripped into him, or the gentle finger that stroked his throat to make him swallow.

'Glucose solution and Rescue Remedy,' Rob said, in answer to Sheina's unspoken query.

Within the kitten was a strong desire for survival that fought against his weakness. The remedy that had been given him stimulated that instinct. It was not enough to counteract the poison that was flooding through his veins. He lay almost motionless.

Sheina put down her empty mug. She walked across the kitchen to the box which Rob had put beside a large radiator. She looked at the festering wound, at the be-draggled coat, and at dull eyes that stared into an infinite distance as if seeing things nobody else could even imagine. She voiced her thoughts.

'It's hopeless, isn't it?'

A strange voice answered her, making her jump. She had not heard Tom come in. She turned to see a small dark man with a mass of thick hair blending into an equally dark beard. Grey eyes smiled at her.

'You never give up hope,' he said.

Topaz was too weak even to hiss as Tom lifted him. The vet looked down, frowning.

'I'll give him a penicillin injection for now. If he's still alive in the morning he'd better come in to us. He needs to be anaesthetised to clean that mess up. Been like it some days,

158

I'd imagine. Mairi's wildcat's kitten, is he?'

'Yes. There are three of them,' Sheina said.

Tom went to wash. When he returned he filled a syringe and injected the little creature. Topaz did not protest. The vet put him in the box again, tucking him up against the source of warmth.

'If he survives the night we may have a chance.' He walked over to Dapple, knelt and stroked her soft ears. 'This one's responding well. We were lucky that she was so young. She had almost no mothering, so she didn't miss it. The kit's several weeks old and as well as being very ill now, he's going to miss his mother and litter mates. If we do get it right he'll be a handful.'

'He'll tame, won't he?' Sheina asked. She was so tired that she thought she would fall over. She collapsed into one of the big armchairs.

Tom shook his head. 'Not a wildcat,' he said. 'They might make small concessions, but you can't ever live with them. He'll need to go back to the hills. It'd be cruel to cage him.'

Rob made coffee for the three of them. A few minutes later there was a pile of sandwiches. 'Tom needs reminding to eat,' he said.

Sheina looked down at the kitten. He was asleep. She voiced one of her fears, wondering if perhaps Hexa and the other two kittens lay dead.

'Can you tell what caused his injury?'

She was still afraid that Rob might have been hiding the truth.

Tom took a sandwich from the pile, and ate as if he had eaten nothing all day, which was almost true. The dogs, now awake at the smell of food, sat on each side of him, their eyes hopeful.

'It's almost certainly eagle talons,' he said. 'I doubt if any of the smaller hawks would try to lift him. They've gone deep. I need to clean that up, get rid of the pus, and probably do some stitching. He's in poor shape for such treatment. I hope the penicillin will help him turn the corner tonight.'

His mobile phone rang, startling all of them. Poco barked. 'I'm on call,' he said as he took it out of his pocket to answer it.

The call was brief and when it was finished he told them, 'Calving over at Jock Cameron's. No peace for the wicked. Sorry, I can't take you home – it's in the wrong direction,' he told Sheina.

He went outside and returned a minute later bearing a small lamb in his arms.

'I'll forget my head next,' he said. 'Born on the hill this morning. The mother died having a second one and nobody got to her soon enough. Duncan said can you rear it for him? He's not the time.'

'Easy enough.' Rob took the lamb from

him and put it in a large cage next to Dapple, leaving the door open. The lamb, only a few hours old and exhausted by his journey, folded his legs beneath him and almost fell to the floor.

Tom went on talking on his way to the back door.

'He had one feed at the farmhouse but Dunc's wife's overstretched, with her own new baby to care for.' He laughed. 'Bad timing. She should have fixed it to be born when lambing was over, but nature isn't always cooperative and even we humans don't know all the answers. I said you'd cope.'

'No problem.' Rob stroked the tiny animal that was too young to have learned fear of mankind. He had never known his mother. 'Don't shut the door. I need help on this one. Can you do the honours before you go? Let her in?'

Tom grinned as he went outside.

Sheina looked up in amazement as Rob whistled. A moment later a huge long-coated black and white dog resembling an outsize collie came into the room and ran up to Rob, delighted to be summoned. Poco and Nin nosed her, and then, on a signal from their owner, returned to their beds.

The lamb bleated, and the newcomer turned to look at it.

'He needs you, girl,' Rob said.

The newcomer walked over to the cage and looked in. She climbed in beside the lamb and curled herself round him. As her warm tongue began to lick him he relaxed, comforted by the dog's warm body.

'Meet Col,' Rob said, looking approvingly at the newcomer. 'Short for Colbern. Her mum was a collie and her dad a St Bernard. She'll mother anything on four legs, and even took over an owl chick once. It fell out of the nest and used to cuddle against her for warmth. It refused to leave me, so lives in an aviary outside now.'

The little deer moved her head to the edge of her cage and pushed against the wire. Col licked her nose through the mesh.

'Dapple thinks Col is her mother too,' Rob said. 'She cuddles up to her just as if she were a deer and not a dog.' He looked at Sheina, his expression anxious. 'I'd better drive you home when this lot's settled. I won't come all the way this time.'

'I'd decided not to go home,' Sheina said. 'My father frightened me. I don't understand what's wrong with the McPhees. No one will ever tell me. It's so stupid.'

'Old sins,' Rob said. 'Maybe something as simple as the trouble between my dad and me. I did manage to make it up before he died ... just. I wish...' He did not say what he wished. 'Running away doesn't solve anything. It doesn't change you.'

He laughed, though it sounded rueful. 'Believe me. Been there. Done that. Got the T-shirt ... and the wounds.'

He made more coffee and glanced at the clock, now reading six a.m. 'Where will you go? Have you relatives? An aunt or uncle?'

Sheina shook her head. 'Both my parents, like me, were onlies. My grandparents all died long ago. I've a great-aunt somewhere in her nineties. Nobody kept in touch with her. I don't even know where she lives – or her surname, as she married. I thought of just going to some big city and getting a job. I could lose myself there.'

'Doesn't sound like a good idea. Big cities are lonely ... and there's some odd people around. They aren't safe these days.' He pushed the plate of sandwiches towards her. 'Go home and think about it. No use trying to run off without somewhere to go. You need clothes. You need money. Or you'll end sleeping in a doorway. No one will take you in without luggage or money to pay. Your old man'll have cooled off by morning.'

He could only guess at what had happened after he had gone.

Sheina wanted to stay for ever, safe in the big kitchen that was the heart of the house. It would be good to help with the animals, to do something more worthwhile than being called in if extra help was needed by her father and Ian.

'I'll run you home,' Rob said. 'But I'll put you down out of sight of the house. No need for your father to know how you spent the night. Any chance he'll think you went for an early morning walk?'

Sheina sighed. 'I don't know.'

She felt, as they drove towards her home, that she was in uncharted territory. Anything might happen. Would her father have recovered from his anger? Would he question her as to where she had been? Would he ever trust her now?

She sat in the Land Rover, unwilling to get out. The sun cast glittering rainbows in the dewdrops on the grass. A bird sang, sudden and high and sweet. She had no choice. She opened the door.

'I want to know about the kitten,' she said. 'Can you tell Mairi?'

Rob nodded. He felt a sudden pang. She was as forlorn as any of his charges and he wished he could help her. 'Want to watch out for the keeper,' one of the men in the inn had said. 'Bee in his bonnet about the McPhees and a temper on him when he lets go ... though, to be fair, he doesna do that often. Bad man to cross.'

Tom's boss had said much the same.

Rob waited until Sheina was out of sight and then depressed the clutch. The sooner he was away the better.

Sheina walked slowly towards the house.

No use rehearsing their meeting. She didn't know what to say if her father asked where she had been. Up on the hills? Without Beulah?

She went into the kitchen. The door was unlocked, so he must be about. The dishes from last night's meal were still on the table. Alastair had opened a tin of corned beef and made inexpert sandwiches. The house was very quiet. Maybe he was out with the dogs.

The light in the den was still on. She could see it under the door. She went into the room.

Her father was lying on the floor, staring at her out of terrified eyes. He tried to speak, but words did not come. He tried to move, but could not even lift himself into a sitting position. He flapped his right hand at her.

She ran to him and put a cushion under his head. There was nothing else she could do. She took a deep breath.

'Don't move, Dad,' she said, knowing her words were daft. 'I'll get help.'

'Stay with him,' Ian's voice said from the doorway. 'I'll see to it.' He went to the phone and dialled 999.

Sheina listened in a daze. 'What's wrong with him?

'A stroke, I'd guess. I don't know for sure.'

'People die of strokes.'

Ian put a hand on her shoulder. 'And lots don't. They recover completely. Stay with him. He needs you. He must be so scared. I would be.'

'Can't we lift him on to the sofa? It seems too awful to leave him on the floor.'

Ian shook his head. 'He may have broken something when he fell – his leg or arm or his back. Moving him would make it worse. There'll be paramedics here soon – they know how to cope. He'll be OK.'

He hoped he sounded more reassuring than he felt. Would Alastair ever be able to work again? If not, how would he and Sheina manage? He waited with her, unwilling to leave her on her own with the sick man.

Sheina held her father's hand, but there was no strength in it. She hoped her touch would comfort him. She could not remember him ever being ill before, other than with winter colds which he always shrugged off.

Alastair tried to speak, but gave up the effort. The words would not come.

'He's so cold,' Sheina said. His hand was icy. Ian switched on the electric fire and fetched a blanket and put it over the keeper. Sheina too was shivering. The room felt freezing, although it had been warm outside.

Ian had work to do, but felt he could not leave them. He made hot tea. Sheina tried to lift her father's head so that he might drink it, but he could not swallow. She felt helpless.

'They're sending an ambulance,' Ian said.

He paced outside the room, unable to settle.

It's all my fault, Sheina thought, guilt overwhelming her. If only she hadn't gone over to the McPhee place. If only she hadn't told her father where she had been. If only he hadn't met Rob. If only he hadn't been so angry. None of this would have happened.

If her father died, it would be her fault.

Ian, as worried about Sheina as about Alastair, hovered between the den, where her father lay, and the front door, watching for the ambulance.

Nobody had fed the dogs. The air was filled with their hungry barking. The waiting seemed endless. When there did come a knock at the door, Sheina jumped. Ian appeared a moment later with their own doctor.

Dr Mac had been part of Sheina's life since before she was born. He was a big bear of a man with a startlingly large corporation and an equally massive beard, once black but now mostly grey. Patients told to slim who looked at his frontage were rewarded with a sharp bark. 'Do as I say. Don't do as I do.' His mere presence was comforting.

'Here's Dr Mac to make you feel better,' her mother had always said, when he visited to see her about her childhood illnesses. He always did.

She remembered him sitting on the edge of her bed, his vast weight bending the mattress. She had had measles, and he made animal pictures wiggle on the wall with shadows of his fingers, trying to make her laugh. When she refused to drink he suggested a small amount of money for every glass finished, and she had fun spending the sum she amassed when she was better. She must have been eight years old. She still had the woolly dog she had bought.

'We didn't like to move him,' Ian said, feeling perhaps they ought to have made Alastair more comfortable. Dr Mac balanced himself on the leather arm of the big old chair. 'Good. You did the right thing.' He looked down at his patient. 'Well, now,' he said. 'So it's come. Told you, didn't I?'

He knelt, a procedure that seemed remarkably difficult. Sheina realised with a pang that Dr Mac should have retired some years ago. She did not like his younger partner.

'A couple of weeks and you'll be on the mend,' the doctor said. 'Then have you up and about in no time. You've been lucky.'

He heaved himself up, using the chair to help him, and nodded to Sheina. She followed him out into the kitchen, where Ian was pouring hot water on to instant coffee.

'Go and sit with him, lad. He'll feel better for company. Talk to him. He can understand, though he isn't making much sense himself. That'll come back. Talk about what you're doing, what you're planning, about the shoots ... keep his mind busy, and focus on getting better.'

'He will get better?' Sheina asked.

'He should. It's quite a serious stroke, but I've seen far worse recover completely.' He did not add that he had seen some die who ought to have got better. Then, to her surprise, he laughed. 'It's the bloody-minded who won't give up and want to prove us medics wrong who do best,' he said. 'And if there's one adjective that would apply to your father, it's that. He and your mam were about my most difficult patients. They had such strong wills of their own.'

'It didn't do Mam a lot of good,' Sheina said.

'No, lass. It harmed her because she wouldn't come for advice. Thought she knew best. Your father did come and didn't do as he was told. His blood pressure was sky high and he wouldn't take the pills. Don't you make the same mistake. No aches and pains yourself, I hope?'

Sheina shook her head. 'It's just...' She stopped.

'Just what?'

'This is my fault. We had a row and I made him so mad.'

'Rubbish. It would have happened if he had spent the day in bed. What were you rowing over? Boyfriends? Late nights?'

'No. Rob Vincent came over for help with his donkey and I went to the McPhee place. Dad and Rob met when Rob brought me home ... and all hell broke loose.' She remembered the shouting.

'That trouble. It was over sixty years ago and should be long forgotten. Never known a man like your father for nursing old grudges. The worst thing anyone of his nature can do is hang on to the past. Besides, the man is only remotely connected with the McPhees and wasn't even born then.'

'What did happen?' Sheina asked.

'Best forgotten. Most people don't re-member it, and it's better not to stir up old wounds.' He glanced at his watch, and then sipped at his coffee after adding four spoonfuls of sugar to it and stirring it as if it were defying him. 'You're a big girl now. Why let that stop you if you want to go over? Rob can do with all the help he can get – nobody wants to work for him. It's not as if you're paid to work here. Your father has tried to get the syndicate to pay you for the work you do on the shoots, but they're mean men.'

He glanced at his watch again. 'I hope the ambulance hasn't broken down,' he said. 'The sooner we get your father to hospital and start treatment the better his chances of a full recovery. And you get rid of those guilt feelings, and start living your own life, lass. Your father has to learn that he can't keep you for ever, and that he isn't always right.'

Sheina looked at him, and he quirked an eyebrow.

'I know. I know. There's none so awkward as those that won't learn ... or some such. I never do remember these old sayings. Mairi is full of them.' He glanced out of the window. The ambulance was drawing up outside. 'At last,' he said.

Sheina went in to sit with her father. She knelt beside him and held his hand but was not sure that he was even seeing her. Ian came outside to the doctor, and stood beside him as they waited for the paramedics.

'Will the old man be OK?' he asked.

Dr Mac frowned. 'We don't know how long he'd been lying there before the lass found him. Speed is important with these things. Every hour of delay can make a difference to his recovery. He may be lucky ... or he may be disabled in some way. Don't tell Sheina what I said. Too early to tell anyway.'

'He hadn't been to bed,' Ian said. 'The lights were still on in his den.'

'So ... it must have been hours.' He sighed and greeted the two paramedics as they came towards him. They paused, listening to him as he spoke in a low voice that Ian could not hear.

The younger man felt useless, and more worried than he had ever been in his life. How would Sheina cope now, and what would happen to her and her father if Alastair was unable to work? The syndicate was not composed of sympathetic men. They were hard and unfeeling taskmasters. Ian himself might be kept on. If not, at his age he could find some other work. But Sheina and her father would lose their home. Where would they go and how would they live?

Even if he recovered, it would be months before Alastair was fit to work again. Life was so unfair.

Eleven

Mairi had a major problem of her own which began the night that Sheina decided to run away.

She was wakened by the kittens' cries. She lay for some minutes trying to identify the sounds. They were calling to Hexa to come and hunt for them. Mairi went to her window. They were in the churchyard, lit by the moon, two tiny versions of their mother, trying desperately to find food. There was no sign of the adult wildcat. Was she dead?

But she must have led the little ones there; they could not have found the place by chance. At times they vanished into the shelter where Hexa lay. There they tried to rouse their mother, but she was cocooned into her pain, and ignored them. She was weak and she was slowly losing interest in the world.

Mairi's chiming clock struck three.

She must silence the cries.

She must also be silent herself. She did not want to wake her lodger. Ian had no time for the wildcats that threatened his own charges. She was not sure if he would shoot them or take pity on them and trap them.

She lay, worrying. There were times when she wished she was on her own again, but her pension had long since ceased to cover any but her basic needs, and she needed extra money. Also, at her age, it was reassuring to have someone who would know if she were taken ill.

Morag had persuaded Mairi to take in Ian's predecessor, a surly and unlikeable young man. She liked Ian, who was more thoughtful, but a young man in his twenties, apt to speed everywhere and take stairs three at a time, was not a restful companion. They ate together in the evening, and then sometimes he would talk, but he too was taciturn.

As soon as the dishes were washed and wiped Ian retired to his own room. He was tidy, which was a mercy as the first man she had taken in had turned the place into a shambles within minutes of arriving for his evening meal.

The wildcat killings made the young keeper angry. He would not tolerate the animals on his land. He had been even angrier when he glimpsed Hexa after the kittens were born and realised she was heavily in milk. How many more to plague them?

Mairi tried to convince him that they could be forced to move if shot at but never shot.

At most he offered to consider trapping them and giving them to someone to look after.

Who would take them in? Could Rob manage them? She did not like to think of them penned for the rest of their lives in a cage.

The cries resumed. The kittens were hungry. Both were trying to rouse Hexa so that she could take them hunting, as they were having little success in the cemetery.

Mairi could not lie still any longer. She crept down the stairs, holding on to the banisters. Old knees did not take kindly to climbing up and down, but Mairi never allowed herself to be defeated. Her own herbal remedies kept the worst of her arthritis at bay.

She reached the kitchen without switching on one single light, able to find her way blindfold. With the door closed and the curtains drawn, nothing could be seen from outside. Light straying across the garden from the window would betray her if Ian woke.

The young keeper was not a night-time wanderer, unless he was patrolling. He and Alastair took turns. But if Ian knew his landlady was awake he might think she felt ill and come down to make sure all was well.

She hoped that he was so soundly asleep that he would not hear the cries. She was sure he would make certain that the kits and their mother ceased to threaten his own world. She did not know that he hated shooting living creatures.

She found a large bowl and filled it. She kept a good store of food so that, should she be unable to shop, she would not go hungry. She opened several tins of sardines and mashed them with bread. The oil would be good for the little ones.

The dark woollen dressing gown, which had once belonged to her husband, now fifteen years dead, was very thick and she did not bother to dress. Nobody could see her. That was as well, she thought with some amusement, as her outfit of nightclothes and wellingtons was strange to say the least.

The churchyard trees, newly in leaf, laced patterns against the moonlit sky. They stood, sentinel-like, branches uplifted, as if praying. Mairi walked softly, anxious not to alarm the kits if they were outside. A small wind rustled the leaves and the dew-wet grass soaked the hem of her dressing gown.

A Victorian angel, battered by time, its imperfections hidden at night, stood guard over a long-forgotten grave. It caught the light and was shadowed by branches, so that it appeared, uncannily, to be moving. Jade, more adventurous than her sister, looked up at it and hissed.

Amber was busy. There was a mouse in the

bushes. Her quick ears heard the rustle as it moved. She sat, watching, her eyes intent, her ears pointing. Mairi, approaching, stopped, hoping the little cat might be rewarded. If they had no mother they needed to hunt or they would die.

Amber sat with one paw lifted, intrigued. She stood, angling her body, ready for her prey. The mouse, young, incautious and intent on his own affairs, came out into the moonlight. Instinct combined with bloodlust. Amber pounced and killed.

Her mew of triumph alerted her sister who, made wild by hunger, tried to steal the trophy. Within seconds they were locked in a fight that was no longer play, but had a deadly purpose. The spits and snarls roused Hexa from her torpor and she crept to the doorway of her shelter, dragging herself along, every movement slow and painful.

Mairi moved fast and spoke softly, knowing that the sound of her voice would startle the combatants and they would take shelter. They broke apart and vanished, hiding behind their mother, who was too sore to move. She lay in the entrance to her den, frightened green eyes staring at the intruder.

Hexa was aware that this was the food bringer, who had helped her before and who had never offered a threat. She felt too ill to do more than give a token hiss.

Mairi saw the cautious movements and

knew that this meant pain. Even in the dim light she could see that the wildcat was injured, a wound on her back bleeding as she crawled. The dense fur had lost its lustre.

The old woman approached to within touching distance. Hexa watched her and hissed again very softly but made no other move. Mairi put the bowl down, as close as she dared, and walked away.

Tomorrow she would add healing herbs to her offering. She didn't want to put in antibiotics as the kittens would eat too and a dose big enough for their mother might well harm them.

She paused under the ivied arch, standing by the fallen gate to watch. Hexa, roused by the scent of the fish, crawled painfully to the bowl. She tested the food, licking it tentatively with her tongue. Pain fought with hunger, but as she tasted, the need to eat returned. The kittens, seeing their mother feeding, came to the bowl too. Mairi waited, and only returned to her own cottage when the three cats vanished to sleep off the first good meal they had had for many hours. They would not cry to the moon again tonight.

With luck they would sleep by daylight and not venture out until dark. If she kept them well fed then maybe they would not call for food at all. But they also mewed to their mother and to one another.

If only they would not make a noise until the night was well advanced and Ian was asleep. Perhaps if she fed the young keeper with heavy meals he would sleep more soundly. She planned steak and kidney pie and suet puddings. He had a very good appetite, like all young men, but she normally tried to give him a healthy diet. She smiled to herself, half ashamed of her plans.

She wondered about Topaz and if he was alive. It was perhaps as well that Hexa only had two now to feed. She needed all her strength, and the little family would suffer through her injuries.

Mairi doubted if Hexa was capable of moving. It might be a week or more before she was fit. If she did recover. There might be far worse unseen injuries. Mairi wondered if she had tangled with the eagle, as that seemed the only creature strong enough to harm her. If he tried to take a kitten ... had she been injured defending Topaz?

More time had passed than she realised. It was not worth going back to bed. She made herself a cup of tea and sat, wondering how best to manage the situation.

By the time she was dressed Ian was about and needed his breakfast. That was the feast of the day, intended to carry him through to evening. Lunch, except on Sundays, was a sandwich snack, which he made for himself. His sandwiches were doorsteps but Mairi

179

felt it wiser to let him fend for himself. He would have to if she were ill.

Sunday was a traditional roast, which Mairi considered a necessity of life. It had the virtue of looking after itself while she was in church – especially now, when she had to travel to the service. Their own little kirk had been abandoned long ago. Soon the graveyard would be full too, and all ties with the nearby village lost.

Ian's mornings always began with a meal that Mairi cooked for him. He feasted. Bacon, eggs, tomatoes, butter and mushrooms all came from the farm shop, as did organic root vegetables and home-killed meat. Home-made oatcakes added to his enjoyment.

Mairi baked her own bread and cakes and made jam, chutney and marmalade. Those too were sold at the farm shop. Twice a week she made batches of small steak and kidney pies and Cornish pasties. Ian relished these as he could take them for his lunch. The profits added to her meagre pension.

Sometimes she varied the morning meal by scrambling the eggs, or adding sautéed potatoes and some of the farm shop sausages. These might be pork and garlic, or pork and leek, or pork and apple. Ian had never tasted anything like them in his life. Sometimes he was given porridge. If Mairi shared it she added salt to her portion but Ian covered his with maple syrup.

He liked his coffee black and strong with three spoonfuls of sugar. His daily walk of many miles over rough ground and hills ensured that he remained slim. He teased his landlady, whose breakfast usually consisted of an apple and a small slice of cheese. She retorted by saying she only had to look at a piece of cake to gain three pounds. Being small, she would not risk looking like a cottage loaf.

That morning she was on edge all the time he ate lest the kittens came out to play and began calling. It was a relief when he drove off.

She was getting her car out of the garage some time later to go and fetch more food for the cats when she heard a siren on the road below. Looking down she saw an ambulance speeding towards Micklemoor House, with a police car following behind.

There was no other residence on that road. Her first thought was of poachers. Had Alastair been injured? He and Sheina might need help. She got into her car and followed them.

She arrived as Alastair was being lifted on to a stretcher, Dr Mac supervising. Sheina, white-faced, was standing beside it, while Ian watched her anxiously. He turned to Mairi with a sigh of relief.

'There's nothing you can do for him, I

promise,' the doctor said as Sheina tried to climb inside. 'He won't even realise you're there. I think he's slipped into a coma for the moment. He'll recover as soon as they start treatment.' He saw Mairi and nodded to her. 'I was going to ring you.'

He turned back to Sheina. 'You can ring the hospital later, and find out how he is. I'll call in on him this afternoon. Just now it would be better if you stayed at home.'

'What's wrong? Do you know?' Mairi asked Ian as the ambulance drove off down the hill. It would be a bumpy ride for the first few miles. It was a poor road.

'Dr Mac says he's had a stroke.'

The keeper did not need to explain to Mairi, who had trained as a nurse. She had been the village district nurse and midwife, but retired two years before Sheina was born. Her nursing skills were often in demand and she could still deliver a baby if the present midwife was delayed.

'Will he die?' Sheina asked.

'Most people don't die. The majority recover.'

For all her confidence, Mairi thought there might be more problems if Alastair recovered than Sheina would realise. Especially if he were unable to continue to work. Strokes often changed people so that they developed totally different personalities. Also, how would Sheina manage if her father were partially disabled?

'Keep her busy,' were the last words Dr Mac said as he climbed into his car. They watched him drive away.

'I can't think how he squeezes in,' Mairi said. 'A man who ought to take his own advice, but how many do?'

'Things to do,' Ian said, unable to handle the situation. He drove off to busy himself with repairing one of the fences, glad to be occupied. There was never any lack of jobs.

Alastair took in gun dogs to train. There were four now in the kennels: three lively springers that were giving trouble and a very well-bred Labrador that seemed to teach himself or to know in advance what was required. Ian wished he could keep the dog.

They were trained to stay still in a huge pen covered in thick undergrowth in which were pheasants and rabbits, running free. These needed feeding as well as the dogs. All needed exercise.

The older man did not trust either his assistant or his daughter with his pupils. Ian wondered if he ought to make a start. He had helped his own father with the dogs sent to him by their owners for professional teaching. He had also competed successfully with his own dogs in field trials. But if Alastair came home fit he might be angry. Nobody could train dogs as well as he. It was an often reiterated comment.

It took much longer than usual to care for the animals single-handed. When the dogs were at last settled and the fence was repaired Ian began to split logs for the range, using the hammer blows of the axe to vent his worry and anger at the trick fate had played on them all.

Mairi made tea and insisted that Sheina at least ate a slice of toast.

'It was my fault,' the girl said forlornly. 'If I hadn't made him so angry...'

'I've been warning him of his high blood pressure for years,' Mairi said. 'He had problems when your mother was alive. It used to worry her. There's no arguing with your father, or reasoning with him. You know what he thought of doctors.' She sipped her own tea and sighed. 'Your mother was stubborn too and wouldn't take advice or go for help, or rest. Look what happened to her. I hope you haven't inherited that streak from both of them. If you have, think about it. Can't do with another like either of them here.'

Sheina bit into her toast, discovering she was hungry. She glanced through the window. A kestrel hovered, standing on the wind. From the back of the house came the recurrent thud of Ian's axe as he chopped the firewood.

Mairi was still talking, partly to fill time and partly to keep Sheina occupied. She knew only too well that Sheina would feel that this, coming on top of the row, was all her fault.

'Alastair's always done as he chooses. He goes on eating all the wrong things, drinking more than he should, never resting, often angry at nothing. You can't go on like that.'

Sheina was only half listening. Her mind was repeating her thoughts over and over. Please, God, don't let him die. Don't let me have killed him.

'When can I ring the hospital?'

'Wait till this evening. That'll give them more time and by then they should know more about his condition. I can drive you down tomorrow. You're not driving yourself. Not while you're worried. That's asking for trouble.'

'I can't ask you to do that,' Sheina said.

Mairi could not forget the wildcats. If they stayed in the cemetery Ian was bound to come across them, or traces of them. Kittens were not quiet.

'You can do something for me in return. Hexa's back in the kirkyard with the other two kits. She's badly hurt and I'm scared stiff Ian will hear them crying to her. They're hungry.'

The thudding axe stopped and she broke off lest Ian came in. He resumed within a couple of minutes and she gave a sigh of relief.

'Suppose we ask Ian to sleep here, as it's too lonely for you by yourself, and you come to me? There's no danger then of him finding them, as he won't need to come down. He can move into your spare room.' She smiled, intrigued by her sudden new plan. 'Your father will be glad to know you aren't here alone. We can come here during the day and eat. Then you can see to the horses. I'm sure Ian would feed the dogs.'

'And Beulah?'

'Bring her with you. She knows the cottage well, and she's no trouble. She can sleep by your bed.'

They looked out of the window at the sound of a car engine. Sheina made a face.

'It's Mr Oliver, the syndicate secretary. He's a horrible man. Do you think he's already heard about Dad and wants us out of here and someone else in?'

She went to the door as the man climbed out of the big estate car.

'Your father in?' he asked.

'He's just gone to hospital. He had a stroke this morning,' Sheina said.

'And Denton? I suppose he's not in hospital too?'

'He's splitting logs,' Sheina said

'Is that a keeper's job? I would have thought he had better employment.'

Mairi came to the door. 'He's been repairing fences and only just come up. Sheina was

186

naturally upset and he's kindly helping her.'

'Who are you? Her grandmother?'

'I'm a neighbour and a close family friend,' Mairi said, her voice icy.

James Oliver walked into the kitchen without being asked and sat himself at the table. Shaggy black eyebrows made dark slashes above angry brown eyes. He was an unnaturally thin man, who appeared to be wearing clothes that had come straight from the shop and never been worn before. Mairi, looking at the creases in his trousers, wondered who had to minister to his needs. She was sure he didn't care for his own clothes. Maybe a doting mother. What wife would do that today?

'I came to tell McNeill there will be no more shoots. The estate is for sale. It ceased to make a profit two years ago. The owners found the shooting sparse and disappointing and have joined another syndicate in the south where they breed pheasants and produce better results than here.'

Sheina stared at him. 'What will happen here?'

'I doubt if it is saleable as it is. One group who are interested would rebuild the house and turn it into a hotel and leisure centre. There's room for a golf course, tennis courts and a swimming pool, if it's bought by the right people.'

Mairi passed him a cup of tea. He added

sugar, stirred it and then drank. 'You might find a job as chambermaid,' he said, looking at Sheina.

She stared at him, furious, but wise enough not to speak. Surely she could at least become a receptionist or assistant house-keeper. Or even a cook. Everyone who came to the shoots praised their food, though rarely to her.

He went on, oblivious to her feelings. 'Denton could be taken on as handyman. By the sound of it your father won't be fit for anything. I had thought he might become a groundsman, but that seems unlikely. Strokes disable people.'

'Many people make full recoveries,' Mairi said.

Colonel Oliver looked at her with dislike in his eyes.

'Where do we go? And when?' Sheina asked.

James Oliver shrugged. 'You can stay here for the moment as caretaker, so long as you pay the rent on time. Nothing definite yet. We expect it to be kept in good order. The horses have to be sold. They cost too much and won't be needed. There won't be any deer shooting. Or trekking, as we'd planned.' There had been a suggestion that they might buy more ponies so that Sheina could run a pony trekking centre. There were very attractive rides.

The visitor stood up and went towards the door, but turned as he reached it. 'We don't pay sick men. Your father's wages will stop if he's in hospital more than a couple of weeks. That will be at the end of this month.'

'Surely caretakers get paid?' Mairi asked, trying hard to control her tongue lest she aggravate the situation.

'She'll have a roof over her head,' the man said. 'Lucky to have that in the circumstances. I'm sending a vet to examine the horses. I hope they're in good shape.' He opened the door and walked out on to the drive.

'I've always felt they were mine,' Sheina said. 'I won't see that foal born ... I can't bear any more.'

Mairi looked at her, for once bereft of words. Nothing she could say would be comforting.

They sat in a silence punctuated by the thudding axe, and listened to the engine sound dying away. Tarn whinnied suddenly, and Sheina thought that she would never be happy again.

Twelve

Hexa was still too sore to move very far from her lair, but the world outside called to the kittens. They were ready to explore. Both were more wary than their brother, and did not stray far. The least unusual sound sent them skittering back to safety and Hexa's reassuring bulk, though she had little time for them.

Mairi put out more food for them before she and Sheina went to bed, so that they were not hungry. Hexa ate, and curled herself into a ball, nose buried in her tail, for a healing sleep. The kittens found another bowl, which contained milk. Lapping was new to them. Jade could not manage at all and contented herself with dipping one paw in the liquid and sucking it.

Amber made several false starts and suddenly discovered the knack, but her small face was covered. Jade licked her clean and then both kits attempted to wash themselves. That was difficult and they fell over several times, having placed themselves in awkward positions.

There was much to explore. The cemetery had been untended for many years, except for a few of the graves. Only four other villagers helped to keep the grass cut and brought flowers for their lost loved ones. There were bushes, weeds and sapling trees, as well as the neglected gravestones. All made wonderful hiding places. The kittens hid and pounced on one another, indulging in mock battles, swiping with small paws, biting and tumbling.

The pink pads were now black, and the blue eyes changing to a soft greenish colour. Both were well-grown, chunky little animals, their striped fur dense. Amber was the prettier of the two, though she was fiercer, and quicker to spark if anything startled her.

It was a wild night. A rising wind chased tumbling clouds across a patchwork sky, where the moon played hide and seek. It rose to a gale, and screamed round the angles of the old kirk. It found its way through broken windows and into the derelict building where bats roosted and two owls nested. Mice darted through the grass, their passage bending the stems. Their small rustles and erratic movements alerted the kits.

One, unwary, emerged from a patch of grass into a moonlit area right in front of Amber, who pounced and missed, falling over. She wailed her frustration. Mairi, hearing the cries, was glad that it was Sheina and not Ian now sleeping in her spare room.

Jade discovered trees. She scrambled up a trunk, using her sharp claws, and walked daringly out on to a branch. A cloud covered the moon as she reached her target, and she crouched, holding on tightly, afraid of the depth below her. She called to her mother. But Hexa could not reach her, although she crawled out of the den. The moon shone full again. Jade half scrambled and half tumbled down from her perch. She fell the last few feet to land, shaken, on grass, and crept to her mother for comfort. Hexa summoned enough energy to lick the small body and be comforted by her daughter's presence.

Amber, playing with a grass head, was covered by the shadow of the hunting owl. He swooped. She remembered her mother's teaching and fled. Soon she was lying in the darkness with her sister, her small heart racing

Within an hour both had forgotten their fears and the outside world was calling to them again. The wind was dropping. Its presence was exciting. It teased so that everything moved, and small paws patted at leaf and twig and shivering grasses. Inept little bodies leaped at leaves that danced in the wind and failed to catch them. Everything tempted them, and there was so much that was new. Caution kept them close to the den.

Amber tried to leap a small log. She landed on top of it and jumped down. The last squalls of a dying wind produced noises that made her dive often for shelter, but she was excitement embodied. She heard a soft slither in the grass, and then came a new smell. She crouched, listening, ears pricked forwards to catch the tiniest whisper of movement.

This was the smell of food. It was throat-tightening, saliva-forming, stomach-tingling. It roused the memory of new-killed meat, brought to her by her mother. It was an intoxicating smell that galvanised every instinct, inciting her to kill.

She mastered her impatience. Hexa had taught her kits without realising that she was doing so and Amber had memorised her actions. Wait. Watch. Keep stiller than the stone behind you. She stalked, all cat, crouched to the ground, each movement stealthy. She did not want to alert her prey. As yet, it was only news on the wind. She had not seen it.

She crept, taking care not to ruffle the grasses. She was a hunter, impelled by age-old instincts. Survival was all. She was aware that she could not depend on her mother. She did not understand why Hexa lay so quiet and moved so slowly, but she knew that she was on her own and had to find food.

The rustling grew louder. This was no cautious beast, afraid of capture. It was an animal that blundered through the undergrowth, hunting his own food. He grunted and grumbled. He came into a small clearing and sniffed the air, lifting his blunt nose to the sky. He caught the scent of wildcat, but that was not his kind of quarry. He marched towards his goal.

He smelled the bowls of food that Mairi had put down for the wildcats. He had a memory of some weeks back, after Hexa had moved on, when they had appeared and stayed untouched.

There was no doubt that this was food. Amber sprang, but missed her target, touching his side with her nose. She cried out in terror as she encountered what felt like stinging thorns. She stared, for now her prey was a spiky ball, with neither head nor tail nor feet.

She sat and licked at herself, then pawed at her face, trying to ease away the hurt. The hedgehog, indignant, thundered off, telling the world of his displeasure. His loud angry grunts died away. He had taught the kitten a new and valuable lesson, and she had survived, relatively unhurt. She would not make that mistake again. Hedgehogs had added themselves to her list of dangers to be avoided.

Jade came out to play, tempting Amber with a slap on the face and a dart into a bush. Her small head peeped out, waiting for her sister to join her again in a romp. Within minutes they were rolling together, engaged in mock battle, fighting with sheathed claws and biting gently at ears and tails.

They explored every inch of this new domain. There were hazards to be learned. They were also learning that their food, which appeared mysteriously, was brought by a two-legged giant, and that it was good to eat. They were entranced by shadows of shifting leaves which deceived them. Both tried to catch them.

Amber found a mole run. Its owner emerged and she prepared to pounce. He caught her scent and dived into the ground, digging fast, sending scattered earth high into her face and eyes. She sat, half blinded, pawing at the unpleasant covering. It was some time before her eyes cleared. Jade helped her sister by licking at her face.

Amber stored the memory and for the rest of her life molehills were given a wide berth. She was learning that both sound and scent, as well as assisting her, were also enemies. An unwary movement and her prey was gone. A change in the wind and everything within range of her vanished.

Tonight the kittens were well fed, thanks to

Mairi, and were playful, though instinct caused them to pounce should anything move that might be edible. Amber, hunting near the wall, found a pheasant's tail feather, long and beautiful, tasting of heaven. The wind teased it, moving it, and she pounced and caught it. She played with it for some minutes, totally absorbed.

Jade tested her climbing and jumping skills. As yet she found both difficult. She patted at a dangling beech leaf, left dry and sere and unfallen from last year, and was startled when it fell. She was entranced by a slug, sliding over ground, leaving a silvery trail. She followed the track, patted it, then tasted it and twisted her mouth in disgust. The slug continued on its way, unaware of the transient danger.

The far end of the graveyard was very damp and here frogs lurked in the grass. This provided fascination. Amber watched as one of them, a small fellow about six inches long, jumped. She put out a tentative paw and patted him, very gently, uncertain of this strange new creature.

He screamed, a small shrill sound, which intrigued the kitten. He jumped again. She patted him again as he landed. She hunted him in this fashion for several feet, interested in his movement rather than in need of food. He found a crevice under a fallen gravestone and crept into sanctuary.

Clouds threatened the moon. It vanished, hidden in their pall. A small rain shower began, the drops rapidly becoming larger, and both kittens fled to shelter. Hexa woke and greeted them with a soft mew, but she was still too sore to rouse herself to lick them. Every part of her bruised body ached.

She, as well as her kittens, was now at risk. Neither Mairi nor Sheina could sleep. Both heard the kittens and both worried. Mairi knew that Hexa could never stand up against a fit aggressor. Both were thankful when the rain began, as it would keep most animals at home. The kittens as yet were at risk from owl and hawk, from stoat and weasel and above all from the foxes, also with young to feed.

Sheina lay, wide awake, worrying. The last message from the hospital just before she went to bed had told her that her father was as well as could be expected, which she found meaningless.

She was exhausted. She had spent the day with the horses, cleaning out the stables, feeding and grooming and polishing the tack, but even so sleep would not come. Every moment she was thinking, this may be the last time. They're going. I won't see the new foal. I won't have ponies to probe in my pockets or greet me when I come home.

Beulah, herself uneasy in new surroundings, could not settle either and jumped on to the bed. Sheina let the dog cuddle against her. Her small bulk was comforting. Alastair would have exploded, but who cared? He wasn't there to know and Beulah was not his dog.

Mairi gave up her struggle to tempt sleep and went downstairs. It was no use spending half the night worrying. The old woman hated lying awake when she could be doing something more useful. She decided to prepare the food for the day's baking, but first she made herself a cup of tea.

She looked up as Beulah exploded into the room, delighted to be up and about and greeting Mairi as if she had not seen her for a year. Sheina followed and fetched a mug from the big old-fashioned dresser. It was covered in an assortment of model animals. There were cats and dogs and owls and a small herd of elephants, two with a calf between them, all standing together, all with their trunks pointing towards the door.

'Elephants hate being trapped indoors so they always have to face the exits,' Mairi explained, her voice amused, as Sheina looked at them, puzzled.

The dresser was also adorned with a number of gaily coloured prize rosettes from the summer shows. Mairi excelled in cake and jam making and in flower arranging, and was seldom beaten.

'We had a dresser like that when I was

little,' Sheina said. 'It was taken away when they modernised the kitchen. I wonder where it went?'

'No heirloom, that,' Mairi said. 'It's from one of the uglier periods. I wonder if anyone will ever make wonderful furniture again. I can't imagine anything sold nowadays becoming a valuable antique. Art today has become perverted. I'd rather have a Fabergé egg than some of the monstrosities they give awards to these days. It's the age of ugliness and nastiness.' She poured tea.

'I can't sleep,' Sheina said. 'All I can do is worry. About Dad. How do I tell him that he has no job and nor do I, and nor does Ian? That we have no home? He has no other skills – and who's going to employ a fifty-year-old gamekeeper who's had a stroke? What could he do in a hotel?'

She refused to think that he would not recover.

Rain lashed against the windows.

'This should keep the wildcats safe,' said Mairi. ' Hexa can't stand up for herself at the moment and the kittens are still very vulnerable. They've been playing. Maybe I fed them too well. They need to be hungry and wary.'

Sheina's mind was on her ponies. 'Who'll buy them now?' she asked. 'They may go to the knacker and end up as horsemeat in France.'

'The night is always darkest before the dawn,' Mairi said.

'And there's a pot of gold at the end of the rainbow and when a door closes a window always opens and pigs might fly,' Sheina said, and then regretted it. 'I'm sorry. I didn't mean to be rude ... it's just...'

'I know. You can't see the light at the end of the tunnel. But often things can be better after what seem like major disasters.' Mairi looked out of the uncurtained window. 'The wind's gone. The rain's stopped and there's the moon.'

The night was rent with banshee screams from the churchyard. Sheina flew to the back door and opened it and vanished into the night. Mairi followed more slowly, wishing she was as nimble as her young guest.

The screams continued. Moccasins were not the best footwear for running on grass made slippery by the heavy rain. Sheina fell heavily, luckily without hurting herself. Mairi helped her to her feet. Beulah raced past them, barking.

The fox, ever an opportunist, knew that Hexa was unable to defend her kittens against him. He had seen her painful efforts to reach the food that Mairi put near the den. He watched the kittens playing. Rain had foiled his early plans but he was patient and he had been unsuccessful that night.

Rabbits and hares were unusually alert and all fled before he reached them.

The wind was his enemy on the hill, betraying him. Here, it was his ally and, when the rain ceased, Amber, tempted by the now bright moonlight, had no warning of danger. Jade curled up beside her mother, too lazy to move. She was warm and had had more than her share of Mairi's offering.

Amber, still hungry, nosed the ground, and watched for movement. A mouse, hearing her, dived into a hole for safety. The cruising owl ignored her, having a rat in his beak. She hid when his shadow fled across the tombstones, and came out again when the threat was removed.

A beetle walked across her path. She pawed it, and then caught and crunched it. It was an unsatisfying morsel, as was the moth that she batted out of the air a moment later.

Her explorations had taken her some distance from the den, and from safety. The wind brought her news. She was overwhelmed with scent.

She knew the smell of rabbit, though this was from a passer-by many hours before. She remembered the smell of hedgehog. That was a warning not to hunt further, as he would cause her suffering. Jade's scent was everywhere, as was her own.

She found a tiny branch, fallen from a tree,

and jumped it. She turned and jumped back again, perfecting her movements. Movement was a delight, and each day both kittens honed their skills.

Amber stood on her hind legs, raking her front claws down the rough trunk of a small tree. She stretched, listening with interest to the sounds she produced. Jade decided to join her sister, and came to the entrance of the den, calling.

Hexa roused. She moved, experimentally. The pain was less, but she was far from being able to hunt. Instinct told her she ought to be protecting the kittens, making sure they were safe. She reached the grass by the den opening and dropped to the ground, listening and watching. She had a vivid memory of another den, high above her, and Topaz lying there, injured and alone. She wanted to return but did not yet have the strength to travel.

Amber, still clawing the tree, turned to look at her sister. She heard the enquiring mew and answered it as she dropped on to all four legs.

The fox sprang.

His flying body momentarily blotted out the moon. Amber ran as fast as she was able, so that his pounce missed her. She turned to face him. He towered above her, eyes glinting, the sharp-toothed mouth open to snatch her from the ground. This was an unknown and terrifying enemy, bigger than her mother, his stench flooding her nostrils. She jumped to one side and turned to run again. He caught her by one hind leg. She screamed.

She twisted, clawing at him. Hexa, alerted by the cries of terror, stood, but was unable to race to help her offspring. Jade cowered in the den.

The fox was faced with a problem. He was afraid to release the kitten lest he lost her altogether. He did not know how fast she could move. He was unable to get a better purchase. He tightened his hold on her hind leg. She twisted, savage claws finding a target. That did not deter him.

Beulah stopped barking, finding she could not do that and run. The fox had heard her when she first came out of the house, but ignored the noise. He knew about dogs. They were locked in at night in shed or kennel or house, or were chained and unable to run. She was no threat.

He was wrong.

Her teeth met in his rump and he dropped Amber. She fled, hampered by her injured leg, to join Jade in the den. They crouched together in the dark and Jade licked her sister's wounded paw. Hexa, her fur fluffed, now appearing twice her normal size, lay across the entrance, snarling, ready to defend them to the best of her ability. She flexed her claws.

Beulah hung on to her victim, who, though he twisted and turned, could not quite reach this tormenting animal. Mairi and Sheina erupted together into the graveyard, shouting. Mairi found a thick stick, part of a dead tree branch. She lifted it and aimed as if it were a gun.

The fox knew about guns. He bolted. Beulah lost her grip as he sped off and dropped to the ground. He jumped the low wall and she gave chase, determined to drive this intruder away.

Sheina called in vain. She raced after Beulah, trying to call her back. She was afraid that if the spaniel and the fox met head on, Beulah would be the loser.

Hexa crawled into her den and curled up round her kittens. She too licked at Amber's injured leg.

Mairi looked at the tumbled rocks. The den backed against the old drystone wall, which had long fallen and never been repaired.

There was no exit at the rear. The rocks formed a tunnel that opened into a small earth-walled cave, long ago excavated by a fox. Mairi blocked the narrow entrance with the biggest stones she could handle, hoping to keep the wildcats safe for the night. She would open their hiding place in the morning when she brought food. The kittens were not big enough to shift the boulders and Hexa had not the strength.

Sheina returned just as she had finished her task. ' Beulah hasn't come back,' she said. 'I don't know where she is.'

'We can't hunt for her in the dark,' Mairi said. 'She'll find her way back. She knows the area.'

'Suppose the fox kills her or maims her so badly she can't get back? Suppose we can't find her at all?'

It was the end of sleep for both of them that night. By morning Mairi had doubled her usual output of cakes and pies and pasties to take to the village. Sheina helped but went frequently down to the graveyard wall and called her dog.

Daylight came with brilliant sun and a warm wind and a breeze that just stirred the leaves. Birds sang to greet the dawn.

Beulah had still not returned.

Thirteen

Sheina could not settle. Her mind was on Beulah. She went to the door at the least sound, hoping to find her spaniel had returned. She drank the coffee that Mairi offered, but toyed with a piece of toast, giving up in the end. A vivid imagination provided pictures of the little dog lying dead, mauled beyond recognition, or trapped in some illicit snare or fallen over a small precipice to lie at the bottom, undiscovered, for weeks.

She did not know where to start looking. The hills stretched before her; miles of wild country without habitation, where people were liable to lose themselves or crash to an untimely death on the savage rocks. Heather and bracken formed dense hiding places. She seemed to be constantly sending unspoken prayers, for her father and for Beulah.

Mairi was very worried about the dog. There were too many dangers on the hills. She was also concerned for the wildcats; she could not keep them walled up for ever. For the moment they were silent, lying curled close in the dark, but hunger would soon prevail and they could hurt themselves trying to get free.

Hexa might well be dying, with internal injuries as well as outward bruising. Amber had limped badly, dragging her leg, which could be broken. If the injury was not treated, infection could set in, as Sheina had told her it had with Topaz, and kill the kitten. They needed more help than she could give and she did not know what to do.

Sheina was just about to go out to look for her dog when a car dew up outside. Both she and Mairi looked at one another in dismay. The last person they wanted at the moment was Ian. The wildcats might well give tongue when they realised they were trapped. The graveyard was only a few yards away.

Sheina's mind raced over a number of horrifying possibilities.

'My father? Have you brought news?' she asked as he came into the kitchen, which seemed to shrink in size with his entry.

'No. The big chief rang last night. I didn't phone as I thought you might have gone to bed early. He's arranged a fishing party. I have to take them out and you have to feed them. Six people. It seems the syndicate is looking for new ways of profiting from the estate to make the sale more attractive.'

'Beulah ran after a fox last night and she's

lost. I can't come,' Sheina said. 'I must find her.'

'I doubt if you have an option. He's not in the best of moods and could sack you on the spot if you fail him. I don't think he wants to sell, but he's been out-voted.'

It had been made very plain to Ian that this had to be a success, and that more fishermen would be coming if that were so. One bad report could sabotage the scheme at the start.

He did not tell the syndicate representative that he was living at Micklemoor House while Sheina stayed with Mairi. Her job as caretaker might then be at risk. Fortunately he often spent the evenings at the house when the shoots took place and his presence was not queried.

The man's last words still rankled.

'Since you can't provide sufficient birds for the guns maybe you'll do better at this,' he'd said. 'I suppose you do know how to fish? I suppose there are fish? And there are boats? In good shape?'

Ian had learned from Alastair that when Colonel Oliver was in one of his worse moods, it was wiser to say nothing. Few people used his title now, but there were times when he behaved as if he were still in the army.

'If this turns out well, there will be deer stalking in due course. Probably for photographers. I expect you to provide all they need.'

Ian wondered how any man could have such a raucous voice and why he did not moderate it when telephoning. The keeper needed to hold the receiver well away from his ear. Even then he was half deafened.

One of the former keepers had christened the colonel 'Jump-to-it Oliver'. Sheina wished she had not remembered that. She was afraid of the man at the best of times.

'I could feed them,' Mairi said. 'We spent half the night making pies and pasties and cakes. Those will be useful. I've quiches and tarts in the freezer.'

'His Lordship's coming over himself to see how things are and expects to be there for lunch,' Ian said. 'His Lordship' was their private code for the syndicate representative. 'I think Sheina needs to be on view. Evidently the syndicate think the lakes could be restocked and provide a big attraction for any buyer.'

'Lochs,' Sheina said, her mind still on Beulah. He always forgot the word.

Ian looked at her, frowning. He knew how much she treasured her dog. He glanced at the clock.

'It's seven now, and they're not due till ten. I brought Craig with me. He's missing your father. He and Beulah are buddies. Let's see if he can find her.'

★ ★ ★

Beulah had forgotten all her training. The fox was an intruder, to be frightened away at all costs. Mairi's property that night was hers, as Sheina was sleeping in the house. The spaniel had chased off foxes before but never tangled with them. Like all springers she was tireless, possessed of immense energy.

Fox scent flooded her nostrils, exciting her. She had never before had a chance like this. Instinct took over.

Her quarry was two years old and knew his territory. He had a mate with three six-week-old cubs hidden in the woods. His rump hurt from the deep bite that the dog had inflicted. A large ragged wound had been left when he pulled away from her teeth. He was intent on escape, not confrontation. He thought Beulah a considerable danger, and was concerned to stay alive.

He sped down a well-trodden deer trail, in full view, his thick brush tempting the dog to run even faster. They were climbing, the graveyard now far below, the house lights no longer visible. Brambles tore at Beulah's fur. The half-moon, softened by a rainbow halo, was hidden at times by tumbling clouds, and then at intervals shone brightly in a star-filled sky.

The dog raced on, determined to catch her quarry. A badger sow hissed at her two cubs to shelter as fox and spaniel fled past. The fox was seeking a track that his own mother had shown him when he himself was a cub. He crossed the stream and plunged into bracken, aiming for the waterfall near Hexa's mountain lair, where Sheina had found Topaz.

The rocky track was slippery, but he kept his balance and vanished behind the screen of falling water, which masked all scent. One moment Beulah could smell him. Seconds later he was gone, not a trace on the air. She tracked him to the water's edge but there his trail vanished.

She cast, nose down, along the bank, where only the day before the water had overflowed. Slipping on the treacherous surface, she fell, landing on a grassy ledge below the waterfall, unable to climb up or down. She was trapped. If she moved outwards, death lay below her in a tangle of rocks thrown up by the careering water. Luckily her run had exhausted her and she dropped to the ground, panting. She drank from a pool of water in a rock that lay on the ledge, then curled herself up and slept, confident that Sheina would find her. Her nose rested against her stump tail. Alastair would not hear of undocked dogs, though Sheina had not wanted the pups so treated.

'They'll be torn by brambles,' he said. 'These are working dogs.'

Beulah slept.

The fox crept out of his hiding place. His back was sore and his leg, which had also been bitten, was stiffened. He made his way painfully up the hill towards an abandoned earth that his mother had once inhabited, where he lay, licking his wounds.

Craig, whose leash had been extended by a length of Mairi's clothes line, followed the track that Beulah had made the night before. Her scent was still fresh on the ground, trapped by the dew. The spaniel was his favourite companion. He needed to find her. He followed her trail with enthusiasm, delighted to be out and working. Ian had helped train him and often exercised him and, though the black Labrador kept his loyalty to humans for Alastair, like the other dogs he knew it was far wiser never to disobey his master.

Alastair was never cruel but he did not countenance disobedience. That could end in disaster, especially with men who might shoot a dog by accident if it ran out. Few of those who came were professionals. Some of their lack of success was due to poor shooting, and many missed birds. The old laird's shooting companions had always been experts.

Tracking was not a gun dog skill, but both Alastair and Ian encouraged the dogs to use their noses by playing hide and seek with them. Ian was sure that Craig would follow the spoor left by his favourite companion.

He was almost pulled over by the Labrador's eagerness. He hoped they were on Beulah's trail and not seeking hare or rabbit or deer. The ground was rough, and he needed to watch his footing.

He was worried lest they take too long. He had visions of the colonel's fury if the fishing party arrived to find a locked and empty house, with no one to meet them and no preparations made. He had prepared as far as was possible overnight, but had thought to fetch Sheina early to deal with the food.

He had slept badly. The thought of losing his job worried him. He did not want to return to the softer downlands where he grew up. He loved the often snow-clad high tops, the vast vistas, the lochs that shone blue in a glow of sun. He did not want to work for a leisure centre. There were fewer and fewer estates now which catered for shooting.

The fishing trip had been promoted in a hurry at a dinner the evening before. Its first suggestion was treated as a joke. Six of the men present were suffering disappointment over the holiday they had planned together in Norway, which had fallen through because the tour company had called in the receivers.

The colonel offered them the chance of fishing in Scot land instead. It did not occur to him that plans had to be made, that food had to be prepared, or that one of his keepers was out of action. When Ian tried to explain, he had exploded in fury.

'You do your job and I do mine, which is to make sure we have facilities to offer when we find a buyer. I expect first-class food and sport and nothing else will do. Understand?'

He rang off, leaving Ian staring at the telephone as if he had been bitten. He was in a strange house and had no idea where Alastair kept his tackle. He felt like an intruder as he opened cupboards, hunting for fishing rods, for reels, for flies. It was too late to ring Sheina, who had had a bad enough day as it was.

Now, plunging in through thick undergrowth in search of a lost dog, he was aware of mounting anger, coupled with the certainty that he could not possibly provide what was expected. He needed a week to prepare, as did Sheina. Alastair sometimes went out with a lone salmon fisherman, but they had never had a party before.

Presumably the group had accommodation? Surely he was not supposed to deal with that? And transport? If only Alastair had not been taken ill.

He tripped and almost fell, and brought his mind back to deal with the present. Half past seven. If they didn't find Beulah soon ... He prayed that she was alive. He and Craig had been climbing, and below them was the cloud-shadowed loch where he intended to spend the day.

Sheina was equally preoccupied. She wanted to ring the hospital. Her father's stroke was a major disaster. Neither she nor Ian knew enough about the mechanics of catering for people such as this. Alastair always did the main part of the work and she and Ian obeyed orders.

She found it hard to keep up, since Ian and Craig were moving as fast as was possible in such tangled terrain. She was worried about preparing meals at such short notice for so many people. Why on earth hadn't the wretched man given them more warning?

She stopped for a moment, almost sure she had heard a bark. Craig lunged forward, having heard it too. Beulah was near. He redoubled his efforts, hunting fast on the track she had left.

The spaniel, having caught her companion's scent on the wind, was barking furiously, determined to attract attention. Ian reached the overhang and looked down. Sheina, arriving a minute later, stared in dismay. Though the ledge was wide, it was more than six feet below them, and the drop was sheer.

'I'll have to go to the bottom and climb up

to her,' Ian said 'If you lie flat and reach down, I think I can lift her high enough. I only hope she doesn't try to get to me as I come up, because she'll fall. Keep her attention on you, for heaven's sake.'

He handed over Craig's lead. Sheina tied the dog so that he was as close to the edge as she dared. Maybe Beulah would stay there as long as she could see them both.

The track down the hillside was slippery, a mud path beaten by the hooves of deer. It was close enough to the waterfall for spray to reach Ian. He noted the fox tracks which led to the stream. The spaniel had lost her quarry there and that was when she must have fallen, he realised, casting around to find his scent again.

The track branched, which enabled him to start climbing sooner than he had expected. He grabbed at a thick bush, aiming to use it to pull himself higher, but it was shallow-rooted and came away in his hands.

He removed his boots and socks. Bare feet would give him a better purchase, and there was less chance of slipping. He could hear Sheina above him talking to her spaniel. She was trying desperately to keep Beulah's attention and prevent her from movements that might send her to her death.

He was within six feet of the ledge and even now he was not sure that he could reach the dog. He had a sudden vision of himself falling, crashing down the hillside, to end on rocks. He paused to take stock. There must be a way up.

Above him, the cliff stretched almost sheer, as it did above Beulah. He had no chance of reaching the ledge itself and standing on it to lift the dog to her owner, but there was a tree beside him. He pulled at it, decided that it was firm, climbed to within two feet of Beulah and anchored himself. He could just reach the dog. He spoke to her softly, praying she would not leap at him, or race towards him and lose her footing.

As she turned, he seized her scruff and tucked her into his zipped jacket. She was exhausted and hungry and too relieved to be rescued to struggle. Ian climbed down, hampered by her extra weight, testing every foothold and handhold. He dared not hurry. One slip meant death. It was going to be hard to arrive at Micklemoor House in time to greet the visitors. Worry flared. He wished they had mobile phones, but there were so many dead spots in the mountain areas where they were useless. There was no point in getting one. He prayed that Colonel Oliver would not be with the fishermen. They might be tolerant when he explained why he was late. The Colonel would not.

At least it wasn't raining. The day was fine, and that would be a big bonus.

He was exhausted and out of breath by the

time he reached Sheina. Beulah leaped from his arms, running at her mistress, crying with joy, her tail wagging ecstatically. The greeting had to be cut short.

Within minutes they were back at the house. Ian sped off with Craig while Mairi and Sheina loaded food into Mairi's car. Beulah curled up and slept. It was not quite nine when they reached Micklemoor House. The fishing party had not arrived.

Sheina found the angling equipment that her father kept stored in a small outhouse. Mairi packed the food.

'I hope there's enough for everyone,' she said. 'It looks as if we'll be busy. Picnic baskets for all, and we have to carry them down to the lochside.'

That chore proved unnecessary as the men, when they arrived some minutes later, were happy to carry their own gear.

'Oliver sends his regrets,' one of the men said. 'Something's come up.'

Ian and Sheina breathed heartfelt sighs of relief.

Sheina checked on the visiting dogs. They would suffer, as they would not be trained today. She let them out to run in the paddock.

'Early lunch,' Mairi said. 'Then there's nothing to do here, so we can visit your father.'

Mairi and Sheina lunched on meat pies

and apple tart. Ian had brought fruit and left plenty behind. Cheese and crackers were followed by grapes. It was a long time since Sheina had feasted on food she had not prepared herself.

Beulah curled up in the back seat of Mairi's small car. Neither Mairi nor Sheina felt like talking. Both wondered what they would find when they reached the hospital. Sheina's mind went back to her mother's last days. She had not visited the hospital since. It was a dreary building, a vast rectangle, which always reminded her of a prison. It dominated the skyline, set on a hill above the town.

It was a hot afternoon. Mairi stayed in the car with the dog, so that she could keep the windows open. Sheina found herself daunted by the need to identify herself, to find her father's ward, and by the smell of disinfectant that dominated everywhere.

His window had a view of the hills, but he lay still, though his eyes followed Sheina as she came towards him. His hands lay outside the bedcover.

'He can't move yet,' the nurse said, in answer to Sheina's question. 'But it's early days. It often takes a week or more for the smallest sign of recovery.'

Sheina sat beside Alastair for some time, wishing she could talk to him. Wishing she could tell him about the imminent sale of the estate, and about the fishermen.

She did not even know who paid for the food. Did they send an invoice to the syndicate representative? Surely they weren't supposed to provide it themselves? Mairi would be seriously out of pocket unless somebody paid.

Her father gave her housekeeping money each week. She had a small savings account of her own, which she had started with the money from the sale of Gwen's pups, but she had spent much of that on winter clothing. Warm outdoor jackets and trousers and boots were expensive and so too were thermal caps and gloves.

She sat, aware of the passing minutes, of the busy nurses and of people in other beds. Meals were brought round in plastic containers, but there was nothing for Alastair. Presumably the drip in his arm took care of that.

She bent over him, but he did not seem aware of her. It was unnatural to see him so still.

'Things could change overnight,' the nurse said, as she passed.

There seemed little point in staying, so she returned to Mairi. They were met, at the end of a tiresome journey, by Ian. Sheina nodded at him, too worried to make con versation. She began to walk towards the stables. She always found solace in the horses and their needs. Ian stopped her.

'Someone's here to collect them,' he said.

Sheina stared at him, white-faced. It was more than she could bear. There was no good news and she felt overwhelmed by the many problems that had surfaced.

How on earth were they going to manage?

Fourteen

Rob was unaware of Alastair's stroke. Once he left Sheina, he had little time to think about her. He drove home to one of the busiest mornings of his life. He had too much to do, very little help and no day was ever long enough.

He heard both dogs barking frantically as he turned into his lane. Dismay struck him as he realised that Napoleon, tired of waiting to be fed, had managed to let himself out of his night quarters. Gates did not deter the young llama. His sensitive lips gripped the latch and opened it.

He explored the yard. The feed store defeated him, as that was padlocked. He put his head over the half-door of Semolina's stable. She brayed, afraid he might harm her foal.

Napoleon spat, filling her eyes. Semolina complained, loud and long.

Rob leaped out of his Land Rover, persuaded Napoleon back into his own field, and raced for water and tissues to bathe the donkey's face. That proved difficult as she was in pain and highly disturbed. He moved Jago to another stall and dodged the kicking hooves. Tied to a ring in the stable wall, Semolina at last stood still while Rob repaired most of the damage.

Napoleon was both hungry and disturbed. He hated changes in his routine and today everything was late. When Rob took out the feed, he too was spat on. Hasty treatment of his old anorak with wet kitchen paper remedied that, but this was a major setback. It had taken some weeks for the llama to accept anyone as friendly; the move had unsettled him. Now Napoleon had reverted to behaviour that Rob thought he had cured. The upsets in routine had disturbed this recent acquisition. Others were not yet settled either and Rob spent much of his time persuading worried animals to eat.

The lamb required a bottle, as did Dapple. Col held on one while Rob fed the little deer. She was standing now, moving awkwardly, hampered by the plaster, but seemed to have energy to spend. She was also extremely hungry and surprisingly strong. While pulling hard at the teat she dislodged it.

Rob sighed and mopped himself, Dapple and the floor before refilling the bottle and starting again. At last both animals were fed and Rob put them in one of the smaller paddocks.

He walked back to the house, aware that he

too was hungry. Any ordered routine for meals seemed to have vanished. He missed his stepmother, who had insisted they ate like civilised beings and not at odd times, or standing while doing something else as well. She had been an excellent cook.

Sandwiches were a godsend as he could pick those up at any time and snatch a quick bite. Mairi brought him pies and quiches and pasties, aware that his time was precious. She also added to his charges on occasion with a baby bird fallen from a nest. One cage contained an owlet whose favourite occupation was sitting on Rob's shoulder and nibbling his ear.

He went back to work. Hygiene was paramount or he would have a sanctuary full of sick animals. Tom might be a friend, but his boss, Fergus Hamilton, who owned the practice, showed Rob no favours when it came to paying bills. Tom might give advice but treatment was often needed at the surgery and drugs and operations didn't come free.

Rob was also very well aware that he needed to make sure he himself was always fit. Nobody else would take this over, he thought, looking out at the occupied paddocks, at the cages of birds, at Tussock, back in his puddle, and at the cats that seemed to proliferate daily. People soon learned that he was a soft touch when it came to any animal at all.

He went back indoors, one of the many kittens sitting on his shoulder, mewing as if recounting a long story. Once inside the youngster jumped down to the floor and then clambered to the chair to cuddle against the hen, who was used to this sort of treatment. His small purr gave life to the room.

The kitchen floor needed cleaning. Young animals had little idea of hygiene. Poco nudged him, reminding him that the dogs too had not been fed. He scooped kibble into three bowls and called Col, who had joined her charges in the paddock and was lying in the sunshine, watching them. She always took her maternal duties seriously, even though these were fosterlings and not her own young.

She was yet another of Rob's rescues. She had a highly developed maternal streak but had been spayed before he took her from the dilapidated though well-meaning rescue centre. The two elderly ladies, both over seventy, who ran it, had long ago lost energy. They struggled valiantly against floods of new regulations, increasing numbers of dogs dumped on them by uncaring owners, escalating bills for food and electricity and fuel and their inability to pay for the many repairs that were needed. They lived near his stepmother and Rob, appalled by what he saw, campaigned vigorously to find homes for some of their refugees.

Nobody had wanted Col who at that time was a skeletal, under-fed animal with a sparse coat and sores all over her, the victim of someone who thought dogs ought to live in sheds and be fed only if anyone remembered. Her former owners would not recognise her now and they had missed out on a terrific character.

Rob did his best to mend the fences and repair the kennels and compounds at the centre before he moved, asking for nothing more than a cup of tea and a slice of rather stale cake. Col attached herself to him as he worked and he could not leave her behind. Every time he saw her now he saw her as she had been and also saw the makeshift runs and the ancient battered feeding and water bowls and wondered how the two owners were faring.

Col's need for puppies led at times to confrontations with the smaller cats who were lifted and taken to her bed to cuddle. Rob bought her a teddy bear at a charity shop, and this was her constant companion unless called in to foster one of the motherless animals that flooded in.

The floor once more clean, he put the bedding from the various animals in the enormous washing machine. He went outside and stood beside the paddock for a moment

226

to savour the sunshine and watch Dapple and the newcomer make friends.

The lamb had yet to find his legs before he could move easily. By the end of the week he would be skipping and bouncing but today he was tentative. The little deer tried to run, but the heavy cast prevented her so that she produced the oddest lag-legged walk, her new companion trailing after her, apparently convinced she was his mother. She butted him away as he tried to suck her tail.

It was eleven o'clock before Rob had time to sit briefly at the kitchen table and eat a large bowl of muesli mixed with two chopped apples. Col was lying outside the paddock, supervising her two charges. Nin and Poco sat, as if mesmerised, eyes fixed on Rob, both drooling.

He drank a glass of milk and tossed them the apple cores. Time to work again. He wondered how Sheina had fared when she faced her father. Maybe he should have persuaded her to go to Mairi and not go home at all.

He wondered why she had not thought of that solution. He wanted to ring her, but that could be unwise. Alastair might answer the phone. He stood for a moment, staring at the mountains, today far away and softly blue, surrounded by a haze. He wondered why he should care at all about someone he had met so recently and so casually. Her face haunted him. He looked up at the soaring peaks and sighed. He longed for a life uncomplicated by emotions.

Sheina was another forlorn stray, tugging at his heart, in need of his care. He mocked himself at the thought. He was an idiot and she was probably thoroughly hard-boiled, very much her father's daughter. No doubt he had seen her in an off moment and had a false impression of her.

He had once been engaged to be married. His thought strayed back to Janet and those long ago days when he thought life idyllic. Till she married his best friend. He had vowed to steer clear of all future entanglements. 'I will lift up mine eye to the hills, from whence cometh my help.'

One day he would find time to climb to the top of the highest peak and look down on the world below. He would stand there, a king over men, high above them all. He laughed at the absurdity.

The grandeur of the mountains dwarfed the petty affairs of men, as did the night sky. Often, when out late, he looked up at the myriad stars and wondered about those unseen worlds and whether other creatures lived fraught lives on any of them. Men and women had suffered under those same stars for centuries and would for centuries more, long after he was forgotten. It dwarfed his problems.

There was a clatter in the yard. The dogs barked to alert him to the presence of strangers. He glanced through the window to see the oddest figure. The old man reminded him of a disreputable pied piper. His red woollen hat came to a point, a bobble hanging from it that swayed as he walked. Tangled grey hair, badly in need of both a wash and a cut, showed beneath it. His long coat reached his ankles. It was shabby and worn, and buttoned up as if it were winter, although the day was so warm that Rob was thinking of shedding his shirt.

By contrast the piebald horse was groomed to perfection, his coat shining, his mane and tail silky, his eyes clear and bright. The cart that he drew was piled high with logs. Rob went outside the greet the visitor, but also to keep an eye on him.

'Thought you could do with some wood,' the old man said, in an unexpectedly soft and cultured voice. 'They've always bought from me here. That Aga of yours has a greedy appetite. I used to come regularly to old man McPhee. Alastair McNeil is another of my customers. Shame about his stroke.'

'Stroke?' Rob asked, shocked. 'When? How do you know?'

'I passed there an hour ago as the ambulance came. I asked Mairi, who went to help. Last night sometime.'

He turned and looked at Napoleon, who

was regarding him with a measuring eye. 'Watch it,' Rob said, unable to prevent the llama from fulfilling his ambition. Luckily the mass of spit fell short.

'I see he likes carrots,' the visitor said. He grinned, showing surprisingly well-kept teeth. 'Doesn't like strangers, though.' Rob could not place the accent, but the old man was not a Scotsman.

'I'm Morris and this is Domino. And I found this on your doorstep. You'll find folk just dump on you. Get a name for caring for hurt beasties, and you'll soon be so full you won't know what's hit you.'

'You can stack the logs for me over by the donkey shed,' Rob said. He took the cardboard box and looked inside at the scrawny, flea-ridden cat. The black coat was patched with sores, the ears folded back from many fights. An old warrior and the last thing he wanted here.

He sighed and took the animal into the kitchen. He put it, still in the box, in one of the cages. It stank and he wrinkled his nose. The cat stared up at him from fear-filled eyes.

'You're in for a considerable shock when we get you better, old son,' Rob said, his voice soft. 'A bath and flea spray. Treatment for those ears. I wonder what you'll make of all that. And Tom'll have to snip you. Can't have an entire male among my ladies, even though they are spayed. You'd be off, wouldn't you?'

He put down a small bowl of bread and milk and closed the cage door. Morris had followed him in and was still talking.

'I miss old man McPhee. Annoy him, which was easy, and he had a temper on him like a March gale, but he always had a cup of coffee and a bite for me. Mairi does too. There's a grand old lady for you.'

Rob hid a grin.

'Made some changes here,' the old man said, looking round him with appreciation. He grinned in his turn. 'I get water from the burn and my kitchen may be a campfire or a primus, depending on the weather. I live on Mairi's pies and home-baked bread. I buy the food,' he added hastily, lest Rob should think him a beggar. 'Live otherwise on fruit and hard-boiled eggs. Got my own hens. Nothing like a new-laid egg and watercress sandwich with farm butter and home-baked bread.'

He sat at the table and stretched out his legs in their heavy steel-tipped boots. For some reason, though the highly polished leather was brown, they were tied with bright red laces. Rob looked at him, puzzled, finding him an odd mixture.

Morris saw the direction of his host's eyes, and regarded his feet complacently. He grinned. 'A sweet disorder in the dress, kindles in clothes a wantonness,' he said.

Rob stared at him in astonishment. 'What's that supposed to mean?' he asked.

Morris laughed. 'I like surprising people. I might have made a head teacher if I had put that element into my lessons.'

'You were a teacher?'

The old man sighed.

'Long ago. I didn't like the children I taught. So few have the divine spark of learning. I wanted them all to take fire from me, to embrace their lessons with fervour, not with disorder and subtle bullying. I got discouraged. Dropped out at forty, due to too much stress, too much wife, too many children, too much booze. Don't drown your sorrows, son. It leads to a lonely old age and rags and ruins and an ancient hut without any mod cons, and people despising you.'

Rob made coffee in two large mugs and brought out the tin of cakes that Mairi, convinced that no male was able to feed himself properly, had left with him.

'Maybe news of the sale of the estate brought it on,' Morris said, his mouth full of cake.

Rob frowned and then worked out that 'it' was Alastair's stroke. 'The estate is for sale, then?' he asked. ' Mairi said it was rumoured.'

'Yes, sadly. It was a shame the old laird

232

died. It was a grand place in his day. Ten years ago now. There's been talk in the village of some millionaire who intends to restore the old house and make a hotel. And a golf course. And a leisure centre. Big tourist attraction. He aims to increase his fortune. The village is against it, and there's a petition in the post office.'

Rob did not like the sound of that. His peace would be challenged if there were a leisure centre and hotel so near. He had no intention of opening to the public; so many of his charges were traumatised, and needed security and quiet. Napoleon would have to be shut away. People did not appreciate being spat at, and the llama had little liking for strangers, though he was less likely to aim at women.

'There's a meeting in the village hall. Wednesday night.'

'I'll be there,' Rob promised. He could not bear the thought of a busy place so near to him, of crowds of visitors, and all the noise and confusion made by humans on holiday en masse. The access roads were narrow, several with passing places only. Would they widen them? Or would they remain a constant hazard? He had begun to love his new home and felt threatened.

Morris seemed unable to stop talking. He rarely had an audience.

'The horses are for sale. I saw a notice in

the paper about them. Sheina'll be distraught. She loves those beasts. She grew up with them, and their predecessors. They were her charges. She always looked on them as if they were hers, though of course they do belong to the estate.'

The old man made short work of a scone and took another, spreading it lavishly with butter and some of Mairi's home-made blackcurrant jam, which Rob had bought in the farm shop. He looked at the label on the jar and nodded. 'You want to try her rhubarb relish,' he said. 'That's nectar.' He sighed heavily. 'Sheina used to come and talk to Domino when she was little. Funny kid. She was alone so much of the time. Most children are scared of me. She never was. Grown into quite a woman. Some man might strike lucky there.'

Rob wondered if the old man were hinting.

Morris seemed to have no intention of going. He helped himself to a second cup of coffee without asking, behaving as if he were in his own home. He added three spoonfuls of sugar and stirred vigorously.

'I may be old, but I'm a good worker, and I'm teetotal, these days. I learned my lesson, though too late. My wife and family were lost to me by then. I grew to enjoy my way of life. No neighbours. Peace. I live as I want and no rates to pay. Nobody has remembered that old shack.' He grinned. 'No use having a drunk in charge of a horse and Domino means more to me than anything else in my life. You need help here. I can fence and ditch and lay a hedge. I took up farming at one time. Never stuck to it.'

'I could do with help,' Rob said, somewhat surprised by the sudden change in the conversation. He was inclined to be cautious. 'Try for a few days and see how we go?'

'Can I unharness Domino and put him in the small paddock to graze? You need help now. Don't want to leave him in the cart all day.'

The piebald, relieved of his trappings, stared at the field in disbelief and then kicked up his heels and cantered round it, tossing mane and tail. He was never free to run. His home was a tethering stake beside Morris's cabin, with a winter shelter built from poles and an old tarpaulin at the back and sides. He was always well rugged in very cold weather.

Rob watched him, half smiling, half frowning. He was pondering the news of the probable changes at Micklemoor House and wondered how Sheina was dealing with the knowledge.

Fifteen

Fortune smiled on the fishing party, which was an unqualified success. The trout were rising. The sun shone. The gourmet food was an unexpected bonus, exceeding their expectations. The men were relaxed and happy, delighted to have found a substitute for their ruined holiday. They decided to extend the weekend to the two weeks they had originally planned.

Sheina felt as if she had taken a train for one destination and discovered en route that she was going somewhere quite different. Her life was unbelievably changed. Her days were more than fully occupied, in spite of the loss of the horses. Bracken's foal was due in a few weeks' time and she would never see it.

Tom had already vetted them. He did not know what to say when he left but eased his conscience by patting Sheina on the shoulder. He would have liked to comfort her with a quick hug and a kiss on the cheek, but was afraid his action might be misconstrued. She said nothing. She had a lump in her throat and a mist before her eyes and was totally unable to speak.

The vet wanted to stay with her, to try and make up to her for everything that had happened, but he had other calls to make. He nodded and drove away. She watched him go, feeling he was her last link with her beloved ponies. She would never be able to own horses again.

The sound of the stable doors closing as the horsebox left was a death knell. She wanted to shout at God and tell him how unfair he was. Nothing was going right. She sat on the low wall that bordered the stable-yard and watched the sun setting over the hills. She needed time alone.

She could not bear passing the empty stalls. No more trusting heads leaning over the half-door, calling to her. No more soft hides gleaming when she groomed them. No more rustling in the straw. No need to fill her pockets with apple pieces and carrots. No more ecstatic animals racing in the paddock, or rolling joyfully in the summer grass, or flying against the wind, manes and tails lifting. The hay nets were empty, the water buckets dry. She felt as if all three had died and grieved for them.

Micklemoor House no longer felt like her home. She was there all day but she did not belong. Within weeks it might be sold to somebody else, might change beyond recognition. As it was, it had already lost its soul with the absence of her father. Even when Ian and Mairi were with her the house felt empty. She listened for Alastair's movements. She expected him to walk in at the door.

At nights, after her visits to the hospital, she lay awake, wondering how a man could so change, wondering if he would ever come home, wondering if he were already on the downhill path that her mother had followed years before. She was haunted by a poem her mother had once read.

Home no more home to me, whither
    shall I wander?
Hunger my driver, I go where I must.

Ian was job hunting, feeling he ought to try to find somewhere else before being rendered workless. Mairi suggested that Sheina moved in with her permanently, but the cottage was small and what would they do with Alastair? There was no room for him and he was likely, after some months, to be able to live some sort of life, though not the one he'd had before.

He did not yet know that the estate was on the market. Sheina dreaded telling him. He was already depressed, aware that the active life he enjoyed was now over, and that would add to his problems.

She signed the petition when she went to the village to shop for the vast amounts of food they now needed. The pages of signatures comforted her. Few of the villagers wanted such a change.

'They won't spend money here,' the village shop owner said. 'They bring their food with them, and they'll use outsiders for the building work. Mess up our lives and we've nothing to show for it but grief.'

Sheina met with more sympathy and friendliness than she had ever known, as everyone was aware of Alastair's illness and asked after him. Nobody wanted the estate sold.

Without her father, there was so much more to do. Ian had to neglect his own duties in order to provide transport and sport for the fishermen, who needed to be shown the best places and also needed a certain amount of supervision as few were experts. Several of their visitors were newcomers to the sport and had to be taught. The dogs needed food and exercise and some training. That she would not neglect.

Sheina went through her father's papers, feeling as if she were committing a crime and invading his privacy. She needed to know far more about the way the estate was run, and also about their own finances, as she could not live on Mairi.

They had to pay their own electricity bills and taxes and keep the vehicles running. The estate did not provide their transport. She discovered that Alastair had a source for both guns and fishing tackle, which he sold at a small profit. She contacted the suppliers, who agreed to continue the favour. She was able to sell several rods and reels and other equipment. She did not buy guns.

It took all her time and Mairi's to prepare the food for the six hampers each day, plus some for Ian who rang the colonel to ask if the two women would be reimbursed for what they spent. They had to produce much more than basic sandwiches if they were to provide an outstanding service. He did not realise that his conversation was overheard by Lee Davison, one of the fishermen.

Lee ran his own small engineering firm and was well aware of costs of all kinds of commodities as well as those of feeding his work staff. His reel had broken and he had come up to the house to see if Ian could lend him a spare. He stood, waiting for the keeper to finish talking, and was dismayed by what he heard.

'Who's paying your suppliers for the food?' he asked, startling Ian who had not seen him come into the hall. He had just put down the receiver, cursing the colonel, who had promised to 'sort something out' but who seemed uninterested in the mechanics of providing even one meal for each of six men for fourteen days. He also seemed to have forgotten that he had told Ian to make sure they were given a midday meal each day.

'I didn't expect them to stay more than the weekend. I thought the hotel would provide them with sandwiches, and they'd pay for it,' the syndicate representative had said curtly. 'I'm sure you can manage, as McNeill did for the shoots.' He rang off.

Ian sighed. 'He doesn't realise that shoots don't go on for two weeks. Rarely more than two days. Mairi and Sheina are working all out every day to provide you with your hampers,' he said. 'The meals they're making take time. None of it's convenience food.'

Lee thought of little salmon tarts, flavoured with some pungent taste he could not identify; of game pies; of meat pasties; of quiches made with unrecognisable but delicious ingredients; of salads packed in their containers, looking like a florist's bouquet; of potato salad, served that day with hard boiled eggs with an exotic dip, and smoked salmon rolls filled with cream cheese.

'They are paid for their work, of course,' Lee said.

'Sheina's paid a pittance for taking care of the house till it's sold. Mairi's nothing to do with the place. She's helping out. She usually makes pies and pasties and wonderful quiches to sell in the farm shop and the local pub and the village bakery, but she hasn't had time to do that this week, so she's very out of pocket. We're paying for the food between us at the moment.'

'That's insane,' Lee said. He was a big man, craggy-faced, with a belly that spoke of his devotion to his food. He appreciated the changing daily menus that the two women provided and the cheesecakes and home-made bread and rolls. Some days there were flasks of soup as well as of coffee.

That night Lee rang the colonel and negotiated a reduction in the cost of the holiday for each man, saying that since the fishermen were expected to provide for their own food, they considered that only reasonable.

Next morning, when Mairi and Sheina arrived to fill the hampers, they were astounded to find a large cheque on the table with a note to say that this was reimbursement for the food they provided as well as payment for their services. It gave them a handsome profit. Each man had contributed his share.

On the last morning of their fortnight Sheina was exercising the dogs when Lee broke off from his fishing and drove back to the house. She had had nothing to do with the men until then. They always ate by the banks of the loch and the streams. The weather had been exceptionally kind.

'We're sorry to hear about your father,' the businessman said, introducing himself. He handed her an envelope addressed to her and Mairi and Ian. 'How is he?'

'He seems to be improving, but very slowly,' Sheina said.

The envelope contained an unbelievably large cheque and thanks from all the men for salvaging their holiday. Sheina stared at it. 'This is too much,' she said.

'Not at all. Divide it between you. They tell me at the hotel you've never done this before, and it was at such short notice. None of the others has guessed we were guinea pigs. We'll be back, believe me.'

'I've never been so busy,' Sheina said wearily to Mairi just after the fortnight ended. 'I never seem to have time even to breathe. I suppose it's as well the horses have gone. I wish I knew where. They're used to good treatment and lots of human companionship.'

She had asked if anyone knew who had bought them, but they seemed to have vanished completely. She prayed they had not gone for horsemeat, which sold well in France.

The colonel was relentless. Sales of big estates took a long time, sometimes years, and he had no intention of letting the facilities lie idle. One party succeeded another, with little rest between. Sometimes there were only four; twice there was a group of ten. The weeks fled by, with only a very slow improvement in Alastair's condition and without any buyer coming forward for the estate.

Lee Davison, a man who had an innate sense of fairness, gave the fishing holiday his accolade. The feeding arrangements still worried him and when he returned to London, he went to see the colonel. He pointed out that if future groups were to be provided with food at midday, then proper arrangements must be made and specified when the parties were booked, so that everyone knew exactly where they stood. It was most unfair to expect Sheina and a woman who was a volunteer to spend their time catering without any recompense either for the cost of the food or their labour. Since Lee intended to return several times, by himself, he would be checking up on future arrangements.

A man well used to dealing with recalcitrant trade union leaders, he made the colonel understand just what was involved. Lee wondered as they spoke if the syndicate's secretary had any conception at all of how the estate was actually run. He seemed to expect miracles, with few people to perform them. His requirements would have been difficult for ten men to fulfil.

After some discussion, the syndicate representative decided that each party should make its own decisions. They could commission Sheina and Mairi or ask the hotel to provide their midday meal. All but one group were grateful to the two women for providing such noble fare. The bills for food went direct to the visitors who paid them and also paid Sheina and Mairi for their time.

The hotel's ideas of sandwiches were very basic, and after two days of indifferent fare the men who had not agreed to the conditions which Sheina and Mairi now imposed were only too glad to pay for a far superior diet.

One fishing group consisted of women only, who surprised Ian by their skill. 'They did better than some of the men,' he said to Sheina as they sat, relaxing, sharing the remains of the lunchtime food.

Sheina grinned. 'Men! So who's the chauvinist now?'

Ian stared at her. Maybe he did need to change some of his ideas. He did not admit that to Sheina.

Alastair continued to improve very slowly. He retained a dogged determination to struggle back to health, and though walking was slow and painful and the exercises forced on him also hurt, he did his best.

He began to ask about the estate. What

were they doing? How were the dogs?

Sheina told him about the fishing parties, but not about the sale of the estate or of the horses. She was afraid it might depress him and delay his recovery. Nobody thought that a buyer would be found for months yet. The committee of people opposing the conversion of the estate into a leisure centre had a good solicitor and were using delaying tactics. Nothing could be done until there was planning permission for such vast changes.

One party of visitors was unlucky as the weather changed to torrential rain and gales which made fishing impossible. After a fight against the wind and the downpour, Ian brought them back to Micklemoor House to eat. Sheina and Mairi made coffee. This was a smaller party. There were only four, all of them newspaper men; a cartoonist; a roving reporter who had been to almost every country in the world; a man who wrote a cookery column, who had been a chef in one of the biggest London hotels; and the man who wrote about fishing for the paper and was intending to write up this particular venture.

Sheina had stored their previous day's catch in the freezer for them. They suggested a cooked meal instead of picnic fare, and turned the day into a party, joking and ribbing one another as they ate grilled trout with new potatoes and peas and carrots.

Their laughter lightened the atmosphere. Sheina relaxed in their company. They prised recipes from Mairi and dog training tips from Sheina and Ian. All had dogs at home, dogs that appeared to rule the family and gain all the attention they demanded.

'Our mutt thinks he's Napoleon,' one of the men said. 'He fetches his lead when he thinks it's time for a walk, and brings his food bowl when he decides it's time to eat.'

'What breed is he?' Sheina asked.

'His mother was a German short-haired pointer. She got out and met a Labrador. He looks pretty weird but he's a fun dog.'

'Our Labrador gets mad if you talk on the phone,' the cartoonist said, dipping a piece of grilled trout into Mairi's special seafood sauce. 'He brings his water bowl and tips it into your lap. We never remember. I spend half my life changing my trousers.'

A helicopter flew over, drowning their words, and Beulah, who was under the table, ran to the door to bark at it and see it off. It flew away and, satisfied that her objections had been noticed, she returned to put her head on Sheina's knee and look at her hopefully.

'Good job your father's not here,' Ian said.

Sheina smiled at the dog. 'I let her in, but I don't feed her at the table,' she said, just as the cartoonist tossed the spaniel a piece of bread.

'Whoops, sorry,' he said. 'I always think everyone else is as besotted with their dogs as I am.'

'She gets what's left when we wash up,' Sheina said. 'Otherwise she'd pester us all the time.'

'Which is where we all go wrong,' the fishing columnist said, and everyone laughed.

A few days later Sheina received a cutting, sent by post. There was a splendid write-up in the paper, with a poem that amused them.

Hidden in the Highlands in the friendly
    kitchen
Men meet and talk endlessly of fish and of
    fishing.
Much time is spent at the end of each day
Telling of trophies that all got away.
Somehow those caught are always much
    smaller
But tales of lost fish become taller and
    taller.
One of the best, for heaven's sake
Is about a boat the pike dragged across
    the lake.
The laughter fills the brightly lit room
The talk dispels the out-of-doors gloom.
The tales come thicker and ever faster
But is fish or man the master?

The meal in the kitchen was faithfully reported and thereafter those who came expected at least one day on which they ate with Sheina and Mairi. It became a last-day goodbye meal, a part of the package.

The holiday mood always prevailed and the laughter proliferated, acting as a counter to Sheina's worries. Most of the men asked if they could explore the old part of the shooting lodge and the ruins of the manor house a mile away.

Mairi's mother had been housekeeper in the Big House and her father the head gardener, positions which gave her some small privileges. They had lived in the lodge, now mostly derelict too. She remembered the laird's family and became the guide, showing them the ballroom, with the remains of gilding high on the one wall that was still standing, and the immense kitchen quarters, dating back to the fifteenth century when oxen had been roasted on a spit in the great fireplace.

It was easy to imagine the days of grandeur, of crinolined ladies and long-haired men dancing the summer evenings away. Mairi had enjoyed the Christmas parties, the huge tree and the luncheon for the staff when their masters and mistresses waited on them, carol singers made music and there were presents for all after the feasting.

'They were good days,' she told her enraptured audience. 'The war changed everything. We didn't have half the stress and worry most folk have today. And few children have anything like the fun I had when I was small.'

The days took on a new pattern. There was so much extra to do. Sheina had never been involved in the dog training before, but there were dogs in the kennels that had to be trained and sent home in a few weeks' time. As she and Ian began to make progress, fascination took over.

There was seldom time for talk but late in the summer they had a free week between fishing parties and were glad of the rest. The Wednesday afternoon was a day from the gods, with a blue sky peppered with baby clouds and enough breeze to make it pleasant to be outside.

The keeper was on his way to clean the minibus the colonel provided for their visitors. Lee had suggested this, as otherwise Ian often had to make two journeys. The businessman had already been back to fish during two weekends. He had a friend with a helicopter who was only too pleased to join him.

Ian paused to watch one of their charges race out to retrieve a hidden dummy.

'I'm getting very good results with this one,' Sheina said. 'I hope his owner will give me a reference. Dad never thinks women capable of anything much except domestic chores. I'd like to show him I can do some things well.'

'He doesn't give me that impression,' Ian said. 'He's proud of you and what you do.'

Sheina stared at him in astonishment. If that was so why did her father never praise her to her face?

'He's always criticising,' she said. Though it had not always been like that, she thought, and sighed.

'I get it too,' Ian said. 'I think this illness may have been coming on for some time. He felt frustrated and that made him bad-tempered. He often moved as if he was in pain. We were handy. Someone to shout at and blame and take out his anger on.'

The keeper was much more at ease with Sheina now. Off duty, she occupied his thoughts, though he never dared to tell her so. He was sleeping in her room, and was reminded of her every time he woke. He wanted to console her.

'These first few weeks must have made a tidy profit, and the dogs look good. Perhaps the syndicate will change its mind and keep us all on to provide more sport for fishermen rather than for the guns. Your father could cope with fishermen. Much easier than hill climbing for the deer, or arranging shoots for the guns.'

'If he comes back,' Sheina said with a sigh. 'Maybe they won't change their minds, and the whole place will be taken over and turned into something all of us hate.'

And we'll be cast out into the cold, she thought. Behind her the ruin of the old house brooded in the sunshine. Their living quarters were on the other side, away from the kennels and training ground. Looking at it now, nobody would dream that there was a very good living space for a family. Sheina had never lived anywhere else. It would be the most tremendous wrench to leave it.

The spaniel found his trophy and returned with it to sit in front of her, offering it. He was black and white with tinges of brown in his slightly curly coat. Long ears drooped on either side of his head and his bright eyes looked up at her, confident in his reward. She took the dummy and praised and stroked him.

'He won't want to go home,' Ian said. 'I know his owner. I wouldn't like to be his dog. Mackie will go back to what he was before he came here – which was an untrained lunatic – in a few weeks, I promise you. Waste of time. Though it's money in the bank, and we've kept our part of the bargain.'

'I'll miss him,' Sheina said. The dog had been with them for sixteen weeks. Worryingly, the owner had not yet paid them. The bills were sent monthly but so far were un-acknowledged. Chase his owner up, Sheina thought. Another job to do. They needed the money. The Discovery was due for a service and MOT and that alone cost a fortune these days. There were always niggling worries. Only now did she realise how Alastair had had to juggle everything to make ends meet.

There were four dogs in for training and Ian and Sheina decided to teach two each. They each had one Labrador and one springer spaniel. They had an unacknowledged competition to see who could get the best results in the shortest time. Ian was reluctant to admit that Sheina was winning. He comforted himself by explaining that he was too busy with the fishing parties.

Sheina, also very busy with the catering, decided to leave him his illusions. As Mairi was an inspired cook she prepared most of the food while Sheina went daily for fresh provisions. They made wonderfully un-usual salads, using vegetables from the farm nursery, and nothing was ever kept over-night.

It was a long way to drive each day to the town with its supermarkets. 'We should have negotiated a deal for petrol spent in going to and fro,' Sheina said, horrified at the need to fill the Discovery's tank so frequently and at the high cost. 'It eats into our small profits.'

She borrowed Mairi's little runabout but even that ate petrol.

She wanted to see Rob. She wanted to know how the wildcats were faring. There was never time.

Rob had his own problems. He was inundated by small animals in need of his care, and though he tried to phone Sheina twice he received no answer. One day, he promised himself.

Morris was now a permanent part of the sanctuary, having proved to have a flair for dealing with sick animals. He had unlimited time and was willing to give up part of his nights to feed the various babies every two hours, while Rob did the daytime feeds.

The two men converted the hayloft above an old cowshed into living quarters that were warmer and drier than the old man's shack. Domino bloomed, benefiting from having a paddock to gallop and roll in instead of his tethering post on the road verge. The piebald was rejuvenated. There was a stable for him at night. One of the ginger and white cats became his constant companion, sleeping on the horse's warm back.

Life was changing for all of them.

It had already changed for Hexa.

Sixteen

Mairi's agitated phone call had not come at a convenient time. Rob thought back to that day. He had been struggling to care for too many animals. Road accidents were too common. Two badger cubs had been found beside their dead mother on the lower road. A lorry driver made a large detour and cost himself a fine from his owners for late delivery, but he could not leave them alone.

Tussock refused to leave his puddle for the little pool, as there was now a swan on it who had flown into power lines and damaged his wing. His mate joined him, and the pair nested on a raft of weeds, challenging all other water birds. The frequent flurries of an enraged cob, wings outstretched, kept the animals near in a state of extreme unrest.

It was nesting time and fledglings had a habit of falling out and were then brought to Rob to rear. He had a variety of small creatures, including four tiny hedgehogs, all in need of two-hourly feeding, as well as a baby owl. Foster parenting was difficult and sometimes unrewarding, as well as being very demanding.

Rob had known it was not going to be an easy task to trap the wildcat and her young, but there was no way he could let Hexa suffer needlessly. If he could cure her, he would. If not, he could at least make sure the two female kittens survived.

He felt like a traitor caging them, but Hexa had little chance of survival if left on her own. She could not hunt. That too might mean the end of the kittens. Nature knew no kindness. If the mother cat survived he would free her and give her back her son.

Topaz, as yet, was too ill to present a problem. He was too weak to do more than give a token hiss and he suffered the attentions of those who tended his wounds. Rob was busy with Topaz when the phone rang. He listened with dismay as Mairi spoke, then he frowned as he turned to Morris.

'The mother wildcat's injured. Mairi says she can barely crawl and certainly can't hunt and the kittens are too young to fend for themselves. She took shelter in the churchyard with her kits. Mairi's walled her up and wants us to catch them.'

That was going to be a major problem.

Morris had taken over the bathing of the still inflamed wound when Rob answered the phone. He wrapped the kitten in a towel, enclosing claws that could still make a sharp scratch, and picked up the feeding bottle.

'What's in this?' he asked, looking at the clear liquid. He wondered if the kitten would yet be able to digest watered milk.

'He's accepting glucose and water and Rescue Remedy now,' Rob said.

Morris constantly surprised him. The man had surprisingly gentle hands and animals trusted him. Nin and Poco adored him so much that Rob felt almost jealous. Domino, if freed from his paddock, behaved like a dog and followed the old man around. They had to ensure that the horse never met Napoleon, who had decided to hate him and aimed large gobs of spit towards him whenever he saw the piebald.

Morris was a major asset. He settled the kitten more comfortably on his knees and considered the problem that Mairi had given them.

'You need to adapt a cage. Make one side movable, and then we can attach a long piece of thick string to it and let it fall when the cats are in. They won't venture in if we're near.'

He did not add that they might not venture in at all. It could prove a frustrating morning with, at the end, no option than to open up the tunnel and leave them to survive as best they could.

He inserted the teat into the now opened mouth, pleased to see that, for the first time,

Topaz was responding to food smells. Rob had crushed one of the pills that Tom provided and dissolved it in the liquid. Morris hoped the smell of it would not drown the smell of the nourishment, but so far the kitten was accepting his feed.

'I killed two rabbits this morning. Both in the shed. Fresh enough to tempt a hungry animal, however scared,' he said to Rob's departing back.

Poco and Nin watched the feeding with interest. Col, who had come in with them, walked over to Morris and inspected the kitten. She reached her head across his hands and licked the small furry face. The smooth tongue was unlike Hexa's rough one, but the warmth was comforting and Topaz did not protest.

Rob, his mind full of engineering problems, turned in the doorway to ask Morris a question but forgot it in his astonishment as Col continued to lick.

'I'll be damned. Our little spitfire's not protesting. Do you think he'd tame?'

'Doubt it. Be like the old tag. "When the devil is ill the devil a saint would be; when the devil is well, the devil a saint is he." Wait till he's fighting fit again and believe me, he'll be fighting us. Better get on with that cage. We don't have that much time. Another batch of feeds due in a couple of hours.'

The preparation of the movable side took

longer than Rob expected but Morris dealt with the feeds and, as soon as those were completed and their charges fed and comfortable, the two men set off. Col was back in the paddock with her two charges, guarding them against mostly imagined hazards. Not even a bird was allowed to land near either the lamb or the deer.

Dapple, surprisingly unbothered by the heavy cast, explored her surroundings with the lamb in close attend ance. Col's sheepdog ancestry kept her busy as she did not like them separated.

Napoleon, who disliked being barked at, did keep well away. Rob locked him in his stable before he left. The llama had his own ideas about mischief and could open too many doors and gates. The feed store was now padlocked. He resented his imprisonment as much as Nin and Poco did theirs. There was no way they could be part of the morning's activities.

Morris packed sandwiches and pasties, bananas and a flask of coffee. They might have a long wait. He had found a new niche in his life and did not intend to leave it. He had thought up many ways of making himself indispensable. He still kept his log round but the McPhee farm was now his base. He left his old home without regret.

He refused wages. It was enough to have food for himself and Domino and a more comfortable home. The sale of the logs paid for his few needs.

The three wildcats were stressed beyond sense. Even through the tunnel walls they could smell the two men. It took time to arrange the cage, to make sure that it was enclosed by rocks so that there was no space through which a kitten might creep and escape, to remove the rocks that blocked the way to the cage and arrange the side so that it was open. The string had to be arranged, so that it could be cut easily. Morris had plaited yards of baler twine, as being the strongest thing they could find around the place. Finally, they settled themselves as comfortably as they could. They expected a long wait.

Morris tested the wind and they moved as far away as possible so that the cats would not be aware of their scent. The rabbit was already on the cage floor, and had been there since the men left the farm.

In spite of all that, fear had come to stay. There was no way the two men could rid the cage of the smell of their hands and of the Land Rover. Man smell.

Fear dominated every moment. The cats had never been so close to anything that smelled so strongly of human before. Hexa knew that men had ended the life of both her mates. She had once hidden, high in a tree, while men tortured badgers with dogs.

She knew the terrifying thunder of the guns that left the deer lying dead to be carried away on horses, or cut up on the spot if it were poachers who were involved. When that happened she found plenty in the parts of the beast they discarded, and profited from their kills.

This was a new form of prolonged fear. It began when the wildcats discovered they could not escape from the home in the graveyard that had become a prison. The penned hours were endless and the only result of their efforts to break free was torn and bleeding paws. The kittens, longing to play and explore, were frustrated. They also wanted to hunt, as Mairi had deliberately given them only a little food. They needed to be hungry when Rob came with his trap.

The smell of fresh rabbit overcame the fear. A raging hunger dominated all other feelings. Mairi's offerings were eaten due to a driving need, but it was not the kind of food that the three animals usually ate. In spite of that, the two men had a long patient wait before any of the three moved.

Rob was uneasy for another reason. He hated churchyards. All his relatives had been cremated. He had a feeling left over from childhood that these burial places were always haunted – though surely not by day. Even so, rustles and unusual sounds alerted him, but he laughed at himself for his fears.

'I spent a night here once,' Morris said, in a soft whisper. 'Got drunk and couldn't get any further. I expected the tombs to open and the skeletons to rise, like the Day of Judgement.' He grinned. 'An owl flew out of a tree. Huge and white and silent and moonlit and at first I couldn't make out what it was. Never been so scared in my life. Paid for my sins. The last time I did that.'

The incident wakened Rob's own memory. 'I trespassed in our own churchyard once,' he said, his mind taking him back to eight years old, and a sudden unexpected recognition of the cause of his fear. 'The boys at school dared me. I couldn't possibly say no. I was scared of them. They were bigger than me and bullied me. I was small for my age and they said I spoke posh so had to suffer. I did.'

He eased himself into a more comfortable position. He wished the cats would move. He needed to get back.

'Midnight, they said, and I got out of my bedroom window and shinned down a tree. Over the grass and in among the tombstones and one came alive and chased me. I ran like hell, and ended up at our own front door hammering on it and screaming. And got lammed for going out at night. Served me right, my dad said.'

'One of your mates?' asked Morris.

'Yes,' Rob said. He had hated Danny

Kernel ever since. Even now he could recapture that nightmare, and the panic that had sent him sobbing and tripping over the fallen gravestones until he found the way to his own home. The churchyard was full and had been abandoned for many years, which made it seem worse. Long ago ghosts survived there as maybe they did in this one.

The cats moved at last. Hunger dominated every other feeling and panic subsided. They had to eat. Jade was first and, as she began to tear at her food, the scent wafted back to Amber, who followed her. Hexa crept out, painfully.

Rob, seated in the fork of a tree, saw the cats feeding. He had made a window of thick plastic so that they could be sure all three were in the cage. He let them eat for a few minutes and then the falling shutter trapped them yet again.

That appalling noise was followed by the overwhelming scent of humans. In spite of the cats' fluffed-up fur and hissing fury, Rob sighed with relief. It was more than time to get back to the feeding ritual. Small animals died if not fed at frequent intervals.

The three cats huddled together, terror escalating. The men smelled of many animals, most unknown to Hexa and her kits. Napoleon had rested his head on Rob's shoulder. A cat had spent time curled up on his knee as he ate his breakfast. He had fed

Dapple and the lamb. Morris smelled of Domino. But their own male scent predominated. A mixture of sweat and food and, in Rob's case, aftershave lotion and diesel fuel, as he had overfilled his engine that morning at the petrol station.

The two men struggled with their burden through the long-neglected grass, trying to avoid the fallen slate slabs. They paused to rest, putting the cage down on the traces of a gravel path. Morris sat on a gravestone. Rob looked at the one beside him. The cats crouched as far away from the men as they could.

'Hannah Marshall. Born 1826. Died 1829,' Morris read. 'Not much of a life, poor little maid.'

Three years old. A little younger than Paul. A carved angel with only one wing and most of her face eroded by time and weather leaned above the grave. Life had been unpredictable then. In many places it still was.

Children ought not to die. Rob sighed, longing for a sane world without war and hatred and the many problems of overpopulation. An 'if only' world.

Morris eased himself painfully to his feet, cursing arthritis, which had taken over many of his joints. It was time to move on.

The cats had a frightening journey. The landscape swung, as the men could not keep their carrier still or level. It was far too heavy, but Rob had not dared bring anything light-weight lest the wildcats escaped. They slithered inside, almost at each step, slipping on the wooden floor.

They reached the gate, long fallen from its hinges. At last they reached the Land Rover. The cage was lifted into the back of the vehicle, which was even more terrifying, as it smelled of dog.

Everything was strange to Hexa and the kittens. The roar of the engine deafened them, alarming them even more. The Land Rover jolted over the potholes, and then accelerated as they reached the main road. The access lane to the sanctuary was not as rough as the river track that Sheina had travelled, but the jolts and bumps were still frightening.

Morris looked over his shoulder. All he could see was six eyes, glaring at him. At first the three had spat and hissed but now they had given up. They crouched, unable to understand what had happened to them.

'I hope they don't die of shock,' Morris said. 'It's not the sort of treatment I'd care for. Must be strange, not knowing what's going on. What do they make of this vehicle? A monster that's swallowed them?'

'Doubt if they'd realise this was the inside of the things they see on the road. I always think they must imagine that cars are raging demons with giant eyes that blind them.

They certainly know they're killers. I've seen crows watching for a road kill as if they knew what was about to happen,' Rob said as he drew in to the side of the lane to allow room for a tractor to pass. The driver nodded to him, acknowledging the courtesy. Morris waved.

'Donald Cameron, from Black Ben farm,' he said. 'Good stockman. His cattle always win at the shows.' His mind went back to what Rob had just said. 'I hate hoodies,' he said. 'Wicked birds. I've known them take the eyes out of a newborn lamb before he stands up.'

The McPhee place was above them. The house stood up against the skyline, shadowed by the dense plantation of trees that guarded it. The engine whined its way up the hill, complaining bitterly when Rob changed gear. Every sound was torment to Hexa and her kittens, as they did not understand the source. Jade and Amber caught their mother's fear and crouched against her, gaining comfort from her presence and the warm contact.

The shed in which Rob placed the cage had been inhabited, up to the day before, by two nannies and their kids. Morris had made a deep frame and filled it with soil as a litter box. The two men hoped the wildcats had the same instincts of cleanliness as domestic cats. Or did that need to be taught?

They left the cats to settle. The terrifying journey had exhausted Hexa. They were drowned in new smells. Even when the trap's door was opened, the three crouched inside their temporary prison, afraid to leave it and explore. There was still more than half a rabbit and another lay on the floor of the shed.

Rob and Morris had made a tunnel of straw bales with a nest behind it. Light flooded their new home as the sun arrowed through the window. The men left the area to tend to their other charges.

Nin, freed from the house, jumped a gate, having decided that it would be fun to play with Dapple and the lamb. The sounds were so near that the cats fled from the cage, desperate to hide and escape from this new hazard. They were sure the dog could penetrate their prison. They ran, keeping to the sides of the big shed until they saw the opening in the straw tunnel. They needed to escape.

Every instinct told them that hiding meant safety. Each crouched low until they were safely out of sight. The smell of the straw drenched their nostrils and tickled their coats, but darkness was safe. Nobody could see them here.

Rob was left with a puzzle. He needed to separate the kittens from their mother and sedate Hexa so that Tom could examine her.

Even in her weakened condition she was dangerous, with claws and teeth that could inflict nasty wounds. Both he and the vet were afraid that she might be suffering from internal bleeding and unseen festering bites.

None of the cats moved until night. Darkness lent a feeling of safety to them. The moon shone across the floor. They could see it through the window, a familiar object that reminded them of freedom. Nobody walked near them in the dark. The noises that they heard were familiar. The call of an owl, the bark of a fox, the grumbling as a roving hedgehog made his way across the paddock.

The owl, with two owlets in the nest, hoped that there might be food left on the dishes put out for Rob's rescued cats, who enjoyed the shelter of the barns, the freedom of the night, and lived their own lives free to come and go as they wished.

Many cats were dumped because they were in kitten. Once the litter was born, the vet made sure there were no more from that particular animal. But many people didn't bother with spaying and neutering. Both processes were expensive. When the inevitable happened they were astounded and dumped their one-time pets, not wanting the responsibility of the kittens and finding homes for them.

There was a colony of cats now living among the many barns, keeping mice and rats at bay and more than repaying Rob for their keep. The females were spayed as soon as the kittens were reared and the male cats were neutered at once, ending their roving days and nights. None of Rob's cats could have a litter or sire one, but the 'rescues' often arrived before their kits were born. He had to admit that he was not sorry. Kittens were always fun, and many did find new homes, though he insisted they were neutered before he let them go.

Two of the older cats were curious about the newcomers and came to the perimeter wire round the compound to stare inside. Jade and Amber, now once more filled with energy, were less wary than their mother. They were exploring their new quarters and hissed. The cats, startled by the ferocity of these tiny animals, moved away.

Thirst was a greater need than hunger. Hexa scented water, but the world around her daunted her, until at last her desire to drink overcame her fear. There was a bowl of water at the back of the cage.

A pony whinnied and was answered. That did not threaten them, any more than did the warning call of a hind to her calf. Hexa moved first and drank, although it was still painful. The need to survive outweighed her fears, and there was nobody near to alarm her. She moved painfully to investigate the fresh rabbit that lay on the floor.

Jade and Amber followed her. Her thirst sated, the wildcat clawed at the imprisoning wire around the enclosure that surrounded the shed that was to be their sleeping place, but it was strong enough for a lion cub and her efforts soon exhausted her.

Hexa was still too weak to stand up for herself or to guard her kittens. Jade and Amber as yet were too young to fight large predators. The eagle remained a threat. He could wing his way to his eyrie with a large hare, and that was several times the size of either of these two little ones. His need was as great as theirs, as his offspring was growing and ever more demanding. Both parents were kept busy.

Play was essential for both the kittens. The need to work off excess energy overcame their fear of their new surroundings and they danced in the moonlight, dodging and hiding, leaping out at one another, rolling and wrestling. Jade found an unusual object in a corner of the shed. It rewarded her by rolling when she tapped it and it became a new plaything which she guarded jealously from her sister. It was Poco's ball, which he had carried into the shed some days before, forgetting it when Rob called to him to come for a walk, an invitation that was never resisted.

The dog loved the nannies and their kids, and visited them daily. Rob had taught the

Labrador to carry apples and carrots for the goats, and also to carry a small bucket filled with their special feed. Poco was also a help when it came to tidying the sanctuary. He picked up paper bags and sweet wrappings that had blown on the wind over the hedges, and brought them to Rob to bin. There was a footpath within a few hundred yards of his boundary and some of those who walked it were careless with their litter.

Animals were apt to eat anything that came their way, especially if it smelled of food. Rob's mother had had the same problem and several of her protégés had been operated on for stoppages in their stomachs, due to polythene bags that had contained meat or cheese.

Botulism was another hazard, as humans often threw away uneaten food, which soon went bad. Eaten by an unwary animal, it poisoned them. Recovery was rare unless the bird or beast was brought in soon after eating. Seagulls were among the most frequent sufferers as they dived at the litter bins and emptied them, looking for anything that smelled as if it were edible. Rob had four seagulls in his care now as well as a cormorant. Though inland, the loch attracted seabirds. Feeding time always amused him, as birds that had been in his sanctuary and released on recovery knew where there was easy pickings, and he sometimes felt as if he fed every bird in the neighbourhood.

Among the most tiresome of Rob's patients was a gull who had been brought in by a couple walking on the beach. He had been almost dead from botulism. He recovered remarkably fast, and decided to stay. Food was on tap here, with no need to search for it. Rob endured him. He was a common gull, and Morris thought that the adjective described the bird very well. 'Dead common,' the old man said with a grin.

The gull explored the bins, pulling out the rubbish in a search for thrown-away food. He undid shoelaces if the owner of the shoes was unwary. He tweaked fur from Semolina, who hated him with a deep intensity and often tried, without success, to kick the bird.

He was fascinated by Morris's long hair. In the end the old man pushed it tightly under his cap, making sure that not one strand escaped. Rob, who had hated the red hat, bought him a much warmer one which had the words 'Head Gardener' written on it. Morris took to it with glee, but the gull was fascinated by the swinging bobble. Once it was removed, Morris was kept safe from sudden mischievous attacks.

'One of the devil's own,' he said in exasperation one lunchtime when the bird swooped suddenly and snatched the food from his hand.

After some weeks the gull acquired the

name Rummage. The morning after the cats arrived he landed on the shed's window sill. Jade hissed and spat. Rummage flew off in alarm, squawking his fury. Hexa and the kittens crouched together. They made themselves as small as possible.

They crept to the back of the cage, away from the light. To the two men who hurried to investigate the uproar they were dark shadows against a dark background, only their eyes alive and intelligent and bright with hate.

Rob wished that Hexa would leave her sleeping quarters during the day, when he could see her. He was increasingly worried about her, and had wondered if perhaps she had died in her bed. Now, thanks to the seagull, she had made an appearance, anxious to protect her kits.

Both kittens were young enough to accept strange events. Hexa, at nearly three years old, had learned far more than they about the world around her. She developed a fierce need to prevent the kittens from becoming too relaxed in these strange surroundings, but easy movement was still very difficult.

'We have to do something about Hexa,' Rob said, on the third morning after their capture. It was a red-letter day, as Topaz had begun to eat on his own. 'But what?'

It was a question that was to plague them for some days, as there was no sign of her.

They could shut the kittens out of the shed in the enclosure, but that got them no nearer their mother. If she were even halfway fit she would be a very unpleasant animal to tackle. If they did not do it, she might die.

Seventeen

Tom solved the problem for them.

He arrived as Morris was cooking the evening meal, and breezed into the kitchen. Rob had a flash of memory. Never once in their past friendship had he seen Tom lose his temper, and the man's presence always brightened any room.

'I began to think you'd left the country,' Rob said. 'I always seem to see Fergus these days. What happened to that night out we promised ourselves?'

Tom looked at Morris and rolled his eyes.

'That from a man who has dedicated his life to two-hourly feeds for every orphan baby within miles. When can you afford time off? I seem to remember offering once or twice ... then I gave up.'

'Six weeks last Friday,' Rob said. 'I was between feeds. For nearly three days.' He sighed. 'Spring is always demanding. You should know,' he added.

'I do indeed,' Tom said. 'Would you believe I'm actually off duty now? I began to wonder if everyone imagined I'm geared to perpetual motion. Fergus has told me to get lost for three days. Can you feed a starving man?'

'Might run to it,' Rob said, grinning. 'I was so glad when you took a job up here and I've seen less of you since we came than when I was down south.'

'Some of us have to work for a living,' Tom said, stroking a half-grown kitten that had followed him in and jumped on the table. Morris made shooing noises and Tom picked him up.

'He'll be visiting you soon,' Rob said. He was stacking an amazing number of feeding bowls into the huge dishwasher. 'Or we'll have another wanderer and kittens on our patch. Few people here bother to have their females done.'

'People like you need banning,' Tom said, scratching the kitten's face. The little animal bent his head to receive further attention and purred happily, enjoying the contact. 'We're overworked as it is.' He leaned against the edge of the kitchen table.

'We all pay,' Rob reminded him. 'Them as don't work don't get no supper.'

'And them as clutters up my space don't get fed either,' Morris said, still busy chopping vegetables and meat.

'I'll pay for mine. In kind. I've been thinking ... no, don't say it. I'm being serious now. Well, I'd better own up – it's Fergus's idea. Comes of being twice my age with a great deal more experience, as he never ceases to remind me.' He grinned as Morris made an odd sound that resembled a snort more than a laugh.

'Let me finish. The cats are nocturnal, mostly. Right? So they ought to come out when it's dark. Hopefully by now they'll be beginning to accept their new surroundings and be hungry. I can tranquillise them with a dart gun, and then have a look at Hexa and see how she's doing. But I need to take my time and make sure I can get at them.'

'I hope it works,' Rob said. His worries about Hexa had grown. She moved as if she were in great pain. He had no desire to keep the kittens in captivity but if she died he would have little choice, at least until they were large enough to defend themselves against predators.

There was a scratching at the door. Rob opened it and Poco and Nin bounded in. They greeted the vet with enthusiasm. Poco jumped at him. Tom ignored the dog and stroked Nin, who leaned against the vet's leg, happily waving his tail, which thudded against the wall.

'I only stroke dogs that don't jump on me,' Tom informed Poco who sat, belatedly remembering his manners. His eyes gleamed and his tail waved gently as he waited for the reward he knew would come when he behaved. Rob had trained the dogs not to jump at people but with his favourites the older dog often forgot. The vet figured high on Poco's list of people he adored, due to his habit of travelling around with a pocketful of all kinds of things that appealed to dogs.

'He doesn't grow up,' Tom said, laughing, as he distributed treats to both dogs. 'And don't you snatch,' he added, as Poco reached for the titbit.

Rob grinned. 'Have you ever met a grown-up Labrador, whatever his age?' he asked. 'Most of the gun dogs seem to have solved the secret of perpetual youth. Wish I could.'

'My mother bred flat-coated retrievers,' Tom said. 'Now there's a permanent teenager for you, but they're lovely dogs. Wouldn't mind one myself.'

'You need the right wife to keep one of those,' Morris said.

'I'll bear that in mind.'

Tom looked again at the old man. He had not seen him for some weeks and was amazed at the transformation. Morris's enthusiasm had been renewed by his improved way of life. He loved showing off his skills at cooking. He had a new wardrobe. The tramp had vanished. Neatly dressed, his beard shaven and his hair cut, Morris was younger than anyone had thought. Late sixties, Tom thought. He had originally imagined the old man to be in his eighties.

'I'm eating properly now. I used to exist on muesli, except when Mairi took pity on me,' Rob said, as Tom dropped into one of the armchairs. The cat immediately jumped on to his knee and settled himself, purring. Poco, jealous, tried to butt him off. Tom pushed the dog away, scolding him.

In spite of the modern kitchen fittings, the room, which had been extended to double its original size, was furnished as a living room and Rob spent most of his indoor life here. The immense Aga provided central heating for the whole house. There were easy chairs and a long pine table with benches either side for eating.

'Pre-Morris, muesli was mostly all I ever had time for,' Rob continued. 'So easy. Cereal, milk and fruit. But boring. Stuck to that unless I shopped for a lot of meals for one, and they aren't the best of diets. Have you eaten? Now I have a chef I can take time off for meals and I'm no longer chasing my tail.'

'Mind you don't get fat on good home cooking,' Tom said. 'Maybe that's what we need at the surgery. I had a couple of sandwiches some hours ago. Just come from Black Ben farm. Nice little calf, after a lot of hard labour for everyone. The cow seemed to leave it all to us. Like to come to us, Morris? A first-class chef would be very much appreciated.'

'I'll be fighting you for him,' Rob said.

Morris laughed. 'I doubt if I come up to Delia Smith standards,' he said. 'But I do make a pretty fair curry. Easy enough to add a bit more of everything. It's a one-pot meal, all going in the microwave.'

'That invention does make life so much easier,' Rob said, producing three cans of shandy. 'We're pretty well teetotal here. Can't afford to take risks due to slow reactions with some of my lot.'

Since Poco refused to be deflected and the cat was angry and hissing, Tom put the little animal down and walked over to look at the latest litter of kittens. Three were ginger and white, one was black, ginger and white, and one looked remarkably like a Siamese. The ginger cat nursing them purred happily. She had soon settled to her new way of life.

'Funny mix of kittens,' he said. 'Two matings? One dad ginger and the other Siamese?'

Rob laughed. 'Not that complicated. Ginger puss has a happy background but her elderly owner died and her son brought her here. The Siamese is the only remaining kitten in a litter of pedigrees. The mother died. She hadn't been well when the litter was born. Three of the kits caught her bug and didn't recover. Reff here is a fosterling and Ginny doesn't seem to mind.'

'Why Reff?' Tom asked.

'Short for Refugee.' Rob drank straight from the can. 'Saves washing up, even with the dishwasher,' he explained. 'It's just a bit full.'

'It's mostly filled with animal dishes,' Morris said. 'Unbelievable the time we spend putting food in them, washing them, carting them around. Some men's work is never done,' he grumbled, grinning, as he chopped more vegetables to add to his curry.

'Plus we have to collect them, and wash and fill water bowls and clean up what comes out the other end,' Rob added, throwing a small piece of bread to each of the two dogs who caught their offerings in mid-air. 'Mairi did help out with pies and pasties and what not,' he continued, anxious to be fair. 'But she and Sheina are going to be fully involved now cooking for these fishing parties. How's the petition to stop the sale of the estate going?'

Tom had two rooms, which had been advertised as a self-contained flat, in a house in the village which also served as the post office and general store. His room had a microwave and an electric kettle and he shared the bathroom.

Hetty McBrae, the postmistress, who was addicted to healthy eating, kept a small stock of organic food, which she induced Tom to buy. She had three grown sons of her own, as well as several grandchildren. Their major treat was to help behind the counter. Hetty added the young vet to her responsibilities and supervised his shopping and diet.

'If ye dinna eat well, then ye'll suffer,' was one of her favourite sayings. She also advised new young mothers when the babies were first weaned. She was getting on in years and the villagers worried. Would anyone take over when Hetty had to retire? 'Everybody's gran, she is,' one of the postmen said. 'Won't get another body like her.' The petition was in her shop.

'Six pages of signatures,' Tom said with satisfaction. 'I think almost everybody's signed. No one wants a leisure complex. But if not that, what? No one seems to want to shoot any more.'

He bent over the cat and her kittens to look closer. The mother cat accepted his gentle stroke, and settled herself more comfortably. The Siamese kitten came away from the teat he was sucking.

'He's younger than the rest,' Tom said, looking at the kitten as he cuddled into his foster mother's fur. The cat held him down and washed him carefully from head to toe. Only his shape revealed his breed. He had not yet developed his black points.

'About two weeks younger,' Rob said. 'He's three weeks old. He has a home to go to if he's fit. He seems a sturdy little animal, which is probably why he's the one that survived. The others died at one day old.'

'He didn't bring the infection with him, I hope,' Tom said, wiggling a finger. One of the ginger and white kittens pounced and caught it. He laughed and picked the tiny animal up. It patted at his hair.

'He was taken away at once, and they hand-fed him till they heard of us.' Rob put plates to warm, and laid cutlery on the table. 'Then someone suggested he came here as I nearly always have at least one cat with kittens and most of them are only too willing to take on extra mouths.'

The microwave pinged. A minute later, Morris spooned curry on to each plate. He brought a bowl of green salad out of the refrigerator. Rob added a jar of Mairi's rhubarb relish.

'Better than any chutney,' he said. 'At least we've all got time to eat in a civilised way for once.'

'I'm off duty for three days, so I can sleep tomorrow,' Tom said, adding a healthy portion of relish to his brimming plate. He began to eat and then gasped. 'What's in here? Volcanic lava?' He took a swift drink from the shandy can. 'It's good, but I didn't expect it this hot.'

'Neither did I,' Morris said, wiping his eyes with a hastily grabbed tissue, after sampling his own share. 'I must've added too much curry powder. Told you I'm no Delia Smith.'

'You can say that again,' Rob said. 'Mind you, it should cure any tendency any of us have for ulcers.'

'Might cure the foxes of bin raiding,' Morris said. Mornings often brought chaos if the lids of the bins were not secure as everything was dragged out and shredded in a search for easily gained food. There were now chains and padlocks but if the men were busy they forgot to secure them. 'They're over-breeding and lazy, finding human homes provide easy pickings. Ian hasn't time to cull any more, and it shows. There'll be a plague by next year. Watch the dogs for fox mange.' Morris took a deep draught of water. 'I'd better stick to the recipe next time. It seemed so little, written down.'

'So you doubled it?' Rob asked. 'I wonder if any chef has ever been sued for producing food that didn't fit the description?'

There was silence for a few moments as the men ate. After a few more mouthfuls Rob left the table to fetch a large water jug.

'It is a tad on the hot side,' Morris admitted, with a rueful grin, as he filled three glasses.

'Have you seen Sheina?' Rob had been wanting to ask all evening. 'How's Alastair?'

'Beginning to recover,' Tom said. 'He's able to creep a few steps and he's determined to get better. So he makes himself walk even if it is difficult, and also does the exercises he

284

has been told to do. Sheina says he's much more cooperative than she expected.'

'Does he know about the sale of the estate?' Rob asked.

'Sheina hasn't dared tell him. She's afraid it might shoot him back into the depression which the doctor thinks was part of his problem. They've been tackling that and she thinks there's a breakthrough.'

'See a lot of her?' Rob asked, wishing he had more time to visit.

'The dogs have had one or two problems. A cut paw, a sore ear, a phantom pregnancy.' Tom laughed. 'Sheina has a teddy bear left over from her childhood. It lies around and she says she can't bear to part with it. She's lost it now, though, as Beulah has decided if she can't have pups to cuddle a teddy will do as well. The thing is nearly as big as she is and she drags it everywhere. She grieves if she can't find it and it's getting filthy.'

Rob and Morris laughed at the picture. 'Lots of Rescue Remedy needed, tell Sheina,' Rob said. 'Though Col's been spayed, she remains permanently maternal. If I don't let her have animals to mother she steals kittens, and that can cause quite a stir as few mums like a large dog making off with one of their offspring. All she does is wash it to death and produce a very soggy little animal.'

'Where is she?' Tom asked.

'Dapple and Splodge are in one of the small sheds and she's decided they need a guard at night so she's curled up with them. Nobody tells Col where to sleep. She makes up her own mind and wild animals wouldn't shift her.'

'Splodge? Odd name.'

'He's the lamb. Don't ask,' Morris said and exchanged a grin with Rob, leaving Tom baffled.

'I am asking,' Tom said.

'He isn't very house-trained. Morris kept saying "That lamb has left us another splodge",' Rob said.

It was Tom's turn to laugh.

'Feeding time again.' Rob gathered up the plates and put them in the sink. He looked at the remnants on all three and decided against giving them to the dogs. 'Like to give us a hand? It's not too bad tonight as most of our present charges are weaned, but there are ten baby birds all demanding vociferously. Can't you hear them?'

Tom had been aware of the growing chorus but had not realised it was due to the approach of feeding time. A few minutes later he realised it was much more difficult than he had imagined to use forceps to pop mealworms into tiny gaping maws that seemed unable to cooperate. It was also time-consuming.

'Our next job is three orphaned kittens,

found on a tip in a bag. They're only a week old,' Rob said. 'One each. My mother had a stock of doll's bottles and they're a godsend. Just the right size so we can't overfeed. Before you start each kit has to be tucked under your chin and purred at, or they won't feed properly.'

'You're joking,' Tom said.

'No way. They lack mothering so we have to be Mum. They like close contact with something warm and if you pull your jersey up to your neck for them to snuggle into you get a funny noise that's a sort of rusty unpractised purr. Once you've done that you can start to feed them.'

Eager little front paws fastened round the hands that lifted them. Rob wondered what an unexpected visitor would think of three large men making soft cooing noises to their charges, each holding a blind kitten under his chin.

Tom discovered that his kitten most certainly did relax after its mothering and fed more eagerly. He looked at the tiny animal, smaller than his hand. As it drank, it held the bottle firmly with its front paws, and its back paws tightened and it its toes spread with each suck. It was so determined to get the milk that Tom had to hold the teat in place to prevent it coming off.

Then came more mothering as the kittens couldn't eliminate without a thorough massage of their underparts, which was usually done by their mother's tongue. Rob had discovered that tissues did not work very well, that olive oil made them greasy and water irritated them. The situation had been eased one day by Poco who came to lick each kit and clean it. They were now used to the dog's big tongue and quite unafraid.

Poco allowed the older kittens in his bed and let them swarm over him and tease his tail when he lay in the yard. Rob wondered if the dog had a sex problem and should have been a bitch, as he was so gentle with the little animals, and rivalled Col at times in his care of them.

Nin was not so sure of very small cats, who were apt to try to swing on his tail and bite it. He played happily with two half-grown kits that were six months old and enjoyed a romp with the dog. They ran up to him, patted him hard and ran off, enticing him to dash after them.

The kittens were returned to the cardboard box beside the Aga, which burned summer and winter. They all gravitated from the far side to that nearest the warmth, then settled in a black bundle to sleep.

Last to be fed were six baby hedgehogs, belonging to two mothers who had ended as traffic statistics. These were old enough to feed themselves. They tucked ravenously into the plates of dog food which Morris put down for them. The sound of contented snuffling filled the kitchen.

'I wish people wouldn't feed them bread and milk,' Rob said. 'It always makes them sick and often kills them. They need protein and lots of it. But I can't spend time digging up worms.'

All three men, once the chores were finished, went out into the night. They hoped if they stayed very still the wildcats might relax.

There was a soft breeze from the south. A jewel-like crescent moon reminded Rob of a brooch his mother had once worn on black velvet. Stars glittered, and then two unexpectedly moved. A plane streaked across the sky, its sound trailing it. Rob looked up, wondering who was travelling and where. So many other lives, so many other needs, all brought together for a few hours in a shell that sometimes he thought was too fragile to bear such a load of responsibility. He hated flying.

There was no movement in the pen. The cats had not left the doubtful security of the cage in which they had been trapped so far that evening. The men had to pass the enclosure to reach a place where they could perch on large rocks, hidden by bushes.

Apart from hisses from the kittens and wildly glaring eyes, not one cat moved. The world around them was strange and smelled of so many unknown creatures. They had eaten the rabbit Rob provided and were not yet hungry enough to be forced to explore in the hope of finding more food.

The men settled for a long wait. Their task might take all night. It might take several nights. If only Hexa would relax and explore her new territory. Or had fear so overcome her that she would not move for several more days?

Eighteen

The cats were aware of the men, but as time went on and none of the watchers changed position, they lost their concern.

Darkness was welcome. The animals that surrounded the cats' enclosure were all in their stalls and stables. Napoleon was the most terrifying. He wandered freely during the day within the confines of the sanctuary walls. He could not resist looking at the the new residents, and had come to the edge of the enclosure soon after they arrived, trying to see them. His overwhelming smell daunted them and they lay still.

Jade and Amber were the first to move. They were young and full of energy. The world around them was new and fascinating, no matter where they were. This was an extension of experience, and the compound was big enough for them to play, run and explore. They both crept out cautiously, ready to react to any unexpected sound.

Life for them was all sensation. They stalked and prowled and ran to hide if there was a shadow that threatened them, or the sound of whispering paws, or the over-whelming scent of some strange new creature that might bring death. They knew how to freeze and sham dead. Twice as the men watched some odd noise startled the two little cats and they crouched against the ground, so still that they seemed more like rocks than animals.

Hexa did not intend to come out. She had known nothing like this in all her life and she still distrusted it. There might be ravening monsters lurking in the undergrowth around them.

She hissed at the kittens, warning them of danger, but they had had to endure stillness too long and were full of pent-up energy. They ignored her.

Tom wanted all three together, lest the sight of her kittens lying still on the ground prevented Hexa from moving at all. They were near enough to the house to hear the grandmother clock on the landing strike two.

Rob had enclosed bushes and a tree. A rising wind excited both kittens so that they chased one another round the bushes, tapping at one another with inexpert paws. They dived under branches, pouncing and rolling, trying to catch a whisked tail. The tree gave them endless pleasure. They stretched and scratched, raking their claws, scoring the bark. They now knew how to come down without slipping or falling.

Explore. Scent the air and scent the ground. Creep and chase and jump and run. Turn and stand on hind legs, tussling, in a mock battle that was practice for a later reality. The two little bodies were lithe and muscled, iron hard, growing stronger daily.

They savoured the texture of the ground beneath their feet, preferring to walk on soft grass rather than hard paths or shale or shingle. Here the earth had been tilled up until a few years ago. It was kind to small paws.

They were thirsty. They had had nothing to drink all day. Rob hoped they would accept the water bowl. They still tested it, with their noses. The metal retained a little scent of Poco, who had drunk from it before it was washed and refilled. There was rescue remedy in it, which added a tempting, tantalising taste. The need for water overcame all fear and they began to drink.

Their mother heard them and her own thirst stirred her to movement. She crept out. The faint moonlight shone on three tabby forms, on eyes that glowed, and on Hexa, lapping. Tom took careful aim.

A minute later, all three lay quiet in the enclosure. The vet examined both kittens.

'Fine,' he said. 'Now for Mum.'

At last he pronounced, 'No real damage. She might have had an argument with a car.

She's very bruised but nothing's broken.' He left the enclosure, and closed the door. 'They'll be round in a few minutes. I didn't give the kittens much. Mairi's herbal brews should see Hexa right. I'd rather not give her any drugs. The pain should be easing now. She's stiff and sore, but I suspect in a few weeks we'll see her restored to full health.'

Morris was on the first three feeding shifts. Rob went to bed. Tom, after some thought, stretched out on the settee, covered by a rug. There was nothing to go home for and he might find happy occupation here.

Walking round next morning to look at one of Rob's recent charges, a discarded race-horse with a major leg problem, Tom thought he recognised some of the animals. He wondered how they had arrived here. He hoped to explore without company, to confirm their identity, as he suspected Rob would be reluctant to answer questions and Morris, asked any question to do with Rob, merely smiled and changed the subject.

'First time I've ever wished I had a real place of my own,' Tom said wistfully at breakfast. 'I don't feel like walking and my two rooms are a base, but not a home. No lawns to mow. No decorating to do. No one to come home to.'

Rob took pity on him and suggested he stayed at the sanctuary.

The vet spent the morning helping with

the feeding rota, which seemed endless. As soon as one lot were finished it was time to start again. Splodge and Dapple both insisted on their bottles, although they were now old enough to do without. Morning and evening they banged against the paddock gate or kicked the inside of their stall, demanding food.

'A bit of a busman's holiday,' Rob observed, grinning as he handed yet another a hungry kitten and a bottle to the vet. Morris had driven off to buy supplies and he returned at that moment, eager to impart his news.

'The estate's sold,' he said. 'In spite of the petition.'

'Who's bought it?

'Nobody knows. But most folk think it's the people who want to turn the place into a leisure centre.'

Rob felt as if his peace had ended already. He could not not bear the thought of hordes of people invading their sanctuary.

He would have to move yet again.

Nineteen

Nothing could stop time passing or allay the worries that beset everyone. Nobody knew who had bought Micklemoor Estate. Meanwhile life had to go on. Tussock's small harem produced ducklings galore. Many fell prey to the hawks that were also busy feeding their own young, and to the opportunist foxes.

The hunting eagle spread his shadow over the sanctuary, where small animals teased his taste buds, though the cages were predator-proof. Rob admired his magnificence and hated his need for prey.

'That's life and no getting away from it,' Morris said with a shrug, when Rob commented. 'We all live on other creatures.'

Spare time had always been a luxury. Now, with every bird and animal producing young, even the little left to them vanished. Rob and Morris worked all hours to build a high wire-roofed enclosure around a large corner of the loch, enclosing some of the land as well. Double doors prevented escape, so that the outer door was closed before the inner one was opened.

Here there were ducklings swimming safely, free from the depredations of pike and hawks and foxes. Each duck had her own nesting box lined with bracken, which the men cut daily. This was piled in the centre of the pen.

Neither Rob nor Morris could resist the evening ritual. One duck swam on the water, guarding the many small families, while the mothers pulled out the old bedding and replaced it with fresh, which they then trampled flat.

Feeding time was a riot. Every bird in the district knew when the two men carried the covered pails of feed to the enclosure. Ducks and drakes flew to them, battering them with their wings, sitting on their heads and shoulders, desperately trying to get at the bounty. Rob had soon learned to empty his first load on the beach and let the birds fight over it while he dived back for another couple of pails.

'Worse than dive-bombers,' Morris said when first introduced to this particular ritual. Both hands were occupied and the men could only dodge the onslaught. Hard beaks added to their problems and the need for bedding for twenty ducks added to their work.

'Wish they'd find a way of piling the mucky

bracken up for us to take away without constantly bending down,' Morris said one evening, several weeks after the cats had arrived at the sanctuary.

Rob laughed. 'Maybe we can train them to use special bins,' he said, as he put a match to the day's pile. 'One thing, this smoke does keep off the midges.'

'The reek is nearly as bad as they are,' Morris said, watching the column rise into the sky from the damp ferns. 'Gets in your eyes. Good job there aren't any neighbours to complain.'

The thought of their future neighbours silenced them both as they paused to watch each duck waddle down to the shore and call her own little brood. One by one the tiny creatures followed their mothers into the nests.

'Never thought ducks could count,' Morris observed as one bird, after bobbing her head eleven times, went back to the water's edge and called, an anxious demanding sound. The drab little ducks were not nearly as colourful as the splendid bright plumaged drakes. The tone of her voice changed, and she swam out on to the water, her young following her. The other ducks led their own families up the hill away from the shore.

'Little one got his head caught in the mesh,' Rob said, a moment later, as he saw where she was heading. He whipped off shoes and socks and waded out. The tiny creature, terrified, struggled harder, so that the wire burrowed into his feathers. It was some minutes before he was free.

There was a fraught and desperate quacking from both mother and baby as Rob tried to release the duckling. At last he was able to join his brothers and sisters. The little file entered the nest box and again the mother counted heads, nod, nod, nod, till she reached twelve. This time she was satisfied. She cuddled down on her new-made nest, blocking the entrance to her home with her body. Fluffed to twice her normal size, she hissed at Rob as he passed her on his way out of the enclosure.

'Wonder if any of them appreciate how we care for them,' he said, thrusting cold wet feet into socks that appeared to have shrunk.

'Ever wondered why you do it?' Morris asked, half an hour later, over a hastily concocted meal of bacon, eggs, mushrooms, sausages and fried-up cold potatoes.

Rob grinned. 'That's easy. Everyone knew me and my mum were mad.'

Morris dipped a slice of bread in the egg yolk. 'My mum used to make me soldiers. Ever had them? Bet modern kids don't even know what they are.'

'Fingers of toast to dunk in your egg,' Rob said. He paused. 'Funny. I wonder why that name? Never thought of that before. You just take things for granted.' He helped himself to more potatoes from the overloaded dish that Morris had put in the centre of the table. 'The salmonella scare probably finished that one. Hard-boiled eggs now. Kids probably just have some sort of cereal for breakfast these days. My little nephew, Paul, eats something disgusting covered in chocolate at breakfast time.'

'Thought your sister was a health freak.'

Rob laughed as he mopped the plate clean. 'She is. But young Paul can be much more stubborn than his mum and she's beginning to learn that a quiet life does have some advantages over a state of constant war.'

'Back to the grind,' Morris said, as he put their dishes in the big dishwasher. 'Nice to have Scruffcat to do our work for us.'

Their latest charge had been brought in the day before by the village policeman, who had found her in a thunderstorm, lying in a ditch beside four dead kittens that had not survived their birth. She was barely alive herself. In spite of that she was heavily in milk and as soon as she was dry and clean Rob offered her the orphan kits, which he put in the box in which she had travelled to them. She accepted them and was soon purring with pleasure as they eased her milk glands.

'That was what she needed,' Morris said with satisfaction as he watched her. 'She's been given a new family and all's well.'

'Wish we could cure them all as easily,' Rob said.

Among their new charges was a very bad-tempered swan brought in that afternoon. He had swallowed a fish hook, and yards of nylon line dangled from his mouth. Tom would have to deal with that one, but the cob would come back to the sanctuary to be nursed and did not appear likely to be an easy patient.

For the time being, the two-hourly feeds were no longer necessary and the days expanded miraculously. Rob decided to override his scruples and called in at Micklemoor House one morning on his way to shop. Alastair was in a rehabilitation centre, and would not be home for some weeks yet. Sheina and Mairi were enjoying a brief well-earned rest, after seeing off the latest party with their food hampers.

Sheina welcomed their neighbour with a smile that made him wish that he had called before. He wished that life was less busy. He wished he had time to talk to her, to walk with her on the hills, to get to know her. Alastair's anger loomed broodingly over both of them.

'I thought you'd forgotten us,' Sheina said, as Mairi got up at once to make another cup of coffee. She pushed across the plate of scones.

'Afraid I might make things hard for you,' Rob said. 'Thought you might like to see Hexa and her kits. They're great fun to watch. Full of baby self-importance and very lively, but we're still their enemies.'

'How is Hexa?' Sheina asked. She was intensely aware of their visitor. Tom, who was a frequent visitor when he had time, did not make the whole room suddenly sparkle with life. Nor did Ian.

'Completely recovered. Within a week or so we'll be letting the family free. Don't know what Ian and your dad will make of that,' he added.

'Can't you take them over the other side of the hill?' Sheina asked.

Rob, busily lavishing his scone with farm butter, shrugged. 'They're likely to return to their familiar places. Topaz will be looking for his own territory, and a mate. We could have an explosion of wildcats.'

'If this is turned into a hotel—' Sheina didn't finish.

'How many fishermen today?' Rob asked, anxious to change the subject. It was no use brooding on the inevitable.

'None. This is a party of amateur wildlife photographers, from some club. Ian's taken them up the hill to try and find the deer. They're here for two weeks. One of these special hobby holidays. They're a nice bunch. Twelve of them, four men and eight women. People like them would be welcome here. They wanted to know if they can come and look round the sanctuary.'

'No way,' Rob said. 'I want peace, not people all over the place frightening animals that already have good reason in some cases to detest the human race.' He glanced at the clock. 'Time I was on my way. I have errands. My lot need feeding. And Morris can't cope all day single-handed.'

An hour later in the post office his worst fears were confirmed. The estate, Hetty said, had been bought by a consortium planning to turn it into a large complex with golf, tennis courts, a children's adventure playground and a baby animal zoo, as well as a conference centre and a hotel paying special attention to fishing parties. The lochs and burns were to be restocked and they were buying a stretch of salmon river.

'We'll be just another theme park. The place will be changed for ever,' Hetty said, stamping a parcel as if she intended to destroy it.

'It will bring work for many,' another customer said.

'The contract is nae yet signed,' said yet another voice. 'There's always hope. They need planning permission. They will nae find it all plain sailing.'

In spite of that, Rob drove home, feeling despair. The mountains mocked him, serene against an untroubled blue sky. On the far horizon, over the highest peaks, a huge black cloud prophesied stormy weather to come.

It echoed his mood. Rob felt as if a dark pall had descended on him. What would happen to them all?

As the days passed the kittens forgot that they had ever been free. The big compound enchanted them. Rob hung a tyre on a rope from one of the branches while the little family was in their sleeping quarters with the door closed. That enabled him to clean out the litter box and put down fresh water. A small trap door allowed him to put in the food, and the bowls were collected when the water was replenished.

Mostly they slept by day and came out at dusk. They could not be handled, but they did begin to accept the two men when they brought their meals. It was fluff and spit and hiss if anyone approached the enclosure.

Napoleon, to his annoyance, had to be confined to a paddock or he kept them in a constant state of arousal. For reasons nobody could fathom, the cats fascinated him.

Rob, walking back to the house one night after his final round to check on all his charges and make sure there was no sign of any intruder, human or bird or animal, hoping for an easy meal, saw a conscious Hexa for the first time. Up to then, at the

304

sound of footsteps or voices, she had always retreated fast to her sleeping quarters, where no one could see her.

She held Amber firmly under one large paw, preventing escape as she washed her protesting daughter. Rob hoped that by now she might accept him without reacting angrily.

She saw the man and leaped to her feet, fluffing her fur, her eyes filled with hate. She hissed, a sound so startlingly loud that Domino whinnied from his stable. Hexa spat, then bounded towards the dark sleeping area where she felt safe.

Rob sighed as he went indoors. 'Hexa's fine, but she still hates us,' he said as he opened the kitchen door. 'There's one that would bite the hand that feeds her. The kittens accept us now. I wonder if they would tame? Topaz is surprisingly docile.'

'Not always,' Morris said. 'I moved fast past his cage today, to answer the phone, and made him jump. He hissed and spat ... real little fury he was.'

Morris had made a late-night drink before retiring to his own quarters. He had shopped that day and called in on Mairi and Sheina. Little fruit tarts were beside the coffee cups, as well as sandwiches, scones and rock cakes, and the freezer was filled with goodies.

Rob picked up a sandwich and began to

eat, his mind on other things.

'We ought be able to release the three cats soon. Also, what about restoring Topaz to his family? I don't want to keep him here for all his life.'

'That could be dodgy,' Morris said. 'Will they accept him after so long an absence? He's been indoors all this while and will smell of us.'

'Can only try. If we put him in a cage in the middle of the enclosure, so that they can sniff him, and he can sniff them? Then if all goes well, we can release him. We can borrow Tom's capturing cage again. I don't want to use ours. It might bring back memories to the other three and undo any good we've done.'

'They're most lively at night,' Morris said. 'Try tomorrow?'

Tom, asked for the cage, brought it himself, hoping to see the reunion. Topaz did not like this new prison, and struggled at first. Rob, wearing thick gloves, persuaded the little wildcat that this was in his best interest, and they finally managed to secure him.

The cats had not yet left their sleeping quarters. Rob had arranged their temporary home so that there was a tiny trapdoor in the wire of the outside mesh, through which any of them could put an arm to close the inside door when necessary. The thin rope attached to the handle of the cage was threaded through the roof and across to their hiding place so that, if all went well, Topaz could be released to meet his family face to face.

When everything was arranged the three men retreated to their hiding place. When they were settled Tom laughed quietly.

'Out there people lead normal lives. They go to bed and get up without interruptions. No pager to call them out at night or interrupt their meals. They work nine to five. They lead busy lives, filled with mundane things like cooking and shopping and cleaning, and they have leisure time. They watch TV. They go to theatres and cinemas, and go out for meals.'

'So?' Rob asked. 'You want to join them?'

'No way. I was just thinking that none of them would understand what induced three grown men to sit hidden in bushes watching a small wildcat meet his mother and sisters. Not to mention leading lives that include night-time two-hourly feeds, being called out when it's dark and pouring with rain to deliver a litter of pups by Caesarean at two a.m., as I did last week, or wrestle with a calf that refuses to be born. Never getting meals on time, and generally dedicating all your life to various animals of one kind or another. Sounds mad, doesn't it?'

'There are others like us, though not involved with animals,' Morris said. 'Policemen, night workers ... doctors ... I wouldn't like to work nine to five.'

'Nor I,' Tom said. 'Though I might just change my mind when I'm fifty.'

'I suppose you think that's old.' Morris stretched. His legs were cramping. 'I'm seventy ... and enjoying every minute.'

It was a wild night, a gale brewing. Rob had long ago invested in a pair of night glasses. Hexa had fed earlier that evening on a rabbit that Morris had shot for them. Her snarls kept the two kittens away. She had no intention of sharing her meal. They were old enough to fend for themselves now and her mothering instincts were fading.

She slept after her meal, unaware that the door to the outside was shut fast. Amber and Jade roused first and scratched at it, trying to open it, while Topaz was put down on the ground, safely shut in his cage. Rob released the inner door and the kits flew out. Hexa followed them at a more leisurely pace.

The kittens, suspicious, nosed the cage. Topaz mewed. Hexa raised her head, listening, and then answered. Topaz cried out to her and she sniffed the newcomer through the bars and then rubbed her head against the cage.

Topaz sprang against the lid. It flew up, startling all of them. He leaped out. The other cats welcomed him, rubbing against him, nosing him, purring their contentment to have him restored to them.

There were only a few weeks left of his kittenhood. He would soon be grown, a male prowling, looking for his own territory and for mates. Now he remembered his early games.

Within an hour of his freedom he was playing with his sisters. The three men had intended to go indoors, but they watched, fascinated. The kittens were half grown, their dense fur tabby-shaded, their tails now ring-striped.

The moving ears listened for every sound. They were never still. They were creatures of the night, revelling in darkness. They behaved as if they were hunting on the hill. Jade stalked a beetle and pounced and caught it. She did not like the taste and spat it out.

Amber succeeded in catching a leaf blown by the wind. It came away from the branch and she stared at it, not sure what to make of it now that it lay so still. She left it, and chased one of the ping-pong balls until it hid itself in long grass at the back of the pen.

The cats loved darkness. They knew the sounds of whispering owl wings, the mournful whoo-hoo of the hunting birds, the grumbling of the boar badger as he foraged, afraid of nothing but men and dogs. No poachers ever came here. They knew the screech of the little owl. These birds were noisy tonight, calling constantly as if trying to drown the sound of the wind in the trees.

The three kittens were dancing shadows, boxing at one another. They leaped and tore round the bushes, delighted to be together again. They hid and darted and rolled and mewed.

Hexa lay watching them, purring contentedly. She twitched her tail lazily and Amber caught it with her front paws. Jade was excitement embodied, the wind ruffling her fur, filling her with a desire to run and jump. She chased one of the ping-pong balls, batted it with fervour, then raced after it. The wind took it, adding to her fun.

She jumped a fallen tree that Morris had dragged home to improve their surroundings. She stood on her hind legs and batted at a feather, hanging above her, which was darting on the breeze. She caught it and it dragged free from the string, falling to the ground, where it blew as if alive.

Moonlight shone in the pen, filtering through dancing leaves. Topaz pawed at the ground, trying to catch the shadows as they moved. Over the men's heads a bat flittered through the branches, producing a noise like that made by a child running a stick along railings.

Later that night, sleep proved elusive. Rob could think of nothing but the impending menace of the leisure centre. Even the fishing and photographic groups would be a nuisance: so many of them, hearing of his sanctuary, wanted to come and see for themselves. He had put a notice on the gate saying 'Private. Keep Out' but even that did not deter everyone.

Often a wife or husband came with a member of the various groups, and sometimes children who were not involved in the day's activities. Their wandering disturbed the deer, and prevented the eagle hunting. There had never been so many people on the hills and this was just a foretaste of the future. The wild animals were constantly disturbed and his own rescues, some of them with bad experiences of humans, became distressed.

'Time to release the cats,' he told Morris one September morning. He wanted to give Hexa and her kits their freedom and give them time to settle again before the sale was confirmed. Nobody could blame him then if they became a nuisance.

'Is that wise?' Morris asked. 'Maybe they're better here than free, with such big changes coming. Will they have keepers to keep the wildlife out, do you think? City folk won't take kindly to deer wandering on the golf course, or fighting cats screaming at the moon.'

'I don't give a damn whether it's wise or not.' The mere thought of the invasion made

Rob irritable. 'They want to come here, they have to accept conditions. This isn't the middle of a big city. It's the wilderness. Can't tame it.'

'They try,' Morris. said. 'Look at all the cases where people have complained about crowing cocks.'

'They can complain all they like,' Rob said, suddenly wanting at least a dozen of the noisiest cocks he could find. 'Do we kill all the owls and the crows and the cooing doves, the pheasants and the bittern, just to satisfy people who seem to think the whole world is dedicated to their comfort?' He strode over to the door, wanting to get outside into the fresh air. The house was stifling him.

'Nothing like a load of drunken holiday-makers to drown the natural sounds,' he said and slammed the door behind him, making the caged animals jump and cry out. Poco and Nin, abandoned, sat and stared at the closed door as if wondering what had gone wrong with their world.

Morris frowned. 'Life just now ain't a lot of fun,' he told the dogs, who happily wagged their tails. 'Have to bear with him, fellows.'

Rob stood in the darkness and stared at the enclosure. He had not yet opened the door of the sleeping quarters. It was now or never, and blow everybody who might object. This was the wildcats' home. Humans were an intrusion. He opened the outer door and went into the house, leaving them free to leave if they wished.

The dogs greeted him as if they were sure they had done wrong and offended them. He looked at the two miserable animals, and gave himself a mental shake.

'Sorry, boys,' he said, and knelt with his arms wide. They raced at him, their world restored to its former security.

He dreamed of dodgem cars and fairgrounds, of candy floss and children running, screaming, invading his paddocks, terrifying his refugees. He dreamed of Sheina, who was saying that he ought not to have let the wildcats out as they would be shot. He dreamed of Ian, aiming with his gun at the four of them as they stood, poised on a rock, inviting destruction.

He woke feeling as if he had spent the night before drinking heavily. He went out to look at the wildcats' cage. There was not a sign of them. The sleeping quarters were as empty as the enclosure. Only their discarded food and water bowls and the litter box testified to the fact that they had ever been there.

Poco retrieved his ball, delighted to see a favourite toy again. Morris stopped beside him.

'Was I right or wrong?' Rob asked him. 'I want them settled before the place changes.

If they have to move on, then it's their decision. They need experience and they won't get it here.'

'We'll have to find out where they've gone and leave food for them,' Morris said. 'They may have forgotten how to hunt and the kits never had enough skill.'

Rob rang Mairi, who promised that she and Sheina would make time to look round the various dens that Hexa had inhabited and see if they could find out where the family had headed. His conscience worried him. Had he released them in a fit of pique, without enough thought, or was he right? Had he condemned them to certain death?

It was no use. He would have to move if the leisure complex was built. Perhaps they wouldn't get planning permission. He looked at the deserted pen with the feathers that had been teased and carried around, at the tyre swaying in a soft breeze, and at the ping-pong balls lying forgotten. He gathered them up. He was going to miss the cats. They had been a source of great interest for so long, even though they had never really accepted him – except Topaz, who was probably even less able to look after himself than his sisters.

He looked up at the hills. Were they roaming there, or had Hexa taken them back to the kirkyard? He hoped that she would still help them hunt. He had interrupted their education.

'Good luck,' he said under his breath.

That night he and Morris listened as the ecstatic animals, free to run and free to roam, cried their excitement to the moon.

Twenty

Ian tore the date off the calendar. Autumn was only a breath away.

'Never known a year go by so fast.'

They all seemed to be saying it, Sheina thought. Morris, Rob, Ian, Hetty. Everyone she met in the village. Time seemed to have changed pace, flying so that the hours vanished.

The sale of the estate was still only a rumour. Nothing was definite. Sheina and Ian both longed for the uncertainty to end.

'The Grant farm has been on the market for four years,' Mairi reminded them. 'This could be as long. Unless an American millionaire decides he wants a place in Scotland.' Malcolm Grant had died when his tractor overturned, leaving his young widow to struggle.

The estate's would-be owners were insisting that planning permission was secured before they signed the contract, not after. That might not be given.

Throughout the summer the colonel had sent a variety of different groups. Some came to fish; others to take photographs of wildlife. A number of small societies heard of Micklemoor House and its facilities. There was seldom more than a couple of days without some visitors keeping the three of them well occupied.

Rob was overwhelmed with wildlife casualties. He and Morris were rare visitors, dropping in for a quick cup of coffee on their way to and from the shopping areas.

The four dogs that Alastair had in for training had all been sent home. Recommendations followed, and the kennels were always full of young hopefuls, destined to go back to busy men who had no time to shape their own dogs. Sheina had to do most of the training as Ian was fully occupied either teaching those who were unskilled or leading the various groups around the mountains.

'Maybe they won't need to sell. This must be profitable,' Sheina said, after an exhausting two-week session with a group of twelve enthusiastic young women, anxious to watch the eagles, to find ospreys, and to stalk the rutting stags and photograph them, an activity Ian thought highly unwise. They were up before the sun, they wanted night-time sessions, and each ate more than any two of any other party. Also they presented dietary problems. Four were vegetarian, which was easy enough, but two were vegan. Animal products turned up in the most unlikely places. One needed a gluten-free diet and yet another was allergic to dairy foods. Sheina and Mairi added to their cookbooks and needed to refer all the time.

'It wouldn't be so bad if they didn't all grumble at whatever we provide,' Mairi said. She had made a quiche, but had failed to ensure that the cheese was a variety suitable for vegetarians.

'We'll deserve haloes when this lot goes,' she said. She was rarely irritated, but after a fortnight during which never a day passed without one or another of the women finding fault, she was ready to yell at the next person who complained.

Ian had problems with them too, as one refused to be parted from her perfume. Any bird or animal within a mile knew that the humans were near, and try as he might to gain a good place for them to watch, the wildlife refused to cooperate. As a result she was unpopular with her companions.

'Funny how some weeks everyone is easy, and in others they all seem to be tetchy,' Mairi said the day before the group departed. She banged down her rolling pin. 'I wish we hadn't started the end-of-holiday party. I've had to change the whole menu.'

'Feed them grass,' Ian suggested. They were all exhausted – it was well after midnight. 'I wonder how the hotel fares with their breakfast and evening meals?'

'Badly,' Sheina said. 'You should hear young Eileen talking about the "English leddies". Picking and poking at the food on their plates and asking about everything that went into it.' She laughed as Mairi attacked the pastry once more with vigour. 'Do you think that will be edible?' she asked. 'Or imbued with your anger and hard as the rocks?'

Mairi sighed. 'Oh, for a group of people who only want bacon sarnies and think that a beefburger in a bun is gourmet food. Where are you taking them tomorrow, Ian?' Her remark was prompted by the pile of bacon sandwiches that he was eating, perched against the window seat.

'It's already tomorrow,' he said. 'They want to see pine martens. Eileen told them Rob has a baby in the sanctuary. The mother was carrying it, and a dog chased her. She dropped it. The dog owner found it, and instead of leaving it for the mother to retrieve, took it to Rob. It was still blind.'

He picked up the king-sized mug that Sheina had given him for Christmas a year ago, saying it would save on refills.

'They're pestering me to make Rob let them visit the sanctuary. I told them it would be better to see the pine martens in their natural surroundings.'

'Are they likely to?' Mairi asked, taking pity on her pastry and rolling it flat.

'With Smelly Nelly drowned in cheap scent? Not a chance. But it will keep them out of harm's way, tucked up, lying there, watching all day. I'll take them to the place where the little one was found. But the mother was probably on her way elsewhere.'

'What will you do while they are tucked up in the heather?' Sheina asked.

'I promised to give Rob and Morris a hand. I can spend four hours there, and it's near enough to check on my leddies, as Eileen calls them.'

The day was unexpectedly successful, although the glimpse the vistors had of the pine marten was brief. There was just a flash of fur as one solitary beast was diverted from its track by the alien scent.

'You didn't deserve that,' Sheina said when he told her next morning. He had the afternoon off, as the women had decided to visit the town and shop for presents to take home.

Sheina was always thankful that they had big rooms at Micklemoor House. The dining room provided a focus for the buffets. This particular feast taxed all their ingenuity. They had learned a great deal about diets during the two previous weeks and, to their surprise, were complimented at the end of the evening.

Next day ten botanists arrived, wishing to explore the hills for rare flowers. They discovered several varieties of orchid that nobody knew grew in the foothills. Late October brought eight eager amateur geologists together with a professor who, they were told, was one of the top authorities in the United Kingdom. They climbed and brought back fossils and rock specimens.

The last-day party had now become an institution. The geologists were so pleasant that Mairi excelled herself. 'You make food to die for,' the professor said. A week later three little parcels arrived with a letter.

This is by way of inadequate thanks for looking after us all so well and making our stay memorable. I hope it will remind you of us with as much pleasure as we will remember you.

The source of your gifts is not Scotland. The stones come from the Anglesey sea bed, and are 600,000,000 years old. They do not occur anywhere else in the world.

Mairi and Sheina each had mottled orange-brown heart-shaped pendants of polished stone hanging on silver chains. Ian's stone was set in a paperweight.

'Maybe the syndicate will do so well from the various groups that they won't need to sell,' Sheina said again.

Nobody answered. It seemed a forlorn hope.

Mairi found more satisfaction in helping with the catering than she did with her pies and cakes for the village inn and the shop, though she kept making for them. She was beginning to feel weary.

'At least I should be able to find a job anywhere as a cook,' Sheina said, one dull day in the middle of November. The current group exploring the hills were on a walking holiday. ' Ian will find something ... but I'm worried about Dad. There's no pension with his job.'

Alastair was due home at the end of the week. He could walk very slowly with help from a wheeled zimmer frame, and was far from mobile. His left hand was almost useless. He did not yet know that they were likely to lose their home. Sheina delayed telling him in the hope the syndicate might decide to function under its new guise.

'Maybe he could find security work monitoring TV cover of some big buildings,' Rob suggested one morning when he had called in for coffee. Mairi and Sheina were enjoying a brief rest. There were no parties to guide and feed. 'He can sit to do that.'

He sighed. 'I won't visit when he comes home. No need to upset him. I wish—'

Nobody needed him to finish the sentence.

'Be Christmas before we know it,' Ian said

on the last day of November. 'The four spaniels can all go home before then. There will just be the two Labs left till the end of January ... if we get that amount of time. Provided the owners keep up our work, they should have good dogs.'

'Clancy's outstanding,' Sheina said, referring to a handsome springer spaniel that had been with them for just under three months. 'I'll miss him. He has a good pedigree and a lovely temperament. Maybe they'll let me use him as stud dog for Beulah in the spring.'

And maybe she wouldn't even have Beulah in the spring. Rob had promised to give the little bitch and Craig a home if Sheina had to take a job where keeping a dog was an impossibility. He too might have to find a new site, but there was no way he intended to change his lifestyle.

Sheina had a sudden unpleasant thought. 'Think they'll let us spend Christmas in peace? Or will we get a Christmas group and have to pull out all the stops?'

'Maybe we could take them to the farms to see if the cattle do kneel down at midnight on Christmas Eve,' Ian said. It was easier to make silly jokes than to brood and grow daily more miserable.

Alastair was due home. Sheina was worried, wondering how they could cope with him. How much could he do for himself?

There was very little spare time with this new way of life and he would have to learn to fit in as it might go on for months yet.

Ian and Sheina changed homes once more. Rob and Morris came to help shift furniture to ensure there was easy access to every room for Alastair. Rugs were moved, and furniture placed to give clear passage. They were watched by two puzzled dogs who could not understand why their favourite resting places had been taken away.

The social services proved unexpectedly helpful, providing handles that Alastair could grab if necessary and blocks that fitted on to the legs of his favourite armchair and lifted it several inches off the ground to enable him to get up from it easily.

During the months he was away, Sheina felt that her father had changed for the better. His illness had distanced him from everything at first, so that he had little interest in anything but his own physical problems.

A change had come in mid-June. When she rang the rehabilitation centre to say she would be late visiting as she had to go to the vet, the receptionist suggested that she brought the dog in. There was no reason why her father shouldn't see him. It might do him a world of good.

The area for cars in the centre was well lined with trees under which she could park.

Visits tended to be short as Alastair tired easily. The dog she had taken to the vet was one of those in training, a recent arrival who, to her annoyance, was suffering from a sore and neglected ear which he scratched till it bled. He could stay in the car, while she took Craig to see her father.

Sheina groomed the Labrador until he gleamed with health. The dog had long ago resigned himself to the absence of his master. He could not believe his eyes or his nose when he went into the room. It took all her strength to prevent him launching himself at Alastair, who was sitting in a chair beside his bed.

Craig unlocked something within the keeper. He sat up straighter. His eyes showed his delight. For the first time, he wanted to know how things were on the estate.

'I think, when you come home, you should have Craig in the house with you, Dad,' Sheina said. 'He's grand company. You won't be able to get around much at first and we'll be busy. You'll be alone so much.'

'I meant to tell you to take the dogs indoors,' Alastair said. 'Protection. It's lonely there on your own.'

'Ian and I swapped homes. I'm staying with Mairi and Ian's looking after our house,' Sheina said. 'They were worried about me being there on my own at night.' She wondered how her father would receive this news, but he only nodded. 'I've been worried,' he said. 'It's a relief to know you're not there by yourself.'

Craig, feeling neglected, pushed his head against his master's knee. Alastair laughed for the first time since his illness. The dog leaned against him, looking at him as if he would never look away again.

Passing nurses came to admire him. A woman in a wheelchair, unable to do more than move one hand and only able to speak in whispers, asked if she could pet the dog. Sheina led him to the chair. The frail hand touched his fur, and her sad face broke into a wide beam.

From then on Craig became a regular visitor and Alastair began to plan for coming home. There were books brought round each week, but those provided bored him. Ian found a supply of dog training books, and the keeper read them avidly, aware that if he did continue to teach the dogs he would need different methods.

He was resigned to the fact that he was unlikely to regain the complete use of his left hand and he would never be able to go out on the hills for long treks.

Late in September Sheina found a strange man sitting with her father.

'This is John, my counsellor,' he said. 'We've been working out what I can and can't do when I come home. I can walk about a bit and shower and shave and dress. I ought to be able to help with the dogs. That'll earn us some money. I expect the estate will sack me.'

'The estate's for sale, Dad,' Sheina said, feeling she could not keep the news from him any longer. 'We'll need to work out a whole new way of living, both of us.'

'A completely new challenge,' John said.

He walked back to the Land Rover with Sheina and the dog. He was a big man who seemed to have been poured into his clothes. Grey hair receded from a broad forehead. Brown eyes smiled at her.

'I've heard a lot about you. Don't worry. Your father's stronger every day and he's determined to make the most of life even if he can't do as he used. It might be as well if he is in completely different surroundings. Nothing to remind him of his past and no room for regrets.'

Sheina told her father about the various groups of people who came, and often had a funny anecdote about one or the other that made him laugh. He enjoyed hearing about Smelly Nelly and her perfume.

The day before Alastair came home Sheina went to the village to stock up with food. She was not sure if she should leave him on his own for long periods.

The post office was buzzing with news.

'No leisure centre. They can't get planning

permission,' Hetty said with a broad smile. 'It's in the paper. The buyers have pulled out. The estate's for sale again at a lower price and they say there's someone waiting in the wings.'

'Going to be a nunnery, I hear,' said a small woman who stood at the back of the queue for pensions.

The man in front of her knew better. 'I'm told it's to be a retreat for a closed order of monks. The kind that aren't allowed to speak. Rich folk will come here to recover from breakdowns and drugs and alcohol, as it will be part of a big medical centre.'

'It's to be a health farm,' Hector McCann from the farm shop said. 'No monks. Taking over the McPhee place too. He's moving out. Furniture vans loading there at the end of last week.'

Sheina felt as if she had been shot. She couldn't believe it. How could Rob move without telling her? Without coming over to say goodbye? His visits had brightened her days. She suddenly realised he meant far more to her than just a friend, and felt betrayed. He could have phoned.

She did not intend to ring him. Obviously she did not mean more to him than any of his other friends. She had thought there might be something between them, though any serious commitment was going to mean problems with her father.

In spite of Rob's defection she determined to ask Alastair, when she visited for the last time, to tell her why he so hated the Mc-Phees. Others would move in and she preferred to be on friendly terms with neighbours.

'Please, Dad,' she said. 'I can't share your feelings, but I would like to understand them.' John was also visiting and she looked at him for support.

'Hate feeds on itself,' he said. 'There's no healing till you let it go. Tell us what happened. Talking about it will help.'

Craig stretched and yawned, a very loud noise that made them all grin. Alastair put out his hand to pet the dog and was licked. He hesitated, unable to know where to begin.

'It happened when my mother was small. She was just six years old. She didn't understand at the time, but she did when she was older. Her anger stayed with her all her life, and she fed it to me. The mere mention of the McPhees was enough to send her into a rage, followed by the most terrible migraine that could put her out of action for a week, and the subject was forbidden in our house.'

He paused as a smiling woman brought in tea and a plate on which were two biscuits. Craig snatched them before anyone could stop him.

Alastair resumed after his lost snack was replaced.

'We lived on the other side of the McPhee place,' he explained to John. 'My parents had a cottage on the hill, and we looked down on the farm. My grandfather and grandmother lived a mile away from us. Both Grandpa and my dad were keepers. I grew up in the job. Grand life for a boy, out on the hills all day.'

He looked out of the window at flowers growing in a small courtyard, where two women sat talking on a wooden bench. He missed the mountains. He wondered if he would ever be able to climb again.

Realising his listeners were waiting for him to continue, he rallied. It was still hard to explain.

'My mother had a sister, eleven years older than her. Ellen was seventeen and the prettiest creature you ever saw. My mother adored her. I once saw her photograph. I thought she was an angel. Remember, this was in the 1940s, just after the war. Life was very different then.'

Sheina knew nothing of the family's past. She had known her grandparents briefly, as a little girl, and had been close to her grandfather, a placid man, who taught her to love animals. Her grandmother had been remote, a cold woman who did not even kiss her and was always critical. Sheina had been six when she died, and did not miss her. She grieved for her grandfather, and her mother's parents who, like Morag, had been warm and outgoing.

'Ellie fell in love with Robert McPhee, the youngest of the brothers. They kept it secret as her parents were strict. She climbed out of her bedroom window and down a tree to meet him. She became pregnant and dared not tell anyone. Her mother would have disowned her. In those days it was a terrible thing to have a child out of wedlock.'

Sheina found it hard to understand such an attitude.

'And?' John asked.

'Ellie didn't tell anyone. She drowned herself in the loch. My grandfather horsewhipped Robert. He served three months for assault. Robert emigrated and died abroad. The two families never spoke again. My mother was always bitter. She had lost someone she loved so much, and lost her trust in people. I don't think she ever let herself grow really close to anyone again. Not even my father. She never hugged or kissed me. I think she had wanted a daughter who looked like Ellie.'

He sighed. 'We were never allowed to mention the McPhees, or acknowledge them if we came across them by chance when out and about. She taught me to hate them. She had little time for men. Now I can't think how she ever came to marry.' He looked back down the years. 'My father never said anything against the McPhees, but he was a man for a quiet life and my mother was domineering. She told me they were wicked and I must never ever have anything to do with them. It was imbued into me from the time I could talk.'

He looked at them and grinned ruefully. 'When I was small I imagined them all with horns and tails. Talking about it now makes it seem tragic, but not a reason for such hatred over so many years.'

John sighed. 'So much unnecessary unhappiness. Mostly it would be better today for Ellie. Young people are often foolish and these things happen, but few take heed now. Though they do in some small villages still,' he added.

He looked at Alastair, who seemed to be thinking of the past. 'Young Rob is barely related to the McPhees,' he said. 'It's time to forgive those long-ago lovers and move on. Tomorrow's what's important and making yourself a life worth living. We can't change the past. We can learn from it.'

'What sort of future do I have? Like this?' Alastair asked.

'When you arrived here you couldn't walk ... now you can get around. That'll improve,' John said.

Ian greeted Sheina on her arrival home from her hospital visit.

'Hetty says the estate has been sold. It's definite.'

They had suspected this as there had been no bookings now for two weeks and no news of any more, but all the same the evening was spoiled.

'Who to?'

'Nobody knows. Lots of guesses. The latest is either a pop star or a world-class footballer, wanting a country retreat away from the fans.'

'Who told Hetty?'

Ian longed to comfort Sheina. He made them both a cup of tea, and sat with her, wishing he could have brought good news. Sheina stroked Beulah, gaining comfort from the dog's presence. Ian wished they were part of his life, but knew that his feelings were not reciprocated.

'Goodness knows how Hetty found out,' he said finally. 'She gets news from the birds. She has her own pigeon post.'

'Don't tell Dad ... not yet. Let him come home and settle in. We don't want to spoil that for him. He's longing to get out of hospital. They won't chuck us out tomorrow, will they?'

She sighed. 'It's going to be hard to act cheerful. I'm not very good at that. I was a disaster in our school plays. In the end I just painted the scenery, though I loved being in the drama group.'

They were all there to welcome Alastair home. The ambulance men helped him into the house, although he struggled to walk unaided, even with the zimmer frame.

Mairi brought a huge bunch of tawny chrysanthemums that brightened the kitchen window sill. A fire blazed in the grate in Alastair's room, which enclosed him with an untidy comfort far removed from the functional hospital ward.

Craig, delighted to have his master home, reverted to puppyhood and spent his time bringing unlikely gifts, of shoes, of a sponge from the bathroom, of a cushion from one of the sitting-room chairs.

Alastair had not realised how much familiar surroundings meant. His room, his chair, his home. The books in the recesses in the wall on either side of the fireplace. Even the mounted specimens of flies, their colours jewel-like, neatly arranged in the display case. Once he had made those for fishermen. He sighed as he looked at them. He doubted if his hands would ever again be capable of such delicate work.

'What future have I?' he asked John, who came an hour later to help him settle in.

'Far more than you had a few months ago,' the counsellor responded. 'Look at the progress you've made. You'll make more. Give it time.'

He grinned suddenly. 'I've had my marching orders too. I'm sixty-five. You're my last patient. Doctor says it's time to slow down but, like you, I'm on my own. No wife now. She died four years ago.'

He paused to waken the fire from a dull glow to a blaze. He had been invited to stay for the evening meal. Ian had promised to run him home. John thought of the dreary flat with its view of an equally dreary street. 'I had a heart attack last year and I'm under orders to work less and exercise more. Five miles a day, the doctor said, but there's no point unless you've somewhere to go.'

He had said nothing of this in the hospital. Alastair realised he had not even wondered about the man who came daily to talk to him, to cheer him, to encourage him. He had taken him for granted, as he had the nursing staff, submitting to their care but bitterly resenting his loss of mobility.

Coming home triggered him to think of others. John was still talking, standing now with his back to the wood fire which, a rare luxury in his life, reminded the man of his own childhood; of coming home to the smell of baking and his mother's hugs.

While Sheina prepared the evening meal, helped by Ian, Mairi made a batch of bread.

'It would be good to walk with you round this place. There'd be purpose. It would get us both moving.'

The keeper realised that John was pleading. He must have been thinking about this for some time.

'I need a purpose in life too. Without that we drift and die of boredom. I can make drinks for you, take some of the chores off your daughter. We'll tackle your walking together ... if you'll agree.'

'The estate's for sale,' Alstair reminded him. 'We may not be able to stay on here. We're just caretakers now for the owners.'

'There's always a way,' John said, refusing to give up his own vision of being needed again, of having a place in the world, which he felt had ended with the loss of his work. He hoped with all his heart that Alastair and Sheina could stay. Here there were wide vistas and soaring hills, ever-changing cloudscapes and vast banks of deep purple heather and the eagle overhead. He loved the mountains. It was another world, far removed from the village street and the constant passing traffic.

'If you do have to leave, maybe you and I could find some place together. Your daughter needs to be free.'

'It's quite a thought,' Alastair said, suddenly more cheerful. He was worried about becoming a burden to Sheina. The only alternative he could see was a residential home and that he knew he would hate.

There was a possible alternative future in

front of him. A country cottage and dogs to train, with John as companion.

The hard chair at the dinner table was too uncomfortable. John and Ian carried Alastair's armchair into the kitchen. Sheina had bought a little adjustable table that held his food, and would also tilt to support a book.

The keeper realised how everyone had thought of him while he was unable to come home. The meal was a celebration, with all his favourite foods. Roast pork was accompanied by roast parsnips and potatoes, glazed carrots and minted peas, all from the organic farm, with home-made sage and onion stuffing and apple sauce. Mairi provided a raspberry pavlova, and there was clotted cream, also from the farm shop.

It was the start of a new era. There were no more visitors to guide and teach and drive around and feed. Ian and Sheina had time to work with the dogs, uninterrupted. They had time to make up for weeks of neglect of the grounds. Mairi came daily to do the housework and cook for them.

John also came every day. He proved a hard taskmaster, forcing Alistair to walk a little farther each day and not give way to a desire to sit and do nothing. Walking was both difficult and painful but slowly the insistence paid dividends and the zimmer frame was abandoned for a walking stick.

Still nobody knew who now owned the estate. There was a very brief letter from the colonel.

For your information. The estate has been sold. The new owner will contact you.

The signature was rubber stamped.

'And thank you all for your hard work, which is much appreciated,' Sheina said when she read it. 'He might have said something, after all these years.'

Alastair insisted Sheina put the rent money away each week. Someone was sure to ask for it. Their only income now came from training the dogs and from the pies and pasties and home-baked bread and cakes that Mairi and Sheina made in greater quantity and sold to the village shop. They added vegetarian and gluten-free meals, which proved a success, as did the sale of goats' milk.

There was no word from Rob, though the postman said that he and Morris and the animals in the sanctuary were still there. Sheina did not like to phone.

Christmas Eve was busy as Sheina insisted that they celebrate in style. John and Ian and Mairi were all joining them, and Tom too if he had time off. The table and counters were piled high with cooling bread and mince pies. Mairi had made a Christmas cake, complete with snow and snowmen, which stood in the middle of the table.

Ian and John decorated a tree. They had more Christmas cards than they ever remembered, from village people hoping that they would not leave. Sheina strung them up, wondering where they would all be next year. They had lived there for all of her life. She could not bear to think of having to find work elsewhere. There was nothing she wanted to do. Everything she loved was here.

The fear marred the day. It formed a background as she filled bowls with glittering baubles to brighten dark corners, and arranged vases of the brilliantly berried holly that Ian had brought in that afternoon.

They had been so busy that they ate sandwiches and mince pies, instead of making a meal. They were relaxing over cups of coffee when Craig and Beulah, now accepted as indoor dogs, barked at a knock at the door.

Rob stood there.

Sheina was unable to do more than stare at him. He was the last person she had expected.

'I hope your father will see me,' he said. 'If not, there's a very big problem.'

Twenty-One

Sheina was speechless. She could not imagine what he had to say. She held the door open, mutely inviting him in. His presence disturbed her and she wished he hadn't come. No doubt he was about to tell them that he was moving away.

Alastair hushed the dogs, who stopped barking and came to investigate the newcomer. They were all staring at him now. He stood, diffident, looking at the keeper, afraid of a rough greeting.

'Come in,' Alastair said.

Their visitor still stood uneasily, as if wondering whether he was welcome or merely tolerated out of politeness. They were all waiting for him to speak. He had prepared a speech, but the words went out of his head. Instead, he blurted out his news, finding it much harder to tell them than he had expected.

'I'm your new landlord,' he said at last. 'I hoped that it would be a wonderful Christmas present ... but I realise now you may not welcome the news.'

There was total silence. They had imagined many scenarios, but not this.

Rob walked across to one of the chairs,
accompanied by both dogs, who were intent
on sniffing every inch of him. He smelled of
an assortment of animals, offering them
unexpected riches.

He pulled the chair out from the table and
turned it round and straddled it, leaning his
arms on its back. He positioned it so that he
could see them all. They were so astounded
that nobody thought to introduce John, who
listened with interest.

'You may not like this at all,' Rob said
again, looking at Alastair. 'I do understand
you have reservations about my family. I
don't know why. I'm not really closely
related to the McPhees.'

'It's long past,' Alastair said, rallying himself. He did not know what to make of the
news. 'Time to close and forget.' He sighed.
'I've had so much time to do nothing but
think and it's hard to understand now why it
influenced me so much. Sheina will tell you,
one day.'

He stroked Craig's head, which was resting
on his knee. The dog sat close, watching
every movement, afraid his master might
vanish again.

'What happens to us now?' Sheina asked.
She could not imagine what Rob intended
or why he had bought the estate.

Her father looked into a bleak future. 'I don't imagine you'll want shooting parties. Do you want us to find somewhere else to live?'

'No. I'm going to realise a dream and hope you'll all help me. I haven't been able to tell anyone that I own the estate as it's been complicated. The contracts weren't signed till yesterday. I didn't want to raise your hopes and then have them crash again.' He grinned suddenly. 'I've been dying to tell you.'

He looked longingly at the cooling food. Mairi saw his glance and smiled. She made him a mug of coffee and passed him several mince pies on a plate.

'My idea of manna from heaven,' he said, taking a few bites before he spoke again.

There was another knock at the door. Tom grinned at Sheina when she opened it.

'I hoped to be here sooner,' he said, coming in to shake hands with Alastair. 'I wanted to be here when Rob broke his news. But cows don't cooperate or obey the clock.'

Rob waited till the vet was also seated with mince pies and a coffee mug. 'I hated the idea of a leisure complex here as much as you did,' he said at last. 'It would be a major invasion. I've no desire or need to open to the public to make money for the sanctuary. It is just that. A place where animals can recover and be freed back into the wild when well, a place where those that can't fend for themselves can find a haven. I want to breed rare birds and replenish the wild places that no longer know them.'

There was passion in his voice. They all saw a man with a vision, planning to realise a long-held ambition.

He stopped to sip his coffee.

'My mother and I operated on a shoe-string. The McPhee heirlooms changed that. I thought of them as money in the bank for future use, selling them one by one to fund my immediate needs.'

They sat listening, unable to take in what he was saying, and wondering what role he imagined they would play in the future.

'I began to look at other places in which to settle. It's a dickens of a job moving all the birds and beasts. It disturbs them, and I need to have somewhere suitable ready when they arrive. It would mean starting again, enclosing paddocks, fencing, making cages.'

He had been sitting sideways on the chair to eat. He now turned it round again and resumed his straddled position. Beulah, who had been watching him hopefully, nosed the ground for crumbs.

'I fell in love with this area when I arrived. With the grandeur of the high hills and the heather moors, with the immense variety of birds and animals. I've never been rich and it hadn't really occurred to me that I was now very wealthy indeed. It was Morris who asked why I have to sell everything one piece at a time. Why not sell the lot and buy the estate? he said one morning. It's not as if you use it, and it takes so much time to keep in good condition. I thought he was kidding but he was serious.'

'The vans were taking the antiques?' Sheina asked, her hopes rising. 'Everyone thought you were moving.'

'I'd have told you,' he said, wanting to add, 'Surely you knew that.' He saw Ian watching him and read the other man's thoughts.

'Tom clinched the matter.' He grinned at his friend. 'He was the genie in the bottle. I told him of our idea but said I had no idea how to go about selling everything at once. His uncle works for a firm of auctioneers specialising in antiques. He visited and nearly had a heart attack on the spot.'

'I only wish I'd been there,' Tom said, holding out his plate for another mince pie. 'Not eaten since lunchtime,' he explained.

Mairi became busy, cutting cold meat, adding pickles and slices of warm crusty bread, covering each with butter that melted as she spread it. Tom was soon feasting. Beulah watched every mouthful intently, though Craig had no intention of leaving Alastair for one second.

Rob laughed at the memory.

'Tom's uncle was lost for words. He began to value everything and then asked if I had ever looked up in the loft. Apparently that's a great source of treasure trove. It never occurred to me, and it hadn't occurred to the solicitors who put everything into storage when the place was rented. It's a huge area, going across the whole building, and was stuffed full of tin boxes of all kinds.'

Mairi refilled his coffee mug. He looked thoughtfully at the picture of a strutting pheasant in courting plumage.

'It was like that TV programme, the *Antiques Roadshow*. All those unconsidered trifles. We carried the boxes down. We were like three kids, delving into them, saying, "Hey, just look at *this*." There were letters from Victorian days. Some were love letters. Letters from the men at the front in World War I. All in their envelopes. All with their stamps still on. There's history in those letters.'

He accepted another mince pie. Mairi decided she would have to make more. These young men had such big appetites – and there might just be two extra for Christmas lunch.

Rob had more to tell. He had been longing to share his good fortune. 'There are also valentines made by hand of lace and velvet with gold lettering. Samplers dating from 1700 on. Dozens of hand-painted postcards dating from the early 1900s, long before towns began to pull down the old buildings and rebuild. Up to then, I hadn't quite enough to cover the purchase and give me a life income. It made all the difference.'

'But buying the estate must have taken ages,' Sheina said. 'When did you start?'

'Way back when the leisure centre asked for planning permission and lost it,' Rob said. 'I thought I might be in with a chance. One of the local councillors told me they hadn't a hope of getting it. The whole village was against it. The syndicate dropped the price, as without that nobody had much future here. They were eager to sell.'

He leaned across and removed a slice of pork from Tom's plate, sharing it with Beulah.

'They agreed to wait, contingent on my getting the money from my own sale. As it happened an American consortium bought all the furniture for a house out there, to open as a musuem. They've apparently removed the building, which was Tudor, stone by stone from a Cotswold village. This ices their cake.'

'I still don't see where we come in,' Sheina said. 'And does it leave you with anything?'

Rob looked at her, amusement in his eyes.

'Any idea of the value of a penny black? There are three of those as well as stamps from all over the world. When those alone are sold I'll have more than enough for the rest of my life.'

'And what happens to the estate and the house?' Sheina asked. She could not imagine what Rob had in mind.

'From now on, this is a conservation zone. I applied for registration as an area of special scientific interest. We more than qualify with so many rare birds and flowers and animals. Those summer groups did a lot of good as they've recorded things nobody knew existed here.'

He drained his mug and put it on the table. 'What's more, I get a huge grant. We let the whole estate go back to nature. We'll manage the deer, and make sure none die of starvation in old age. The hills are for the wildcats ... and the hawks and pine martens and the eagles.'

He laughed at their expressions. 'There's work in plenty for Sheina and Ian. Mairi can come and cook for us all. You don't have to move. Alastair can train all the dogs he can find time for ... and if he will help when we've loads of baby animals in need of feeding it would be a benefit.'

'Is there a niche for me?' John asked, envious of them all. 'I'm useful with tools, can mend fences, and I expect I could feed a small animal if it came to the pinch.'

'We'll need all the help we can get,' Rob said. 'I can pay high wages, offer accommodation, and I can't wait to get started.'

He suddenly looked anxious and turned to Alastair.

'Here I am ranting on. It's up to you. I'd like you to stay on here, rent free, as part of the deal. During the months ahead we can tidy up the old part of the house, and use it for cages. I can take more animals in. There's a huge supply all the time, and I can't always make room. Morris and I have been clearing the fields for paddocks for the horses.'

Tom looked across at Sheina. He, like Ian, had had hopes, but he was aware that she had never stopped watching Rob.

'If you go over to Rob's place, you'll meet three old friends,' he said. 'They'll be delighted to see you, and there's a nice little filly foal.'

'You bought our horses?' Sheina couldn't believe it.

'Couldn't let them go just anywhere,' Rob said. 'I usually go to the sales and bring home one or two, to make sure they at least have a good life for the rest of their time. The horses are your reponsibility if you agree. I never get time to groom them.'

Sheina wanted to dance.

Rob looked at them all, hopefully. Each had a vision of an entrancing future.

'You'll need time to think.'

'No,' Alastair said. 'I'll never be able to work as a keeper again, but this is possible ...

I'd given up hope. You don't need to ask Sheina,' he added, suddenly light-hearted and laughing. 'Just look at her face. She's been offered heaven on a plate.'

'I'm on,' Ian said. 'And if Mairi wants to come, we can go to work together. She can drive over with me.'

John, thinking of his dreary home, looked anxiously at Rob.

'You said accommodation?' he asked, afraid he might be wrong.

'I don't use half the rooms,' Rob said. 'There's a sitting room and bedroom for you, and we can put in another bathroom. Since this house is mine now,' he added, turning again to Alastair, 'I'd like to improve your bathroom and bring in mains electricity. The syndicate should have done it long ago.'

Tom vanished briefly to return with a bottle of champagne. 'I didn't bring it in, just in case,' he said.

'To the future,' Rob said.

Glasses were raised.

Alastair relaxed, the thought crossing his mind that he was like a poacher who had turned gamekeeper. He now had a very different role. He realised that he would enjoy it. He looked at his daughter, but she had eyes only for Rob. Tom and Ian, also watching, said goodbye to their own dreams.

Far away, on the hill, Hexa and her family

hunted and played, unaware of their new status as treasured animals to be protected at all costs. Soon other wildcats would join them and each of her youngsters would start a family.

Years later, Rob and Sheina would take their own children up the hill, and hide, watching wildcat kittens playing together and crying to the moon.